A VAMPIRE'S FATE

THE ORDER OF THE BLACK OAK - VAMPIRES

MARIE-CLAUDE BOURQUE

SEA STORM PUBLISHING

This is a work of fiction. Names, characters, businesses, places, events, locales, and incidents are either the products of the author's imagination or used in a fictitious manner. Any resemblance to actual persons, living or dead, or actual events is purely coincidental.

No form of AI was used in the creation of this content. All content authentic human-created.

A VAMPIRE'S FATE
The Order of the Black Oak Series - Vampires
Copyright © 2023 by **Marie-Claude Bourque**
Sea Storm Publishing
P.O. Box 15531, Seattle WA 98115

Edited by Jennifer Bray Weber
Cover Design by Frauke Spanuth
ISBN: 978-1-956115-08-6

"Bourque develops a world of mages and sorceresses unlike any other."

-- Night Owl Reviews
www.marieclaudebourque.com

To Logan and Finlay, for family.

CHAPTER 1

Briac Falls, Québec, Canada
Present Time

Rosalie Gauthier clutched the crisp stems of her bridal bouquet as she stared at the striking immortal vampire she was about to marry in front of her whole wolf-shifter pack.

The summer sun streaming through the stained glass of the St-Anne-des-Pins chapel bathed the altar in suffocating warmth.

The groom she barely knew didn't seem to suffer one bit from the sweltering heat of mid-August.

Meanwhile, her organza gown stuck to the lower part of her spine, and her breath felt heavy behind her thick wedding veil.

"Do you, Rosalie Marie Gauthier," Abbé David began with the vows, "take Renaud Callan St-Amand for your lawfully wedded husband, to have and to hold…"

St-Amand was listening to the priest with polite attention, the expression on his handsome features unreadable in the local church adorned with white satin bows and pale iris-flowers arrangements.

Her husband-to-be had been around Briac Falls for as far back as she remembered but she still knew little about him. A fixture at her dad's tavern, he was known as the protector of the pack—the powerful immortal who had been indebted for centuries to her alpha family.

"*Je le veux*," she declared.

She peered at the pew and took in the happiness of her father, Alcide Gauthier, alpha leader of the Domaine-Lassalle pack. Beside him were her younger siblings, Delphine and Liam, all decked out in formal attire— Delphine having made the fashionable dress herself especially for the occasion.

Behind the front row were her many cousins, including adult ones such as Don, sitting with his pals Nick Pelletier and Gabe Beaulieu. And the other wolf-shifter families, like the Pelletiers, Beaulieus and Fortins, as well as the Merciers —a family of crafty healers. A few humans were in attendance, too, like the Leclercs who owned the local gas station.

Practically everyone who made the tight-knit community of Briac Falls her home had come to witness the unexpected nuptials.

On the groom's side of the church were only two people. Two men—no, two *immortals*—who seemed to fill the entire space with their powerful aura. One was Cass St-Amand, the well-known rock star and Renaud's sibling. The other was also a St-Amand brother, though she couldn't recall his name.

Both wore their dark hair a little too long and neither had dressed for the occasion. The musician sat back in a black jacket over a black T-shirt, a silver cross dangling from his neck. The other slouched over his knees and fidgeted with one of the leather-bound church missals.

They wore slightly bored smiles as they watched their brother respectfully nodding at the priest of St-Anne-des-Pins who was proceeding with the service.

"*Je le veux.*" Renaud St-Amand's voice echoed in the tall chapel and his rich tone struck her straight at the center of her chest, sending tingles all the way down to the back of her knees. She swallowed at the jittery sensation.

This was real. In a few minutes she would be married. Her carefree life as a nursing student in the city was over.

She had returned to Briac Falls just after graduation when her father had been hit with a frightening heart attack. He had recovered now, but she was to take over the leadership of the pack from her father. *She* was to be their alpha.

Inheriting from her father, as previous ancestors of her family had done before her.

Dad hadn't wanted to wait for her little brother Liam to be old enough to take the lead. His health forcing him out, he had chosen her with pride.

She loved her people, but this town was still steeped in tradition. Female alphas were rare.

And to ensure the respect she was due, Dad had asked his best friend—the vampire who had protected their village for centuries—to take her as his wife.

Her father had been worried that there might be some pushback at a female alpha, but he was sure that now with St-Amand by her side, the villagers would accept her as their leader.

"The rings," Abbé David called.

Her little cousin Hugo approached with the small white pin cushion where rested the two rings signaling their fate.

She wondered what St-Amand thought. What man would give away his freedom like this to honor a friend's wishes?

He looked calm and composed in front of her, showing

3

no anguish nor pleasure. Like a dutiful soldier. The warrior who looked after Briac Falls out of some oath he'd made to her ancestor before even her great-grandfather was born. Their few phone calls to arrange their union had been so brief, she still didn't know how he felt about this arrangement.

"Renaud," the officiant prompted.

The immortal she was marrying seized the ring and took her hand. The warm, manly touch sent further shivers up her exposed throat and she looked up at him, trying to catch some sort of emotion in his eyes—perhaps a glimpse of her future ahead—as their gaze finally connected.

But there was nothing. He was a closed book.

"Rosalie Gauthier, with this ring…." His deep voice repeated the vows after the priest.

What had made sense just a few minutes ago—as her aunt Camille had rearranged the long veil over her hair before Rosalie could proceed down the aisle—now constricted her throat with apprehension.

She had a duty to her pack. But she *was* tying herself to a stranger forever. Soon, she would share her life with him, a home. Oh god, would he also expect her to share his bed?

Driven by fear for her father's health, she had gone along with this without qualms. But right now, with this stranger's strong hand holding hers, and as the gold wedding band met his diamond engagement ring on her finger, an irrational panic turned her mouth dry.

She took a deep breath. *Wait, Rose.* She shook herself. *This has to be weird for him, too.*

"Rosalie." The elderly priest who'd known her since she was a little girl, cast her a benevolent smile and she nodded back, the sudden trepidation gone.

She took the offered thick gold band on the cushion,

cracked a grin at little Hugo who looked adorable in his pint-size tux, and with confidence in the future, she slid the wedding ring on St-Amand's calloused finger.

As she took notice of the solid forearm under the dark tuxedo sleeve, her pulse began to race faster.

Her groom was an attractive one.

Relief spread over her. This marriage was a good thing. Dad would retire from the minutia of the town's leadership that had caused his heart attack, the burden gone now and allowing him to focus on running his beloved tavern.

The worry lines at the corner of his eyes would ease, confident in the knowledge his daughter had everything under control.

And she knew she could do good. As Abbé David proclaimed them husband and wife, she stole a glance at the crowd.

She cared for every single one of the town's residents. She'd known them and their concerns her entire life, from Mrs. Savard's ailment to Mr. Fortin's worries about the general store. She knew the old Leclerc sisters were gathering funds for a new roof for the parochial school and that Sabine Beaulieu was pregnant. Rosalie had already stepped in as the woman's nurse practitioner even before her new clinic was finished.

In less than two weeks, she would officially lead and protect her pack after the coronation ceremony held on the next full moon.

Filled with her usual optimism, she turned her gaze back to her brand-new husband and beamed at him. *Yes, this will work.*

"You may kiss the bride," Abbé David finally announced.

St-Amand—no Ren, she corrected herself—drew up a corner of his mouth in a hint of an amused smile, revealing a reaction for the very first time since they'd agreed to this plan.

And this was it. They were married, about to start a life together.

Her heartbeat hammered in her chest, and she gulped with nervousness. She had just broken up with a boyfriend in the city. She was no blushing bride. But this was a man she barely knew. A tall, wide-shouldered man who may expect intimacy this very night.

She swallowed once more. Her strapping groom was much more than a mere man. Dang it, he was a centuries-old *vampire*!

She pondered if he was an old bachelor set in his way, or perhaps had antiquated views about a woman's place.

With heart palpitations, she braced for his kiss but relaxed as he gently took hold of her bare upper arms. This didn't feel like someone who would want to control her. In fact, his touch was both respectful and enticing.

She leaned toward him and as he lifted her veil, she realized he had no intention of taking her lips but was about to drop a chaste kiss on her forehead.

A crash at the church's entrance made them both jump before he had the chance.

"My, my, what have we here? Our future alpha!" The wolf-shifter who had flung the doors open—Charles Bouchard, local property developer—was now striding his hefty bulk down the aisle, two of his cousins behind him.

Ren tensed and spun toward the newcomer, keeping his body slightly ahead of her in a protective stance.

A gasp scattered among the attendees at the rude disruption, the St-Amand brothers perking up at the intruder.

"Charlie Boy." Her father stood from the pew, followed by her cousin Don, Max and Gabe. "You're late. You missed the wedding."

"Sorry, old man." Charlie sneered at her dad, before stopping at the altar steps below her and Ren. "So, *this* is to be our new alpha."

She shuddered under his cold devious gaze but said nothing, her spine straight.

"Rosalie, yes," Dad declared.

"A woman," he spat.

"Yes. And a fine one at that." The pride in her father's tone was obvious to all.

"You up for it?" he asked her with a leer.

Ren drew himself taller at the unspoken threat, his quiet strength unmistakable.

She inhaled slowly and flexed her fingers a few times, feeling awkward to be confronting Charlie in a delicate wedding dress.

"Why wouldn't I be?" she answered him.

"What if the Val D'Or alpha descends upon us, challenges you?" He puffed up his burly chest, barely contained by the tight polo shirt, and cracked his knuckles, one after the other. "Can you take him on?"

"Not every battle is fought with fists." She leveled with him, steadying her racing pulse.

"What? You'll reason with him? 'Please don't hurt me, I'm a nice girl'," he mocked before turning to the wedding attendees. "Is this who you all want to protect you? A little girl in a frilly dress?"

She blinked a few times as she felt the wolf inside her wanting to emerge at the insult. She had always controlled that side of her, shifting on demand when she wanted to, but her anger favored an impulsive shift.

Epinephrine rose in her veins as her senses turned keener. She could hear her foe's heavy breathing and detect his faint predator scent.

"Bouchard." Ren's tone was as deadly as his stilled posture beside her. "Get out."

"Oh, that's how you want to fight your battles, sweet pea?" Charlie scoffed at Rosalie. "You'll send your vampire after me. Like a pet dog. So, we have vampires in charge of protecting us now?"

"You heard St-Amand, Charlie. Get out of here," her father ordered.

"Alcide, you got old. You forgot what we wolves, stand for," Charlie hissed. "That freak has been fighting battles *we* should have fought."

"There's no more battle, son," Rosalie's dad retorted. "Go home and worry about your real estate properties. I heard they're in need of repairs."

"I will not stand down. As long as you were in charge here, Alcide, I let things slide," Charlie rambled with a jeer. "Out of respect for your family. Used to be the Gauthier name meant something. But now, you want to put your daughter in charge. Fuck, it's pathetic. Led by a girl and her housebroken vampire. Am I not right, folks?"

Shocked, she saw Julien Lambert and Danny Fortin nod at him.

Damn.

Ren's features were turning stark. He would pounce at Charlie if just given the word.

But this was *her* fight now.

If she was to lead this pack her way, this here was her test. Oh mercy, the ink on her wedding certificate was barely dry.

She stepped down to the aisle and stood right in front of her foe, muscles tight and ready for the confrontation. The wolf-shifter was a good head taller, with massive hands that would crush her in an instant.

"Charlie," she said. "You know me, we were at school together. You know I'll give my heart and soul to meet the pack's needs."

"Needs? What they need is better protection than you and your...husband." He spat the last word.

"Like Dad said, there is no war. I'm set to meet Rémi Desmarais at the wolf's council meeting next month."

"A council meeting?" He stared down at her with an arrogant expression, reminding her that he'd always been a bit of a jerk even as a kid. "What if he brings his whole gang with him? Can you take them down yourself? Or are you going to ask your pet to do it? At least your dad could fight his own battles."

Ren snorted behind her, and she glanced back to send him a pacifying look.

"I don't need to fight," she said. "We're all past that now."

A familiar pain deadened her chest. Her mom had given her life to protect her family against the very last attack from coyote-shifters mercenaries hired by the Great Lake Boreal pack down south. They were all at peace now, but it would never bring her mother back.

"You're a girl," Charlie continued. "You can't best Rémi at combat."

"I don't need to." She knew very well that her mother's death had secured the Val D'Or pack allyship. Rémi Desmarais had instigated the peace treaty for all shifters.

"Do you hear this, folks? She admits she can't fight for you."

"Aye," someone shouted from the pews while Ren took down the steps to stand by her side.

"Is this your answer to everything, Charlie? Fighting?" She took a deep breath. "What about the land dispute with *Bois-Franc Village*? They want to sell to some German company who'll build a frickin' amusement park. It's the pack's land. You can't *fight* your way out of that."

"She's right there, man," her cousin Max and Ren's

9

best man, agreed. "We need to protect our territory from all these newcomers."

Charlie pursed his thick lips and took another step forward. "I can do that, too. I have money to buy lawyers."

"I heard you got busted with tax fraud last year," Rosalie rebutted. Despite being away, she'd kept up with the news of the town. "Not a good look when you plead our case to the Mount-Tremblant County board."

"Fuck all this," Charlie shouted. "We're not pen push-ers. We are *wolves*! And you, missy, are no *alpha*."

"Alphas have always been Gauthiers," her dad said. "Would you go against tradition, pal?"

"Tradition? I tell you what tradition calls for." He was now towering right in her face, his pupils starting to dilate. "I want an actual combat!"

"What?" Her sister blurted out from the pew. "No, you can't."

"Oh, I can, cutie." Charlie shot Delphine a lecherous leer that brought a shudder through Rosalie's spine. "I want to fight your new alpha, Alcide. It *is* tradition."

"Not while I stand," her dad barked. "You will *not* fight my daughter. If you want a fight, you can have one with St-Amand. But it didn't turn out so well when you tried to take down his brother a few months ago, did it?"

She'd heard about Charlie's fight with Justin St-Amand at her dad's tavern. The wolf-shifter had been left barely conscious by the immortal and had needed two men to carry him off the premises.

"Vampires and immortals have no place in Briac Falls," Charlie ranted. "I will *fight* her. If she wants to be alpha, she has to prove she can protect her pack. In about ten days. Just before the full moon. We'll see then who will be coronated."

She swallowed. Yes, she could fight. She could easily

take down any human opponent and was well matched to her cousins. But Charlie, dammit. He was massive.

She stared around at everyone's eager faces. She had felt their support earlier. But while her best friend and maid of honor Caro Mercier and her human parents in attendance were shaking their heads at the idiocy of this combat, some of the wolves—especially the younger ones outside her immediate family—seemed keen to what Charlie was suggesting.

The tension in the air was high. It was her job to diffuse it. This was a wedding celebration, not the beginning of a civil war.

"Fine," she finally replied in a clear voice. "I'll fight you."

"You can't do that, Rosie," her dad said. "No one has battled for the alpha claim in over a century."

"Rosalie?" Ren frowned at her, his rich tone addressing her for the first time since the nuptial vows. He laced his palm at the middle of her back and a shiver spread down to the bottom of her spine.

"I will, yes," she announced, trying to drown the little panicked voice in the back of her mind warning her that this was madness.

But she was only agreeing now so her opponent would leave her wedding.

She narrowed her eyes at Charlie. "If this is what you need, I'll fight you. The Gauthiers have always led this pack and I'll show you why."

Would her heritage truly kick in? She had at least ten days. Enough to figure out a better way to win over her people.

"Maybe it's time for the Bouchards to take charge." Charlie wetted his lips as if anticipating crushing her. He turned to the attendees to thrust both fists into the air with zeal. "A fight!"

"Fight, fight!" his minions chanted behind him, fists pumping the air. Julien Lambert and Danny Fortin got up from the pew despite the dark look from their dads and joined Charlie's supporters in the aisle.

They marched out of the church and just before they reached the door, Charlie turned back to her.

"I will see you at midnight two days before the full moon at the old playfield by Beaver Woods. And I will beat you, sweet pea. I will take down the Gauthier line." He chuckled unpleasantly. "Just as it used to be done in the good old days. This will be a fight to the death!"

"Daddy! No," her teen sister screeched and brought both fists to her mouth.

Rosalie had no time to respond. Ren had taken off down the aisle.

Holy hells! She jerked back in shock.

In a flash, her new husband had Charlie by the neck, his fangs out, his handsome face turned into that of a vicious killer.

His grip securing her challenger's throat, he stared at her, waiting.

She just had to say the word and her rival would be dead, bled dry. She had married a stone-cold executioner. And she had mere seconds to decide. A quiver clenched her stomach.

"Stop!" Her palm shot flat out in front of her, her spine ramrod straight.

Everyone was now looking at her, holding their breath at what would happen next. This moment would either make or break her claim to the leadership of the pack.

She could order Charlie killed on the spot or do it her way. With diplomacy.

"Let him go." She forced as much resolve in her command as she could, her head held high. Filled with uneasiness at the combat she had agreed to, she slowly surveyed the crowd with an air of confidence, despite the turmoil boiling inside her. "This is not the way."

If she was to lead, she couldn't let Ren fight her battles. Even if he was now her husband.

She would have to deal with Charlie herself.

CHAPTER 2

"Are you insane?" Ren stared in shock at his new bride standing poised at the base of the altar's steps in her elegant wedding dress.

Summoning all his control, he released Charlie. The scumbag stumbled on his feet while Rosalie marched up the church's aisle toward them.

He heard a faint chortle from the pew and caught his brother Cass's amused expression at his predicament. But damn, this was no joke. Ren was now lodged deep into wolf politics.

Charlie's little gang was right beside him and the big wolf waved them aside, shooting Ren a look full of hatred before smirking at the group of villagers that surrounded them in the atrium by the heavy doors of the chapel.

"This is our wedding, honey," Rosalie said, continuing the pretense they had married for love. She looped her arm around his, her feminine scent crashing into him and making him dizzy with mixed emotions. She held her head high in the regal posture of a queen by his side. "There is no place for bloodshed."

"Of course, love," he reluctantly agreed.

Someone opened the doors and her veil fluttered gently in the summer breeze. He cautiously led her outside while keeping an eye on her challenger. Her spine was unyielding, her lithe body remaining graceful in the white dress.

She cast him an intense gaze of the purest amber, the shade scattered with specks of sapphire. The deep desire that had not left him since he first saw her walk down the aisle shot straight to his groin. He had the hots for his arranged bride and had no idea where it came from.

But here he was, her husband. Ready to kill for her.

"A fight to the death?" He scoffed, trying to play it cool, but his blood was raging inside. Someone had the audacity to not only interrupt the wedding, but challenge to fight a woman—and his bride at that.

This was Alcide's daughter, the one he had last seen as a gangly young girl with an efficient bounce in her step just before she left town for college. She was all woman now, and dammit, she was also his *wife*!

He turned from her to stare at Charlie who was swaggering down the church's steps to his massive truck, a brand-new white Silverado glistening under the bright afternoon sun. His minions—all wolves below the age of twenty-five—surrounded him while gleefully pumping the air and high-fiving each other.

Oh, Ren knew Charlie alright. He'd been beaten to a pulp by his brother a few months ago and had been vocal about his hatred for the immortal brothers since.

The shifter was a drunk at the time, but it was different now. He'd gotten cleaned up, started to lift regularly. Pumped with steroids, muscles bulging out from everywhere, he was not someone the Gauthier girl—his wife, he reminded himself—should be fighting.

"I'll take your place." Still staring at Charlie, Ren tilted his head toward her. "I'll do this fight. Isn't it why your dad arranged our marriage?"

"I will fight my own fight." She turned to her sister. "It will be okay, Delphine. Don't you worry."

"You can't fight him, Rosie. He's freakin' scary strong." Rosalie's sister was white as a sheet, sniffling, obviously in anguish. She was a nice kid, but a teen girl still prone to drama. And this today was beyond drama.

"I can but I might not have to." Rosalie left Ren's side to go pat her sister's cheek. "Anyone have a tissue or something? Come on, sis. Your makeup is going to be ruined."

Someone—Mrs. Mercier, one of the town's matrons— passed Rosalie a tissue and just like that, as if she hadn't just agreed to a trial by combat, she fixed her teen sister's face.

"Alcide." Ren addressed his old pal, the middle-aged man still looking dignified with his salt-and-pepper beard despite the recent health scare. "You're not agreeing to this fight, are you?"

The current alpha looked down at his young son. The boy of ten had his eyes glued to his device's screen, engaged in a tiny battle of his own with a video game.

"*I'll* have to do it," he said.

"Dad, no!" Rosalie protested with agitation. "Your heart. You can't be fighting."

"Barely felt it." Her father shrugged. "I'm still the alpha of Domaine-Lassalle. Right, people?"

"Yeah, you are, Gauthier," an older man—Mr. Fortin —agreed. One of his children had left with Charlie, but the owner of the local grocery store was still a hundred percent behind Alcide. "Disrupting your little girl's wedding like that, you go tell that punk what's what."

Rosalie pursed her lips and shot Ren a deadly look. A ping strung at his heart to see the strain in her gaze. They had agreed to marry over a simple phone call. This had to be hard on her.

"I'll do it," he reassured her.

"No." She shook her head. "They'll want a Gauthier to put Charlie in his place."

As she wrapped a loving arm around her sister, her expression was full of resolve. And the reality of their wedding suddenly hit him.

This strong-headed woman was about to enter his life. She would be in his cabin in the woods, using his modest kitchen, his shower, and dammit, she might be in his bed this very night. They hadn't even yet talked about *that* part of the deal.

His heart pulsed faster. It was all going to be very different than he'd imagined.

He had sworn an oath to protect the Gauthier family when her ancestor had saved his life. He'd cut himself off from his own kin to move here among the pack. The wolves' world of honor and duty, their black-and-white views, called to his straightforward personality.

Where his own St-Amand family dwelled in shades of gray, the wolves' strong sense of justice had made him feel right at home. He had a place here, he was their protector, a right-hand man to their alpha. But never in a hundred years, had the alpha been a determined, yet sexy, woman of twenty-six.

"You won't win this fight, Rosalie," he told her. A part of him shuddered to think of that bastard messing up her pretty face.

"I will if I have to." She lifted her chin at him before turning to her father's supporters, the locals all dressed in their formal best, eagerly looking at her. "Dad will not fight this one. I will. I'm to be your alpha."

"Oh, *ma chère*," Mrs. Mercier replied with alarm, "you can't be fighting that big brute. You're just a little thing."

"Yeah," Ti-Jo Leclerc said. "He'll kill you, girl."

"That boy was always trouble," his wife added with a huff. "No one wants death here. Rosalie will be a fine

18

leader of this town. You look very pretty in your dress today, sweetie."

His bride's tight expression relented. "You're too kind, Mrs. Leclerc. Léa Pelletier made it for me, she's very good."

"Louise is right, kid. You should let your husband fight that one." Old Simon, the town's elderly postman, was resting a sympathetic gaze on her.

"I'll sort this out," Ren told everyone. "It's not a problem."

The townies looked at him with a mix of relief and horror. Yes, there were some strong fighters in the village—he cast a quick glance at Nick Pelletier and his best buds, Max and Don Gauthier standing stiffly at the back—but most were regular people who had no taste for bloodshed.

They obviously loved Rosalie—she had that warm way about her that endeared her to all here. He recalled her as the stern teen with baby Liam in her arms at her mother's funeral, little Delphine hanging around her ankles. Responsible even then. She cared for people, he could see it now in the way she cooed to her sister, who was still sniffling and dabbing her tissue delicately at her eyes.

"You can't just go and kill Charlie, Ren." The way she spoke his name so easily made his pulse speed up and reawaken the anger inside him.

He wanted to run after that son of a bitch. Bouchard had threatened her life. He was fair game, just a bully ready to kill a young woman, traditions be damned. Only her keen resolve for peace was stopping him.

"Why not?" he griped. "It would solve your problem."

"These folks here, sure they may accept us. But not everyone in town is that loyal to our family."

"Yep," Alcide said, cursing under his breath. "There are already some young pups challenging my authority."

"I have to win them over the right way," she added.

19

"Win them over?" Ren blinked with disbelief. "By dying? Alcide, sorry man. I get that Liam is too young to take over, but what about Max? He's family."

"Rosalie is what this town needs," Alcide insisted.

"Not everything is solved by fighting." Her jaw was set. "Sometimes diplomacy is better."

"Diplomacy, with that asshole? He won't back down."

"I know." Her brow furrowed as she mulled this over. "I'll have to convince him."

"You can't fight him, Rosie," Delphine blurted, tears welling again in her pretty eyes.

"I won't fight him, sis," she uttered softly before turning to Ren. "Promise me you won't go hurt him behind my back."

"I can't promise that."

"Aren't you bound to my family?" she said, as if he was indeed some kind of pet.

He let the insult slide. The poor woman was in way over her head. First their fake marriage, now this.

But it was all simple, really. She would go talk to Bouchard, the creep would send her packing, and then Ren would go beat some sense into him.

"Technically, I still answer to your father," he answered with a slow smile. "Even if we're married, *honey*."

Emphasizing the term of endearment, he lifted his hand and rested his thumb on the new thick gold band on his finger to remind her of their status.

She looked down at her own slim version next to the diamond ring he had gifted her just three weeks ago and seemed to realize that this was indeed her wedding day.

"Of course, sweetie!" Her vexed features turned into a beaming smile as she addressed the wedding attendees. "Don't you all worry. We have this under control."

She gave her sister a warm squeeze before letting her go to loop a confident arm under Ren's elbow. Her fresh feminine scent enveloped him at once, sending a rush of blood below his belt.

"We have a party waiting for us at the hall," she added with eagerness. "Nick and Don's mom and the *Cercle des Fermières* have spent all week preparing it for us."

"Alright," Nick shouted with a laugh. "We all need a drink."

Ren's pent-up tension released, and he figured he would deal with this pesky Bouchard problem later. It wouldn't be the first time he had to go on a little hunting excursion to keep the peace. He wouldn't need to kill the big wolf, just make him and his pals see reason. There was no need to ruin her wedding day.

He gave her an easy, reassuring smile, nodded at Alcide that all was well, and took her down the steps as people cheered while raining confetti over them. The church bells remained silent, forgotten in the midst of all the drama.

Her body was warm and supple at his side, her presence loosening his dark mood. Maybe he could make this union work, make her warm up to him.

His gaze suddenly narrowed on the lone figure of a man advancing toward them from the parking lot. He frowned at the newcomer, who looked out of place in a fancy summer linen suit and neat haircut.

Rosalie, who had been waving and shouting back at friends and family with a warm smile, froze beside him. Her tone shook as she spoke. "François?"

Ren stared at her, then back at the stranger.

"Rosie, someone told me you were getting married today." The young man's distress was obvious in his pleasant-looking features. "I told them it couldn't be true."

"We broke up." Rosalie tensed as she dropped Ren's arm. "Remember?"

"But that was just a small quarrel, *chérie*." The man's

head flinched back. "I didn't expect you to pack up and leave Toronto so soon. Let alone get married!"

For the first time today, she seemed tongue-tied as she tugged uncomfortably at her veil.

Nick and Max eyed the man before both turning a puzzled look at Ren.

A sudden primal growl resonated from deep inside him. She was his wife!

A stranger, yes, and for convenience, sure. But they were bound to each other under the Almighty. He didn't expect her to have someone else in her life.

He carried this intense, inexplicable attraction to her, which he fully intended to investigate further. And this puny human facing them had no rights to his new bride. His fists tensed with irritation and an irrational sense of betrayal.

"Uhm, Ren, meet my boyfriend..." She shook herself uneasily, apparently still filled with feelings for the man. "I mean, my ex. Dr. François Beaumont."

CHAPTER 3

The wedding reception had been tense, that was the understatement of the year. Rosalie's stomach churned with anxiety.

She folded and unfolded her hands on her lap over her organza dress as she rode the passenger seat of Ren's truck driving down the dirt road leading to his woodland property.

Her skin was clammy from the heat, still relentless in the evening. His windows were wide open to the fragrant air and, as the gentle summer breeze stroked her heated body, the scent of pine meeting her nostrils filled her with melancholia.

She had missed that woodsy fragrance of the mountain and the way the tall trees reached the star-filled sky.

No one had seen her turmoil tonight. She had danced with her new husband, her father, and some of the elders in town. Plastering a beaming smile on her face, she had reassured the few who worried about her impeding combat.

She'd stopped occasionally to briefly talk to François who she'd introduced as a doctor friend from Toronto.

He'd been surrounded by local women, shifters and human alike, some—like sassy Émilie Fortin and fun-loving Jade Leclerc—her former high school pals.

She obviously hadn't been clear with François when she'd told him their relationship was over on the day after her dad's heart attack.

She'd had no choice but to drag him to her wedding reception today, promising him an explanation later. He was all set to stay at Mrs. Beaulieu's B&B down the road for the night.

He had mingled well with the people in town, oblivious to their supernatural nature. And his laid-back manners made her wonder what life would have been if she had not returned to Briac Falls.

Practicing her career alongside her talented partner in the city. Saving lives. Not risking hers.

She gave a tiny sigh as she stared at the sliver of the waxing crescent moon above the trees.

"You still love him?" Ren spoke for the first time since they left the reception, his tone detached. She'd have to get used to his silent, taciturn demeanor.

In response to his inquiry, she searched her current feelings for the men in her life and found nothing but confusion.

"I don't know," she answered him quietly.

"I heard he's staying in town." He shot her a small, tight smile.

"Yeah," she muttered. "I didn't have the heart to send him packing without a good talk."

"Does he know everything?" He gave her a slight shake of his head.

She surveyed his handsome features and noticed the strong jaw above the collar of his tux, with the bow tie hanging loose over the fresh white shirt. His brooding gaze indicated a repressed passion under the stern warrior.

She found her chest expanding with unexpected heat again.

"That we're wolf-shifters?" she answered. "No, François doesn't know anything about that."

"How long has it been?" He probed, his expression easing.

"What?" she replied back, confused.

"Since you shifted." He had dropped the talk of François, as if the whole subject of her ex was inconsequential and had nothing to do with him.

Yet here they were, married. She felt slightly hurt that he didn't even act a teeny bit jealous.

"A while," she told him.

"In the city?" he inquired casually.

"Many times. Full moon, mostly. I'd run to High Park at night. Shift and howl to feel connected to that side of me." It was quite the cliché, and the pack did have complete control over the time of their shifting.

She didn't need to wait to shift but howling at the full moon, away from the bustle of the city, was something she always had the urge to do. It connected her to that primal side of hers, made her feel whole.

"And fighting?"

"Not since I left," she told him. "I used to spar all the time with Max and Don. Aunt Camille has trained me since Mom died. I tried a local dojo in the city for a while, but I was swamped with my nursing program."

"Look, Rosalie," he started, calling her name in that rich, sexy tone of his. "We know this marriage is for looks only, but you can't have a boyfriend caught in the middle of it all."

So her ex *was* on his mind. She nodded as he took a sharp turn from the dirt path into a long driveway bordered by a singing brook.

"I know," she said.

"You need to talk to him and send him back to Toronto." His voice held nothing but certainty while his gaze remained fixed steadily on the small lane. "The townies will start talking, diminish your authority if they realize it's fake."

"Yes, I know," she repeated.

"You want me to talk to him?"

"No!" He truly did appoint himself as her fixer. She got why but it was still odd to be partnered with this near-stranger.

A small smile appeared at the corner of his mouth. "You really don't like anyone doing things for you, do you?"

"Ever since Mom died, I'm used to being the one who takes care of things." She winced. "And this talk with François, it'll require some finessing."

"And you don't think I can do that?"

"You're the tavern's bouncer," she chuckled. "So no, I don't think you use finesse."

"Depends on the moment." He raised a brow and his gaze descended along her body in the fitted wedding dress, sending shivers from the center of her belly all the way up to her chest.

She'd always seen him as Dad's immortal bodyguard but now, things were changing fast. They were bound to each other.

He had returned to watching the path ahead while she studied his hands on the wheel and swallowed.

Dang it. This was their wedding night. In just a few moments, he could be running his calloused fingers along her body in the most intimate way. Neither one of them had dared to have *that* conversation.

She cleared her throat with unease. "Ren, about tonight, I—"

"Oh boy. Is someone here?" He stopped his truck in

26

front of his log cabin next to her own vehicle parked in his driveway.

"It's my jeep." She couldn't help but be relieved to postpone the touchy topic, if only for a little while longer. "Delphine brought it over for me. She just got her license. She's so excited she wants to drive all the time."

He stepped out of his truck where she remained seated admiring the ruddy but inviting home bordering the river. The single-level timber construction was simple but substantial. A small series of steps leading to the entrance was flanked by a sizeable wrap-around porch.

He opened the passenger door for her. "Your car's packed to the roof."

"Well, I *am* moving in." As they'd discussed on the phone, everyone had to believe their union was real.

Rosalie took his offered hand and gathered her heavy satin skirts to come down from the high step of the truck. She jumped to the dirt ground in her small heels. Everything was quiet here, aside from the croaking of bullfrogs and the gentle sound of the stream hitting the rocky shore.

The sky opened to the stars above and a handful of fireflies danced in front of her in the moonlit night. They were far from civilization despite being just a few minutes' drive from Briac Falls.

"How much stuff did you bring?" His expression seemed genuinely baffled.

She walked to her jeep and retrieved a canvas overnight bag prepared for the occasion. She would leave the rest for later. "Well, I have a few small pieces of furniture, bedding and linens, kitchenware. Decorative pillows."

"What on earth are decorative pillows?" He chortled taking the suitcase from her.

"Uh, to decorate?" She gave him a light shrug as she followed him up the wooden step onto the bare porch which was lit with the simple glow of a floodlight.

"Decorate?" He opened the screen door to let her in and cocked an amused brow at her.

"I see," she mumbled as she took in the interior of the cabin.

The place was sparse, with nothing in the open floor plan that was not functional. A plain brown leather couch, sound system, and TV were placed next to large sliding doors heading to the back deck. A wooden kitchen table and two chairs sat on the other side, leading to a small galley kitchen. The few windows were adorned with basic canvas curtains. There was no AC, the simple fan running in the corner barely strong enough to dissipate the stifling heat.

He stared at her deflated look. "You don't like it."

"It's…nice but, it needs a little sprucing up."

He sighed and silently dropped her travel bag on the bare table.

"You didn't think much about what this marriage means, did you?" She leveled with him.

He walked to the fridge and took out two bottles of beer. He twisted them open and passed one over to her. "No, not really."

"You just did what my father asked."

"Damn hot this week." He skirted her observation as he sat his beer on the table to pull off his bow tie. He removed his tuxedo jacket and folded it over the chair before unbuttoning his shirt completely to let it fall over his well-defined chest and stomach.

She took a welcomed sip of her cold beer, trying to keep her racing heart in check and avert her gaze from his enticing exposed flesh. He'd been alive for centuries, yet his body was one of a late twenty-something virile man, a very fine man, well-proportioned and with muscles in all the right places, his skin a pale golden hue.

He turned around to move her bag down to a chair

and the shirt shifted to expose his side covered in scars.

A large part of his flank was marred by a crisscrossing of raised fibrous tissue, lighter than the rest of his skin. The marks seemed rough while also holding a shiny texture that broke the perfect lines of his body. What could have caused this substantial injury?

Unaware of her appraisal, he grabbed his beer again. "It's cooler by the water. Let's get some air."

He slid the screen of the patio door open and stepped onto the porch.

Still in her wedding gown, she was dying to change into something less formal, but not sure where she fit in his house. So picking up her silk skirts with both hands, she just followed after him.

She breathed more easily as the starry sky above welcomed her, the gentle flow of the running river below soothing her frayed nerves.

He pulled an Adirondack chair out for her before sitting on a plain plastic garden chair by her side. He dug the heels of his leather dress shoes on the wooden deck and took in the river in the dark, still remaining silent with his beer in one hand. He had yet to comment on why he'd agreed to this union.

"Why did you marry me, Renaud?" She wanted to know.

He shrugged. "It's the right thing to do."

"You always do the right thing?" She was dying to know more about his mindset.

He leaned back and took a swig of beer before turning a straight-forward gaze toward her. "Yes."

"Always? For your whole entire life." She had heard the legends about him from the pack's history, yet it was hard to believe that he'd sworn an oath to them more than a century ago, when he was right there next to her. Looking so normal. And her husband no less.

"All three hundred years of them," he added, stretching his powerful legs farther. "It's not that hard."

"Is it that simple?" She pressed doubtfully. "Have you never done the wrong thing?"

"Sometimes you have to do the wrong thing for the right reason." His indiscernible expression gave nothing away.

"Like us getting married?" she probed.

"It's the right thing for the right reason." A certainty was setting on his handsome features, his jaw set.

"Which is…"

"Duty." He turned an unfaltering look upon her.

"Uh?"

"Strong-headed Rosalie." He slowly shook his head. "You and I are actually driven by the same thing. You have a duty to your pack and your father. I also have a duty to your family. To aid and protect the alpha. Your ancestor saved my life."

"And condemned you to an existence here."

"I like life here, I chose this. I like the pack, the mountain." His features eased as he took in the shadow of the woodland-covered slope on the other side of the river in the darkness. "It's my home."

"Mine too," she said, wistfully. This here, the land, their people, it was her home. Her calling.

"So, there you go. You want to do good for your pack. I saw it today. Your father's right. You care for them. You are the true alpha," he affirmed. "Not someone like Charles Bouchard who's doing it for power and status."

"You're not just following my dad's orders?"

"He thinks me marrying you will help your claim to take over for him. I haven't heard of a female alpha since Rémi Desmarais' mother in Val D'Or in the sixties. Your dad does fear for your life. Since your mom was killed, he's been more protective of you all. He knows you're not invincible. I trust his judgement. So, I agreed to this fake union. I was always the right-hand man of the Domaine-Lassalle pack." He paused from what must have been the longest explanation he'd ever given her since the wedding ceremony. His gaze on her remained heavy. "Your alphas always had me at their side. The other packs know this. It's not new."

"But marriage?" she countered.

"How do *you* feel about this? That poor Dr. Beaumont. He doesn't look like he'll go away easy."

"I realize that."

"Look, we *are* married." He underscored their agreement. "I don't expect us to be married in all the sense of the word, obviously, but it's not a good look if you have a boyfriend on the side."

"People here wouldn't like it." She nodded before fretfully digging her teeth on her bottom lip at his mention of the physical side of their union.

"They expect us to be a loving couple. If you don't appear to honor our commitment, it defeats the whole reason why we had to marry."

"When we talked on the phone about this arrangement, we never discussed…" she couldn't finish.

"That other part?" His lips curled in a playful twist.

"Right."

"Look, *ma belle*, you're a very attractive woman, but I don't know you."

"Oh." Her heartbeat stopped for a second, leaving her surprised at her reaction to his dismissal.

She didn't really want to sleep with him on the first night. No, she didn't.

She fingered the band at her hand. Or maybe she did? Get it over with. She certainly expected him to press, though. It was unsettling that he didn't.

She had a sudden urge to slide his dress shirt off his

shoulders and run her hand up his corded neck. She wondered what it would feel like to pull him toward her and drop a kiss to his decisive mouth. She repressed a sigh of unexpected longing.

"I cannot father children. You know that, right? Mag tried everything. Aside from our birth father—whatever he is—immortals just can't," he continued, unaware of her inner turmoil. "The marriage is for your protection. It will not last for your entire life."

"So, you plan to divorce me?" Why was she crushed by the news? She should be thrilled.

"For sure. At some point." He observed her quietly. "If you want to continue your Gauthier line, we'll have to."

She flattened the silk skirt over her thighs to compose herself. It seemed she, too, had agreed to her dad's plan without much thought. His heart attack had scared her to death, and she had told him she was coming back home right away.

She had already taken over the old tannery building in a quick deal to start her own health clinic for a permanent move to Briac Falls when her father had prompted the news that she was to become alpha and suggested she marry St-Amand.

Still in a state of panic over his health, she had gone along with her father's plan, skipping over most of the details. After seeing the gaunt features of her dad, his once strong body hooked to a heart monitor and IVs, with Aunt Camille's anxious manners as she silently stood guard by his bedside, Rosalie had sworn she'd do anything to ease his pain.

Ren and she had talked a few times on the phone as she'd packed her old life away. He'd sent her the diamond currently adorning her hand just a week later.

"Did you and my dad really go over all that planning?"

"Plans? Your father was in no shape to plan after he

left the hospital. Once he decided the town was better with you as alpha, he was keen to see you safe. He knows I can protect you. Not sure his thoughts went beyond that."

"How long should we stay married then?

"Oh god, Rosalie. I'm not sure. I'm a pretty simple guy, you know." He stretched an arm along the armrest of his chair, his beer bottle dangling above the deck. "I tend to live day by day. I keep to myself and deal with trouble when it shows."

She sipped her own drink, the cool, bitter liquid fresh in her throat. She listened to the bullfrogs' calls for a moment, her eyes lingering over the flashes of a few fireflies dancing over the porch.

"We do have trouble," she said, the altercation in the church giving her spine a nervous shudder.

"I'll deal with it, I told you." His gaze turned dark. "It's nothing."

"You can't kill Charlie." With one hand, she edgily rearranged her long dress over her thighs.

"I won't kill him," he insisted. "Just make him understand."

"You'll beat him up, you mean." She took a sharp inhale.

"Yep." He lifted his beer in some sort of salute.

"We can't do that." She'd used the "we" on purpose.

"And why not? I've known plenty of men like Bouchard. Fighting is all they understand."

"I have a better way."

"Oh, you do?" The corner of his mouth rose with amusement.

"Negotiation," she said.

He pursed his lips with doubt. "I grant you that diplomacy might solve your Dr. Beaumont problem. He doesn't seem the physical type."

"He's not," she informed him. "But he *has* saved countless lives."

She saw him flinch. "Lucky him," he snorted.

"He's a fine doctor and a nice person," she defended her ex. And in truth, François *was* all that. He treated her respectfully. And everyone at the hospital loved him. She had caught the envious look of her colleagues more than once.

"Well, maybe he can wait for you to establish yourself here. We could divorce a few years after your coronation. You'll still be young enough to carry his children by then."

"Years?" The breadth of her commitment to her town suddenly hit her.

"Why, is that too long?"

"For you, maybe not. But me?" She hadn't really thought about it all. In fact, until a few minutes ago, she had vaguely expected to be bound to Ren for her entire life.

A blink for him, but forever for her. But he was right, perhaps after a while, her status would be unchallenged, and she could leave him.

Marry for love. Have that Gauthier heir. But with François? Would he actually wait for her? Could she explain her true nature to him? How would he react to that?

And birthing a child, oh mercy. Human-shifter hybrids were a rarity.

And it wasn't entirely up to her to carry on the line, after all. Delphine or Liam had a chance to give them the next alpha. Could she not pass on the tradition to a niece or nephew?

"I know it sucks," he said, interrupting her troubled reflections.

"What?"

"This." He glanced back at his cabin. "This is enough for me. But no place for a woman."

"I can fix it up." She shot him a hopeful gaze, happy to have found a distraction from her gloomy thoughts.

"Oh god," he groaned.

"Well, it would make things cheerier." Her spirits lifted at the idea of tackling a simpler project.

"Cheery?"

"Yes, you need some color in here. Some comfort."

He snorted but a genuine smile appeared on his lips.

"Comfort." He shook his head, amusement lighting his eyes. "You have a meathead wanting to fight you to the death and you're thinking about bringing my place some comfort?"

"We all need comfort."

"Do we?" He was still smiling.

"Yes," she insisted. "Life is short for me compared to yours. I don't want to just exist. We have to make it nice looking and cozy in here."

"Sure." He shrugged. "This is now your home, after all."

"So, I can bring my things in?"

"Knock yourself out," he grumbled, placing his empty bottle on the deck at his feet.

"Great." She would deal with François and Charlie soon, but at least she could entertain herself with a little housekeeping to keep her mind off them for now.

But there was one more thing to settle first. She took a hesitant sip of her beer to mask her discomfort.

"So, that's that." An apprehensive tingling rose from the back of her spine as she stared at the attractive man that was now her husband—his bare, well-sculpted chest flexing as he leisurely leaned back to cross his hands behind his head. "Now, what do we do about the sleeping arrangement?"

35

CHAPTER 4

"*S*o, are you going to kill him?" His brother Cass tugged at the Celtic cross at his neck and stretched back under the starry sky on the wide balcony of Chateau Briac—their sibling Justin's stately hideout at the top of the mountain—where Ren had run to in the middle of the night, leaving Rosalie sleeping alone in his bedroom.

"Which one?" Ren took a slug from his beer can as he rested his gaze on the valley below, the shades of the tall pines silhouetted on the dark golden background of the moonlit night.

"I vote for the boyfriend." His other brother Griffon reached for the cooler at their feet to help himself to another drink. The wayfarer sibling had recently returned from his travels and both Cass and Griff had taken over Justin's place while he and his wife were away in Europe.

Ren had left his silent cabin to drive up the mountain late in the night. He'd been edgy at having Rosalie sound asleep in his bed, his usual peaceful retreat making him feel claustrophobic.

After tossing and turning on the couch, surrounded by the fancy pillow collection and matching throw she had brought inside for him, he was left wondering what the heck his loyalty to Alcide had gotten him into.

Her fresh feminine scent had been everywhere. And he grudgingly acknowledged that it was not the pillows, or even the vanilla-scented candle she had lit on the kitchen table, that bothered him, but seeing her in a short nightgown padding from the bedroom to get herself a glass of water.

Calvaire! Those curves were all just *there*. He got that the night was hot, but damn, he could see her nipples poking through the thin pink cotton and his desire for her had again rushed straight through his groin.

It was just physical, he told himself. He could handle that. He *had* to handle it.

But she was his wife, goddammit. Surely, he had the right to his own bed. The right to *her*.

But his sense of honor had prevailed, and he'd done the gentleman thing by giving her his bedroom until they had a chance to discuss their relationship further.

"I can't kill the boyfriend," he stated. "He's a freakin' doctor."

"And…"

"Oh, come on," he grunted.

"You want to, though." Cass nodded at him.

"Do I?" Ren cocked him a smirking brow.

"What on earth possessed you to get married?" Griff wondered.

He shrugged. "People get married all the time."

"Not us." A dark shadow passed across Griff's forehead. It was well known in the family that Griff's wandering way had never led him to start a serious relationship.

"Val did," Ren pointed out, mentioning their brother now living in the States with his wife, the high priestess of a powerful coven. "Hells, even Justin."

"To Emme. She's one of us. Not the same thing."

"What about Mag?" Ren countered. "He's getting married soon. And Nyssa is human."

"Under the protection of our mother," Griff stressed.

"And, sorry dude," Cass added, "but Mag and Justin are actually in love."

"Same with Val," Griff said. "He moved to that New England witch town to be with Maisie."

"I know." Ren cringed. He hadn't married for love. But could he fall for Rosalie? He experienced a strong lust, no doubt, but love?

"So why did you get sucked into this?" Cass drew his brows together in concern, his bantering turning serious.

"Alcide. I owe the family."

"Still? It's been centuries since the wolves saved your life," Cass said. "Surely that debt is paid now."

"It's not just the debt. I like Alcide," he admitted, his tone lightening. "He's a good man."

"You do like it here," Griff agreed, understanding him better than anyone.

"Yeah, you get it, bro. There's more out there in the world than bloody vampires."

"Except that Griff has been on the trace of *the* vampire," Cass said.

"Our dad, you mean?" Ren's tone darkened, glad for the change of topic.

"The freak is not our dad. Papa Antoine was," Griff grumbled, mentioning the stern but responsible man that had married their mother while she was pregnant with them.

"Then why have you been on his tail for the last century?" Ren asked.

"While I was traveling to explore new lands," Griff explained, "I came across these tight-knit communities everywhere. Not knowing our entire blood ancestry eventually really got to me."

"It's been over a hundred years," Cass said, "and you haven't stopped searching. It's messed up."

"Not as much as our buddy, here." Griff tilted his beer at Ren with a smirk. "Will he kill the boyfriend, or the contender?"

"I don't care about the boyfriend." Ren attempted a casual shrug, even though the thought of Rosalie with the sophisticated doctor bothered him. A lot.

"But Bouchard," he added. "Yeah, maybe. I could go down to his compound and smack him around a bit."

"I could go with you," Cass said. "But it's not like I spend a ton of time in your reckless world. It might not look good in the tabloids if someone finds out."

"Sure, Mr. Hot Shot." Griff offered him a half-smile. "Worry about your image."

"Hey dude, we're not all world-weary travelers like you. I'm actually an artist."

"Artist?" Griff snorted. "You gotta be kidding me. You love the limelight, man, you always have."

"Hell yeah, bro," Ren added. "I keep seeing your face on the magazine rack at the corner store. It's freaky."

"I like making music." Cass pursed his lips. "It's how I process things."

"Process?"

"Look, ever since Mom took off when Papa died, we all had to deal with this undying thing our own way," Cass said. "Justin got himself a million college degrees, Mag built up his club like a shrine. You, Ren, eventually came here to hide with the wolf pack."

"True." Ren shrugged. "Val locked himself in a cave and, sorry Griff, but you just took off."

"I did stumble on a clue about our birth father soon

after I docked on the coast of Brittany," Griff informed them. "Remember that scroll I found."

"Romania. *Calvaire*." Ren said with a disbelieving shake of his head, mentioning the revelation Griff had made years ago. "Our father, something like a real Count Dracula."

"Actually, he's from the daemon world," Griff said. "Exiled apparently. He just passed through Transylvania for a short generation."

"For real?" Cass's interest was piqued.

Ren didn't care one bit. Papa Antoine had been his real dad. Ren loved his father's sense of justice and the moral compass he'd instilled in his boys.

The fact that their immortal birth father had impregnated their mother just before she crossed the ocean from France and had never bothered to find her after their encounter, showed that the mysterious immortal was an absolute scumbag.

Ren had no place for jerks like that in his life. He could never understand Griff's obsession with reconnecting with him.

"Forget the bastard," Ren snapped. "I have a real problem here. What do I do with Bouchard?"

"You won't touch the boyfriend?" Cass asked.

"No." He paused with a pained look. "Rosalie can handle that one. She knows that if she's seen with him, the townies will dismiss her alpha claim. She cares too much to take that risk."

"He's still in town," Griff reminded them. "Mrs. Mercier dropped by earlier to check on the house and she asked us about him being here. She wondered what you thought of that?"

"I think nothing of that," Ren replied in a huff. Which was not entirely true.

He hated the fact that the good doctor was the one

who she probably wanted in her bed. Hells, even if they did get around to consummate this joke of a marriage, she'd probably fantasize about him.

Dr. Beaumont was everything Ren was not. Well dressed, college-educated and more, someone who helped others, saving lives. Ren hadn't missed that the women of Briac Falls, young and old, were all over him earlier at the wedding reception.

He tugged at the plaid shirt he'd slid on before heading out of his cabin in the dead of night and dug the heel of his work boot on Justin's deck. He had stopped going to school at the age of fifteen, learning everything he needed from life experiences, more interested in setting fur traps with his father, and later running the woods with his companions to trade goods with the First Nations.

It was a hunting expedition that had sealed his fate. When an incensed mob of new settlers had attacked their camp, his pal Pierre had not survived. And Ren wouldn't have either if it hadn't been for Joseph-Marie Gauthier and the Domaine-Lassalle Pack.

Fucking narrow-minded humans. Mom had been long gone by then. But as soon as the group of newly debarked colonizers had heard the words "witch's son" while gathering for a drink at Mag's inn, Ren had been a target.

He was the only St-Amand brother on the premise that night—Mag had already retired for the evening—there for one last whisky before heading into the woods with his friend Pierre to set new traps.

The cowards had been too scared to confront him on the spot and instead had marshaled in a small raiding party that had followed them into the wilderness for days until the surprise attack.

Burn the witch! they'd heckled into the frigid night.

Ren tightened his grip on the beer can at the memory of the horror they'd unleashed on him and his best friend.

Ren's grief and shame at his failure to protect Pierre had haunted him ever since.

And now, he had to do good by his oath to Joseph-Marie and his descendants. He would take care of Charles Bouchard properly.

He'd seen the envy in the big shifter's eyes. That wolf hated the Gauthiers. Rosalie's rival would not let it go. He could really kill her to become the next alpha.

"I need to deal with Bouchard," he told his brothers.

"Let's do it then." Cass stood from his deck chair, ready for action.

"We could go to his place now." Griff stayed put but mulled over the suggestion. "Impress upon him what will happen if he hurts Rosalie. He'll see that there's not just one immortal he has to deal with."

"Not yet," Ren stopped them.

"Why not?" Cass sat back down and crossed his arms at his chest.

"If we beat him up, we prove his point. That Rosalie can't defend herself and that she needs us to do her bidding."

"The pack has a problem with our family?" Cass asked, still unconvinced.

"The majority don't care," Ren explained. "I get along well with some of them, even the younger ones. Like Nick, Don. Max. When that supernatural hunter came to town in the spring and Justin and Emme got rid of him, the locals were grateful. That damn scum had shot Max with a silver arrow and taken Mrs. Mercier hostage here at the Chateau."

"LeGall?"

"Yep."

"Have you seen that psycho since Justin turned him?" Cass asked. "Is he still alive?"

"Don't know," Ren said. "He's a vampire now, so he's

in hiding. Nick saw some animal carcasses left behind in Beaver Woods. He thinks he found the bastard's cave."

Cass shook his head. "You should all have left him for dead."

"Well, it was Emme's decision in the end," Ren justified. "I bet she left the scumbag alive because of Justin. He was freaking out."

"Justin? Not the type to freak out."

"He's never killed a human." Ren took another slow sip of his beer, remembering the look on his scholarly brother's face after Justin had drained LeGall to the brink of death, showing that when someone threatened those they care about, the St-Amands were predators at their core.

"Neither have I," Cass commented.

"Well, I have." Ren winced.

But not in time to save Pierre, he reminisced, again clutching his beer can tighter at the pain of the tragedy still rattling his bones centuries later. The righteous group of settlers had been after Ren. And Pierre had paid the ultimate price for being his friend.

But he *had* been avenged. After Joseph-Marie Gauthier had nursed Ren back to health, he had found every single one of his friend's murderers and enacted his own justice.

"Griff?" Cass turned to their brother. "Have *you* killed anyone?"

"No comment." Griff shot his brother a dark look.

"Right," Ren said. "One day, you'll have to tell us all you've done."

"You'd have to get me drunk," Griff teased with a chuckle.

"We can't get drunk," Ren pointed out.

"But at least we got sorcery skills," Cass snorted. "Ren, do you still practice Mom's magic?"

"Oh hells no." Ren's connection to witchcraft had seen

his best friend killed. He left the spellcasting to Val and Justin. And there was no real need for it here with the pack. "You?"

"I dabble," Cass replied. "Griff?"

Their brother murmured something under his breath and flicked his hand at the collection of lit candles on the balcony's accent table. The small flames started to flicker and dance before growing into a shimmering ball of twirling fire. The sphere rose in the starlit sky as it expanded in size.

As Griff casually lifted his finger, the apparition coiled and rearranged to develop a scaly head and sharp talons until a fully-formed golden dragon appeared above them. The majestic glowing beast spread its wing wide and took flight over the mountains.

Griff turned a satisfied smile to his brothers and crushed the beer can in his other hand. He dropped it at his feet before forcing his conjured dragon to dissolve into a spray of sparkling light.

"I'll take that as a yes," Cass grumbled at Griff's obvious magical talent. He nodded to himself and turned to Ren. "Do you need my help, *frère*?"

"No." Ren cut the discussion in the bud.

"You won't make Bouchard see reason?" Cass insisted.

"Not right now. I can't get in Rosalie's way." Ren leaned forward in the wrought iron chair with resignation. "She has to make that call."

"And she won't?" Cass asked.

"I doubt it," Ren groaned. "She's more the diplomatic type."

"Really?" Griff said. "People at the wedding reception said she was a decent fighter."

"She might be," Ren noted, "but honestly, most people see it her way. There was a lot of bloodshed in the eighties. And her mom got killed in that coyote raid ten years ago. It hit everyone hard. People don't want that kind of violence here. It could start an all-out civil war if we just go in and beat Bouchard up."

"So, you'll let her fight?" Griff asked.

"*Calvaire!* No." He jolted with dread at the idea of Rosalie facing that brute in combat. "I'm the one who should fight this trial. I'm the Gauthiers' protector, not just her husband."

"Shit, man," Cass suddenly lifted a concerned brow as he set his drink aside. "This is your wedding night. Shouldn't you be with her right now?"

"I'm sleeping on the couch."

"Dude." Cass shot him a pained expression.

"Yeah," he rasped as longing took hold of him.

His breathing deepened and he imagined how he could slide between his sheets next to her enticing body and explore every curve he should be calling his. Take her as she cried his name in the depth of passion.

"So, you haven't…" Griff started. "Never?"

"No." He cleared his throat and dug his nails into his palm, not wanting to discuss the matter further.

"Don't you want to, though," Griff said. "She's quite attractive."

"Dude, she's his wife."

"Well, apparently not," Griff retorted.

"Not in that sense, no," Ren huffed.

"Why the hell not?" Griff picked the crushed can from the deck and passed it to Cass who had started to pick up the empty drinks.

"Well," Ren started, "first I barely know her. And second, she has a boyfriend."

"Ex," Cass corrected, dropping the dead beer cans into the brown paper bag marked with the logo of the Fortins' grocery store.

"Whatever," Ren said.

"So, you two will just like, live together. But…nothing?" Griff asked.

"That's the plan," Ren acknowledged. "This is a fake marriage. We'll just divorce in a couple of years."

"Fucking messed-up plan," Griff smirked.

"Yeah." Ren shuddered with discomfort. "My cabin is pretty small."

"Years?" Cass said.

"Oh, I don't know," Ren grumbled. "Until she wins over the pack."

"But years living with a stranger in that tiny space," Griff countered, "how is that even supposed to work?"

"I don't know." Ren shrugged hopelessly. "I haven't thought that far."

"Man, that loyalty of yours will be the end of you," Cass noted.

"I don't want to move somewhere bigger," Ren huffed with restlessness, "but we might have to."

"At least build up the cabin," Griff suggested.

"Maybe." In fact, that was not a bad idea. Something to keep him occupied.

Ren shrugged some more at his brothers, and with a deep exhale, he took in the emerging dawn. She was down there at the bottom of the mountain, in his personal space. He couldn't ignore her.

"I should go back." Resigned, he shook his head.

"Yeah, bro," Cass stated. "This *is* your honeymoon."

"Yep." Ren rolled his eyes, wondering how that morning conversation would go. "Some honeymoon."

CHAPTER 5

*I*t took her a minute to realize where she was when she opened her eyes. The early morning sun poured through thin bamboo blinds, and she remembered. She was not in her apartment in Toronto and not in her childhood bedroom at her father's. This was Ren's cabin and she had woken alone, in his bed.

Right. What now?

The whirring of the fan by the bed reminded her they would have to install A/C—the summer air already stifling at daybreak. Perhaps as an immortal he didn't feel the change in weather, but as a wolf, she did. She would need to talk to him about it.

She fidgeted with the ring set at her left hand. So here she was, married.

Strangers, but definitely joined as a couple under the Almighty.

Jumpy, she stretched her muscles twitching with nervousness, speculating on what to do next.

Despite her mixed feelings, she would have to make this a good day. She leaped from under the thin cotton sheet, her naked feet meeting the hardwood floor. The room was spotless but stark. A bed, chest of drawers, and an old wooden chair with a plaid shirt draped over the back, that was it.

The outside wall looked like it'd been erected from logs centuries ago. She bet Ren had raised his cabin himself. There was no doubt from his strong build that he had worked with his hands his whole life.

She mused over when he had finished this place.

A hundred, two hundred years ago? Sometime in the eighteenth century, she recalled. Old Simon, the postman, loved to talk about the legendary days when her ancestor had found the immortal barely alive in the woods behind her family's property.

Despite its age, like many ancestral homes in their small town, the cabin was sturdy enough to withstand the worst of their winters. And Ren had taken the time to add modern touches like plumbing and electricity. She noticed the rudimentary heater boards along the wall and smiled.

He'd surely be okay with air conditioning.

Her husband was a stranger, and she chewed over how they'd settle into a life together. They had to fool the town, so she had no choice but to stay here.

There was no doubt both had blindly followed her dad's request without much thought on the actual logistics. Dad was reassured of her safety now, and with his precarious health, that made her happy. But what about tomorrow, next week?

How was today supposed to go?

Ren seemed easy-going enough, and certainly loyal to her family, but they couldn't spend the next couple of years with her in his bed and him on the couch. They needed a plan.

She surveyed the area as she discarded her sleep shirt to put on yoga pants and a sports bra fetched from her small suitcase. While tidy and functional, his surroundings could do with a little joy. Some color. If she invited people over, they'd expect tokens of a happy marriage scattered in their home.

Flowers would be a good start. She would gather some wild ones after her morning run.

As she sat on the bed to lace her sneakers, she pondered how much more she could make this place hers. They needed cheerier surroundings, but she wasn't sure how he'd take her input.

It would be awkward and unpleasant, but a good talk was what they both needed. They'd discuss their living arrangements and figure out how to deal with Charlie.

She'd known her rival all her life. He would have to concede. He liked to boast in front of people, but if she could just talk to him alone, he would see that he did not need to fight her to the death and take over the pack to achieve his deep-seated desire for status.

Maybe lowering Ren's involvement and the immortals' ties to the pack would be enough to keep him satisfied. Charlie liked his money and thrived on success and making deals. If she could help finesse the land agreement with *Bois-Franc Village* so he could build his dream golf club for tourists and lord it over them all in that space, he might drop his alpha claim.

Yes, that should work.

But first, let's deal with Ren. She took a deep breath in anticipation of meeting with her new husband.

But as she stepped into the living room, she found it empty.

Her heart fell to see her pillows neatly arranged on the couch, with the pretty magenta blanket folded on one of the cushions.

There was no sign of him.

Barely sunup and he was gone. No coffee on, no signs of breakfast. She noticed the beer half drunk on the living room table and questioned if he'd actually spent the night or had left.

A bit disoriented after he'd informed her there would be no wedding night, she had quickly retired to his bedroom. Drained from the nuptials and finally free of the heavy bridal gown, compounded with the confrontation with Charlie and the shock of seeing François, she'd fallen sound asleep as soon as her head hit the pillow.

Weary, she furrowed her brow at the unexpected complications of yesterday. She would have to deal with those two men as soon as possible. But first, she needed to find her husband.

She stepped onto the back deck and was met with the cheerful sound of the river and the morning chatter of the birds. She walked around the porch to the front of the cabin hoping to find him.

But his truck was gone. Just like that, with no explanation.

Dang it, he could have left a note.

She sighed with frustration, taking in her solitary jeep in the gravel parking spot. She felt clammy under the shaded deck. This would be another scorcher. She'd better get on with her run before the heat worsened.

Getting the endorphins going would set her day right.

Trying to push away all her problems to later, she took off at a leisurely pace on the dirt path leading back to the main road crossing into the forest of Domaine-Lassalle.

Her racing mind wouldn't stop.

She wondered where Ren could be. It was too early for hanging out at Alcide's Tavern, or even visiting her father at home.

Her heart seized. He hadn't been so rash as to go find Charlie, had he? Damn, that would wreck everything.

She really didn't know him. And she *had* to rectify that. As soon as her run was over, she'd make breakfast and text him. This was their honeymoon. Not a traditional one, granted, but they needed to take the time to know each other for people to believe it was real.

She'd seen the canoe tied to the small dock by the river. Maybe they could go for a paddle later, or coffee in town, or even just sit on the porch and take the time to figure something out together.

She continued to pound the gravel of the dirt road, her pulse fast but regular. The familiar scent of honeysuckle rising in the warming air filled her with hope for the day ahead.

She was just about to take the next turn toward the road when a massive white truck screeched to a halt right in front of her.

She stopped mid-step and caught her breath. *Oh snap!* The glistening new paint and jacked-up tires were unmistakable. Charlie.

He stepped out of the vehicle, two of his gang—his cousins Tom and Hubert—following behind him. Hubert was swaggering his barrel chest while Tom shot her an eerie leer.

"Where's your bodyguard, alpha girl?" Charlie licked his thick lips as he rolled his overdeveloped shoulders in the too-small company polo shirt.

A sick feeling overcame her, making her overly conscious of her bare stomach below the sports bra. When had Charlie turned so creepy?

"I'm not the pack's alpha yet." She squinted cagily at him. "My dad is."

"And so it should be," he boasted. "Women don't become alphas."

"You forget Nicole Desmarais." He should need no reminder of the woman who had led the Val D'Or pack when her son Rémi had been a child.

"She didn't last long," he grunted at her.

"But under her rule there was peace and prosperity." She exhaled deeply to settle her hammering heart and heard the motor of another vehicle behind her.

She glanced back to see a run-down Chevy Blazer come to a full stop. This was the Lamberts' truck.

The door opened to a skinny pale form in frayed shorts and white socks. Yep, Julien Lambert.

"This little girl looks lost," he said in that nasally voice of his while his pal Danny Fortin stepped out from the passenger's side.

"Want us to help you find your way, missy." Charlie advanced toward her with a chuckle.

Her gut slowly tightened. She was trapped on the road between the vehicles, the five men circling her.

"I'm good, thanks." She jutted her chin at him.

"You don't look so brave when your dad and cousins are not around. Or your *husband*." He chortled on the last word. "Alphas stand alone under threat, *fille*."

"What are you saying?" she spat back. "Is this a threat?"

"Could be. If we need to." He rolled his shoulders again, cracking his knuckles one after the other.

"Tom," she addressed one of Charlie's cousins. "We did our homework together when we were ten. Would you really hurt me?"

"That was a long time ago, Rosalie." Tom smirked, still eyeing her up and down. "Things have changed."

"Oh really. What about you, Danny," she asked the Fortins' son from the general store. "My dad helped your father rebuild your house when you guys had that big fire, doesn't that count?"

"That was your dad."

"And what about your sister?" She turned to Hubert. When Noémie Bouchard's small Toyota had been hit by a construction truck on the highway to Montreal, Rosalie had visited her bedside almost daily to offer comfort.

Hubert looked at her blankly with his pug face and said nothing. She remembered how grateful he'd been the day his sister was released from the hospital. Thanking her profusely for her help. It'd been the reason she had wanted to pursue nursing.

"That's not enough," Charlie crowed, dangerously closing the distance between them. "Look, sweet pea, I don't want to kill you. For old-time sakes, let's say. But you got to back down from the alpha claim."

She pursed her lips at the command. Her blood started to boil under the menace, and a low growl rose from inside her as her wolf nature coiled in self-defense.

"It's not my call," she seethed under her breath. "My dad decides."

"You'll die, Rosalie," he doubled down with less furor but the threat was still unmistakable in his tone. "And I don't want to kill you."

"Right," she smirked. "Not a good look, is it? Killing the alpha's daughter."

"They like me as much as they like you." He waved a hand in dismissal.

"It's not a question of liking." Maybe she could help him back down. He couldn't be that driven to hurt her. "It's not a popularity contest."

"Oh yeah, then what else is it?" He was back to posturing, thrusting his wide chest at her.

"Leadership. Taking care of our town."

"I can do that just fine. Right, boys?" He grinned at his pals.

"Really? You'll sit with Old Simon when he gets gloomy about his time in the military? Organize the *épluchette* fundraiser with the *Fermières*?" she countered, mentioning the huge corn shucking party the pack hosted every summer.

"Oh fuck that," he barked. "See, that's the problem right there. When have wolves been about baking sales? You belong in the kitchen, Rosalie. If your freak husband can't keep you there, we will."

"Yeah!" Julien Lambert shouted after him, his bare scraggly forearms tensed with zeal.

Charlie's four men advanced toward her again, Tom wetting his lips and staring at her chest. "She needs to be shown, boss."

She shuddered. Tom had always been a perverted jerk.

"Yeah. She doesn't get it," Julien said, his small beige canvas shoes kicking dirt.

"Come on, cutie." Tom somehow managed to get close enough to grab her ass and she smashed her arm back to strike his hand off.

"Ow!" he screeched. "That hurt, bitch!"

Her heartbeat had ratcheted higher. Epinephrine raced in her blood vessels.

Her senses turned keener, her muscles rearranging as her body called the wolf inside her. She stood ready to squat, just like her aunt Camille had trained her to do at her Wolf Kung Fu studio.

It'd been a while since she had sparred with anyone, but she was prepared to fight. They would not see her back down.

She was still in human form but not for long.

"Oh boy, is she shifting?" Julien scoffed, looking at Charlie with excitement as he swung his skinny legs into some sort of martial art stance.

Charlie snickered at her. "You really think your little wolf can take all of ours?"

Goddammit. She surveyed her surroundings for an exit.

There were the two trucks and five men—Charles and

his two loyal Bouchard cousins, that annoying Lambert guy, and Danny Fortin who looked at her then back at the others with hesitation. He didn't seem ready to hurt her.

She would go for Danny first. He might not fight her back and she could take off through the woods and run all the way to her jeep. She was fast enough.

She prepped herself to settle in a crouching fighting stance, ready to bend low to the ground with one leg extended in front of her, waiting to see if anyone would make good on their threat.

"I'll go last," Charlie was scoffing. "Tom, you want her, right?"

"Uh-huh," the sick creep replied.

"You gotta know who's boss, *fille*." Charlie rolled his neck with a crack before nodding at Tom. "Sorry but it's not personal."

"Come on, sweetie. No one has ever complained," Tom leered. "I'll be gentle."

"I won't," Julien said with a weaselly snicker.

Tom didn't wait and lunged for her, grabbing her wrist.

She plunged low to the ground before leaping up in the air. Swiveling in a full half-turn, she jammed her extended leg down right across his forearm as she landed.

She heard the crack as he howled with pain.

"Bitch!" Tom screamed. "My fucking arm!"

"Well, that's it!" Charlie roared and swaggered forward.

Damn. Her muscles remained still for a second. No one had shifted into wolf form yet, but they were ready to beat and rape her.

Except maybe Danny. He still looked unsure. He was her way out.

She was about to bound and topple him when the skid of tires on the road made everyone stop and freeze.

Everything after that happened in a blur.

A menacing form soared over Charlie's vehicle, slammed two of his gang on the way and the next thing she knew, her brand-new husband stood before her, with Charlie in a chokehold against his chest, his fangs already deep in her enemy's throat.

Blood splattered on the shiny white truck. The other shifters were motionless, their jaws dropped. Tom cradled his broken arm to his chest with a dazed expression.

Goddamn! She bolted to Ren and shoved him hard in the shoulder, trying to get him off Charlie.

"Ren, stop!"

But the immortal kept Charlie secured at the crook of his elbow. Both were matched in height, Ren's sinewy muscles against Charlie's burly shoulder.

The wolf's body jerked back as Ren siphoned his blood, his jaws dug deep into the hefty neck.

"Why?" Her husband leisurely lifted his lethal fangs from his prey, his bearing deadly, the blood of her attacker dripping along his chin. "Takes no effort to finish him. Your problem gone."

For a moment, she wished she could let him do just that. But killing Charlie and his gang would not go over well in the village.

These were not some strangers attacking her.

All of them were people she knew from childhood. She knew their moms and dads, their extended families.

"Charlie." She approached her rival and eyed him harshly. "You got to let your claim go."

Her foe said nothing. He blinked a few times under Ren's grip. His reddened face remained filled with rage.

Her heart sank. There would be no diplomacy now. She might actually have to fight him.

"You just made everything worse," she told Ren with a huff.

He shot her a look so dark that she flinched back. Oh

hells. He had just saved her and here she was, criticizing him.

Damn it all, making everyone happy would be the hardest thing she'd ever done.

Being the pack's alpha would not be easy.

"Let him go. Please." She cast Ren an insistent look. He was acting like her sworn knight in shining armor, and she had no idea what to do with that. "You and I need to talk."

CHAPTER 6

"What's there to talk about? You nearly got gang-raped!" Ren angrily paced the cabin's back deck.

People would now be glad to see that fucker dealt with. Why was she making things so damn complicated?

Fresh from the shower, she was toweling her damp hair and looking at him with a thoughtful air. Barefooted, she wore a small blue cotton top above frayed denim shorts, the tiny straps at her shoulder revealing the white lacy bra underneath. Her face, devoid of makeup, was dewy from the muggy heat.

"We have a lot to talk about." She shot him an accusatory frown. "First, where were you this morning?"

"Does it matter?" He stopped marching to stare at her with a blank look.

"Well, yes. I woke up and you were gone." She shook her head with impatience. "No note or nothing."

He leaned back on the banister of the deck. "Were you worried?"

"No, but we're in this together," she insisted. "That's what being married means."

"Together." He narrowed his eyes at her, thinking about what that actually meant.

"Yes." She dropped her towel on the deck chair and waved her hand at him, making her diamond shine in the late morning sun.

"You want an account of all my movements?" He frowned, frustrated. "This is not a real marriage."

"Has to look like one. You said so yourself!" she countered. "You could have left a note or a text."

"I was at Chateau Briac. With my brothers," he grumbled. "But what about you, though? You were alone in the woods, an easy prey to those power-hungry idiots."

"I still can't believe it." She wrapped her arms under her chest, the lift of those sexy curves prompting a surge of lust deep within him. "They were really about to attack me."

He exhaled slowly to curb his rising desire. Her distress made his heart melt. "Rosalie..."

She looked at him and he saw anger in her gaze, not fear. She favored negotiations but she was also strong as hell.

"Bastards," she muttered under her breath.

"*Calvaire.*" He seethed, his duty to her returning full force. "I should have drained him raw."

"A century ago, maybe. But now?" she disputed. "The others might back down. But if words get out that you murdered Charlie, it'll bring the *Sûreté du Québec* police to town. And you can't just kill everyone threatening me."

"The police don't bother us," he said.

"The regional authorities don't. Something else I'll need to deal with. Dad is tight with Captain Akande, but she has to report to her superiors if things get out of hand." She chewed over that, mentioning the sensible officer of the SQ Montreal-Laurentides region. Akande gave a wide berth to supernaturals as long as they remained on the right side of the law. "I have to assure her there will be no trouble when I take over."

She rubbed the back of her neck and, with strain visible at the corner of her eyes, took a seat in the Adirondack chair facing the river.

Drawn to soothe her, Ren crouched down to her level to reach for her hand. A mix of desire and protective feelings rose inside him at the touch of her soft skin. "They could have seriously hurt you, Rosalie."

Her face turned grim. "I was about to shift."

"They would have, too. Even in wolf form, could you really take the five of them?"

"I'm not a weak little flower," she insisted.

"You're not." He smiled fondly at her resolve. With her chestnut hair damp and down to her shoulders, her face natural, she looked vulnerable. But there was a determination in her that didn't go unnoticed.

"I'm their alpha. I really am." She parted her lips slightly and unwelcome cravings shot straight down below his belt. He bit the inside of his mouth hard to repress it. Going there with her right now would be all kinds of complicated.

He nodded. Alcide had faith in her. He had to trust his current alpha.

And there was no denying that she was standing her ground when he got to her earlier. She would have fought.

But for how long?

He stared at the smooth, tanned legs below the frayed hem of her shorts, dying to trace the shape of her thigh with his palm.

Horror crawled down his spine to think they would have touched her—worse, *violated* her.

Sinking his fangs in that scum Bouchard had felt good.

He really should have gone all the way. Bleed the bastard out.

He'd ended a few wolves during the eighties war and later had gone with Alcide after the punk coyotes that had killed Rosalie's mother in that cowardly attack in the middle of the night.

But Rosalie was right, it had been a while since the pack had seen any violence.

As if reading his thoughts, she said, "It won't look good if you rough up Charlie for me. He is well-liked by some. And they wouldn't respect that he had to be taken down violently without a proper combat so I could take over."

"He promised to kill you."

"He's just hot-headed." She shook her head, casually dismissing the threat. "I've known him since we were kids. He hasn't gotten over your brother giving him a beating in front of everyone at Dad's tavern."

"It wasn't pretty." Ren chuckled, momentarily distracted from Rosalie's predicament, as he recalled how Justin had left Bouchard beaten within an inch of his life. So out of it that his minions had to carry him out of the bar.

"So I heard."

"Justin said he was bothering Emmeline."

"His wife?"

"Yes. She might be a deadly vampire, but my brother has a weird sense of loyalty. He had to step in."

She smiled. "Didn't you do the same today?"

He shrugged. "Maybe."

"The St-Amand brothers…" She pondered with a raised, amused brow.

"What?"

"Oh nothing. You've all been alive for what? Hundreds of years?"

"At least three hundred and fifty," he grumbled.

"Long time." She nodded to herself, and her gaze turned inward as she considered the difference.

He patted her hand once more before letting her go to sit in the deck chair beside her. "First wolf I met was your great-great-great-something-grandfather."

"Joseph-Marie?"

"Yes."

"The elders say he saved you."

Ren agreed. "He did."

Had Joseph-Marie not known to bury Ren deep in the soil of Beaver Woods when he'd found him unconscious, still tied to the tree and burnt beyond recognition, Ren would have desiccated into nothingness, a living corpse for eternity.

"So now you're stuck marrying me because of it."

He burst out in a low laugh. "Stuck is not quite the word."

"Then what *is* the word?" She peered over at him through her lashes.

"Honored." He held her gaze steadily. "I have the honor of marrying the future alpha of the Domaine-Lassalle pack."

"You make us sound important. We're just a small town."

"Maybe, but in the world of wolf-shifters, your family is highly respected."

"Because of Dad."

"Yes. He manages to rally together not just the Val D'Or pack but also the Great Lake Boreal and the Laurentian Timbers. Even those crazy hardhearted Labrador shifters."

"And now, *I* have to do that, too," she stressed.

"You worry about it?" he asked, genuinely concerned.

She stared at him, deep in thought. Then as if she'd decided to trust him, she admitted, "I do. I don't know if I'm up for the job. Sometimes I think my cousin Max would have been a better choice."

"Because he's male?"

"There's that. But I did leave Briac Falls for college." She crossed her strong legs, making his heart race with lust again. "Three years, things have changed. I should have stayed here."

"You wanted to become a nurse," he said, carefully keeping his desire in check.

"I wanted to help. Three years is all I would allow myself away from the pack," she explained. "I actually really wanted to be a doctor, but it would have meant years away from here."

"A doctor, huh? Like your boyfriend."

"Yeah, him." She seemed lost in thoughts once more. His heart fell that she did not correct him and call the man her ex. She had to still be in love with the worldly city physician.

"So maybe you're right. We do need to figure stuff out." He leaned toward her. A tingling teased his senses as he caught her captivating clean scent again. "The attack is one thing, but there's us."

"Us?" She jerked her head back. So he *was* ready for that conversation.

"Yeah, you and me. What do we do? We're married." He was unable to tear his gaze from her. "You want me to report to you when I'm not around?"

She winced. "I'm not your boss."

"You are. A little bit. You'll be my alpha."

A slow smile lit her face. "You really see yourself as one of the pack, don't you?"

"I do, yes." And he was. He'd seen the comings and goings of all these wolf-shifters for decades. Had hunted alongside the Gauthiers, but also the Beaulieus and Pelletiers. Hells, even the Bouchards. Charlie's ancestors were not as pigheaded as their descendant, that was for sure.

"You're my husband now."

"That I am." His grin was getting broader by the minute as warmth expanded in his chest.

He couldn't remember a time when he'd actually enjoyed the company of a woman as much as now. Her gentle presence had a soothing effect on his usually grim disposition.

"You can't be sleeping on the couch forever."

"I only have the one bed," he pointed with amusement, leisurely stretching back on the wooden deck chair in the midday sun.

"We could share."

"Is that a proposition?" His brow rose as he became strongly aware of his racing pulse. His mounting hunger for her would not leave him.

"We could *sleep* in the same bed. It's big enough." She had emphasized the sleeping part, while his mind—and body—went much beyond that. He wondered if he could actually lay beside her without wanting to take her in his arms. And more, cup her waist and spread her wide. Sink himself into her sweet curves, take her over and over as she bucked against him and panted with pleasure.

He let out a slow, controlled breath to ease the tightening in his pants.

"Maybe." He choked on the word. So much for his habit of sleeping naked.

"And we could do couples things," she added with eagerness. "Show ourselves in town together."

"Couples things?" He could only think of one couples' activity he'd want to do with her. *To* her.

"Oh, I don't know. Dining out, maybe? Or go on a

hike. Bring a picnic to the falls. You know, like newlyweds do on their honeymoon. People will expect something romantic."

"A picnic?" He tilted his head to the side with surprise at the suggestion.

Her face fell. "It's a bad idea, right?"

"No. It sounds great." His heart turned lighter suddenly, and he felt compelled to be truthful. "You're a very pleasant person to be around, Rosalie."

"Pleasant?"

"And attractive."

She said nothing but her skin flushed under his appreciative gaze. If he could actually break through her composed and friendly attitude, she might eventually see him as more than her bodyguard.

Maybe they *could* make this marriage real in the physical sense. Before the time came for him to divorce her.

There might be something there. Their union could eventually turn into more than just a duty to the pack.

Hells, they'd have to share a bed for a while, at least until he built an addition to his cabin.

A light-headed feeling emerged inside him, and he suddenly wanted to do all those things with her, picnics and drives down the country road, take her along the river and up the mountain. He'd never been the wine-and-dine type but why not? Taking the time to woo her would be worth it.

He yearned to get closer to that nurturing streak she possessed. Get to know her fully.

"We could go to the swimming hole today," he suggested, mentioning the rocky flats below the Briac Falls cascade where people liked to hang out in the summer. "With this heat, everyone will be there."

"A swim! Yes, that's a great idea. It's so freakin' hot right now."

Oh god, he hadn't analyzed this through. His way of rushing into things without thought was becoming a problematic habit. A swim meant her in a swimsuit. He wasn't sure if seeing more of her bare flesh would be good or bad. Would he be able to control his powerful desire for her sexy shape?

But damn, his body just couldn't say no to seeing her wet and free, frolicking in the local lagoon.

He leaned back, trying to appear casual. "It will be good for your claim, the locals seeing you there with me."

"Good point." She rose from her seat with excitement, tying her hair up in a high ponytail. Her tank top lifted with her movements to expose her bare waist and he had to tear his eyes from her to control his lust.

"There's only one problem," he said.

"What?"

"Your boyfriend. He's still at Mrs. Beaulieu's B&B." He hoped she'd just send the guy packing with a quick call.

"Right." Her arms fell to her side. "He's my ex, remember?"

"He doesn't seem to know that." Ren smirked, pleased to hear her finally addressing the man as a former partner.

"I need to talk to him."

"You have to do it soon," he insisted.

And he admitted that there was something else bothering him. Ren just didn't like the competition sticking around.

Since he had finally decided that he could no longer ignore his pangs of lust for Rosalie, and that, *calvaire*, they were married, he was set on seducing her.

But that could not happen with the ex-boyfriend hanging around.

"Fine," she relented. "I'll have him meet us at the falls. I'll talk to him there."

"Sure," he grumbled, frustrated.

Here he'd thought a carefree afternoon would loosen the tension between them. But he'd just made things worse by reminding her of the bloody boyfriend.

He thought of his brothers' earlier suggestion with a grim smile. He couldn't just kill the guy now, could he?

CHAPTER 7

"*H*ey Rosalie. Ren!" Her cousin Max called out to them from the busy creek's shore as she ambled over from the parking lot where they had met her ex. Ren and François were walking along at each side of her. "I can't wait to see you kick his ass."

"Ren's not fighting Charlie, Max," she told him while scanning the area for a shady spot to hold a heartfelt conversation with François. The heat was torrid, and her ex looked uncomfortable in his light-colored linen suit and button-down.

The Briac Falls swimming hole was packed with locals taking the afternoon off to escape the swelter, from the middle-aged in casual T-shirts and shorts to the bare chests and bikinis of the younger crowd, many inked with artwork chosen in tribute to their wolf's nature.

She caught friendly waves from most people, and downcast looks from a few others.

"Fight?" François turned to her with a frown. The whole thing was awkward.

"I'll explain later." She leaned uncomfortably toward him.

She had sympathy for her confused ex-boyfriend, but here in her hometown, it was obvious that her relationship with the doctor was doomed even without the arranged marriage to Ren. It had made sense in the big city, but not here. He was an amazing, compassionate physician but not the type who could have easily assimilated with the pack once she'd explained what her kind truly was.

She hadn't been keen on dealing with François in front of the town, but she wanted their difficult misunderstanding resolved as soon as possible, at least for Ren's sake.

"I was talking about you, Rosalie," Max continued. "You will fight, right?"

"What, not you, too?" She stopped mid-stride in surprise. "You want me to fight Charlie?"

"Isn't that what alphas do?" he said. "Plus, Mom said you can take him. She didn't train you for nothing."

She wrinkled her brows with disquiet, wondering if she hadn't been too rash in the church when she'd publicly agreed to a combat with Charlie. People were now actually anticipating it.

"Rosalie?" François leaned in toward her proprietarily.

Ren groaned beside them.

She rolled her stiff neck with frustration. This was a right mess.

"Look, Max." She stared at her cousin with as much confidence as she could muster. "There will be no fight. Tell everyone."

"But—" he protested.

"No buts," she snapped before skimming the area again.

She noticed the Mercier brood at a picnic table. The grandkids were in their swimsuits, chomping on thick sandwiches and washing them down with lemonade. Mrs.

Mercier waved at her, and she waved back at the matron, forcing a cheerful smile.

"Check around you, Max." She relaxed her stiff stance. "No one wants this fight."

"You'd be surprised, coz," Max countered. "I think some expect it."

"Rosalie, can you please explain what's going on?" François asked, with a brittle laugh hiding his uneasiness.

"Village business," Ren spat, his irritated tone surprising her. "This has nothing to do with you."

Oh boy. She shot him a quieting look and smiled warmly at François, racking her mind about how to best deal with this. What had seemed simple on the deck of Ren's cabin—with the mid-morning sun and cheerful bird-songs—was now turning into a nightmare.

"Rosalie," François insisted, "what's this about you kicking someone's ass?"

"I'll explain," she said.

She narrowed her eyes to Max. "I will handle Charlie." Still rattled by the confrontation on the dirt road earlier today, she was no longer sure how. "But not his way. You'll all have to trust me."

"Maybe." With a raised brow, Max nodded at Ren who had returned to being silent. "The fact that you have *him* doesn't mean you don't need to prove yourself."

"I will. I promise." She exhaled slowly as Max gave her shoulder a supportive pat before he turned to join his brother Don and their pals, Nick and Matt. The squad of wolves loyal to her family was lazily taking the summer sun on a large blanket by the water amid a few local women, humans and shifters alike.

Winning over the locals might take longer than she thought. Max was family, he and his boisterous crowd might not require an actual fight, but they would need something from her to prove she was worthy.

Maybe she could convince Mrs. Savard to sell her old property in town so Nick could expand his motorbike shop. That would earn her his full support. The flower store had been closed for a year and Nick had been attempting to buy the place for a while now.

"I don't get any of this, Rosalie," her ex interjected again, glancing around the townspeople for an answer. "I thought you were here just to help your dad after his heart attack."

"Look, François. We did split up," she reminded him, trying to be kind. "You shouldn't be here."

His face fell and her heart broke. She cared for him. Truly. She didn't know what to say to make things easier for him.

She glanced at Ren. His features were stoic as he watched François. The man had lived for centuries. She wondered if he found her predicament merely amusing, or if he was annoyed that her ex was here with them.

They were married, and he came from a time when arranged marriages were common, with women having little agency.

Although, she reminded herself, wolf-shifter females had always exerted their power. But not many had become alphas. She only knew of Nicole Desmarais in Val D'Or who had briefly led alongside her son a couple of decades back. And there was no denying that there was a time not too long ago when brute force was all that mattered to the pack.

"Let's talk." She gently took François by the arm and motioned to a quiet area farther back from the water. "Ren, you mind?"

"Not at all." He grinned a half-smile and she cringed. He was obviously not upset but entertained by her predicament.

Of course, the mighty immortal probably thought little

of the city-dwelling François. But she did. The man saved countless lives in the ER every single day and she had seen him cool under tremendous pressure.

But this here, her town, would never have been a place for him. She cast a glance at her best friend Caroline Mercier distributing small bags of chips to her young nephews and nieces. The healer with the magical craft, Caro was the type who was needed here.

Someone who could deal with wolves and was not afraid of a little spell or potion.

Most people went to Caro now that her *grand-maman* Mercier had gotten old.

As a nurse practitioner, Rosalie was hoping to become her friend's partner. The next line of care with her modern clinic if Caro's magic required more traditional medicine.

As she led François to the shade, with Ren following closely behind, a few locals accosted them. They all wanted to ask about Charlie, but she stopped them with a shake of her head. She owed it to François to end things right.

"Not now," Ren cautioned the bystanders, acting as the staunch bodyguard.

François looked more and more confused but kept it together.

"Here." She sat on a flat boulder under a fragrant pine tree and patted the top to invite him over.

She watched the kids splashing each other under the cascade next to the giant Briac waterfall, letting her gaze linger on the small bubbles floating away at the surface of the clear water pool. The smell of tree bark was mixing with the coconut scent of sunscreen lotions, the familiar summer fragrance boasting the courage she needed to explain herself.

Ren stood further down, daring anyone to come talk to her.

"Your husband." François dipped his chin at him while

sliding the sole of his leather shoe on the carpet of pine needles at their feet. "This is really weird."

"It should be," she said gently. "It all happened very quickly."

"Why didn't you tell me you were getting married?" His expression turned slack. "Were you two an item while you were in Toronto?"

"No, I wouldn't have done that to you." She looked at the rings on her middle finger, the large diamond still feeling foreign on her hand, wondering how much to tell him. A clear and clean break was the simplest. "Look, François, you're a great guy."

"But you're not into me," he said with a grim twist of his mouth.

"Kind of." She winced.

"So you just moved back here and married this…" He glanced up at Ren in his plain jeans and white T-shirt, who stood guard, his chiseled body hinting at the warrior he truly was. "Stranger."

"He's not a stranger," she told him. "Look, you might as well know. We can't tell anyone but…"

She had to come partially clean to François. They had wonderful memories together. She didn't expect him to still be around in ten years like Ren suggested, but she did owe him part of the truth.

"It's an arranged marriage," she added.

"Arranged?" He shot her a look of disbelief. "Are you forced into this?"

"No." She smiled. "Nothing like that. It's just fake. Politics are weird here. My father is sort of the mayor of this town."

"Sort of?" His brows furrowed deeper.

"Yes, like I said, it's complicated. He's officially a councilman of the county. And now with his heart attack, it's too much. I need to take over."

76

"You need to get elected in his place?"

"Yes, elected." She didn't need to reveal that the election was actually a wolf-shifter coronation ceremony held at the next full moon.

"Why the arranged marriage, then?"

"People really respect Renaud. Dad thought that me being married to him would help me gain everyone's approval."

"Why didn't *he* run?" François gave a small shake of his head. "Why does it have to be you?"

She thought about this for a moment. Why *did* it have to be her? What if she let Max take over? He was a strong shifter. He had survived the silver arrow of a supernatural hunter not too long ago. He was family. He would be able to take down Charlie.

She pressed her lips together. Would his heart be into it though? As much as hers was?

When he was not working at Nick's shop, Max liked to hang out at the tavern and ride his motorcycle with his pals. Hunt through the seasons and drive his skidoo in the winter forest. Would he think about the school that needed fixing? And the water supplies that had to be surveyed regularly. Or make sure people like Charlie kept their real estate businesses up to code for the safety of the locals?

Brawn may be required within packs but how about dealing with the outside world? Dad had both. And so did *Grand' Pa* Gauthier. In previous generations, they'd been able to keep to themselves, but now? They were more and more connected with the rest of the world. And there were the others. They had just made an alliance with the Order of the Black Oak, with its witches, warlocks, and daemons. This all needed someone with a diplomatic mindset.

"I'm the best person for the job," she finally told François with quiet determination. She knew she was right.

Not in a brash, defiant way, but with serene certitude. The village was her calling and they needed her.

"Who's this Charlie?" François inquired with concern etched on his forehead.

"Oh, just my rival." She shrugged. If Max would not be a good leader, Charlie would be a terrible one. He'd been known to cut corners with his business dealings and the confrontation this morning in the woods made it obvious that he would always be fists first. It wouldn't take long before he'd drag the pack into some unnecessary war.

"And you have to *fight* him?"

"Max's just kidding," he said casually, trying to make light of the situation as she hid the truth. "I have to beat him at the polls, that's all."

"Oh," her ex's breath eased. "It sounded much worse."

François was too perceptive. She had to get him out of Briac Falls soon.

"Look, François," she started. "You have to understand, my life is here now."

"I was told you're setting up a clinic in town."

"Yes, I am. I never meant for us to happen." She let out a slow exhale. "But it did. I'm sorry."

"I thought you really did like me." His plea cut straight to her heart.

"I did." Fondness warmed within her as she recalled their first few dates—nice restaurants, movies, a musical. "I still care for you, but not in the way you deserve."

"I intended to propose." His voice cracked on the last word. "I truly thought you just needed a break from us because of your dad's health."

Oh mercy. Married to the empathetic doctor instead of the aloof immortal. She wondered what that would have been like. A completely different life. Companion to a selfless physician, opening her own practice in the city. Maybe for children. She'd always been interested in pediatrics.

There'd be no coronations, and vampires, and pack of wolves who wanted to assault her.

She sighed wistfully.

But she was a gray wolf-shifter of the Domaine-Lassalle pack. And she liked who she was.

She was a Gauthier. And that spelled duty. Caring for the people here.

"I'm truly sorry, François." Her features softened as she lightly touched his arm. "This was not meant to be."

"Do you actually love him?" He tilted his head to the side, his eyes dull. "Even a little?"

She stared at Ren, in a firm posture a few feet away, and a turmoil of emotions rushed inside her. He had saved her earlier and was now respecting her space. He was her father's most-trusted friend. The pack's strongest ally.

He was a constant presence here. Solid and silent—like the million-years-old polished boulders surrounding the lagoon—he had always looked the same.

While she'd cared about François for his compassion and warm-hearted disposition, she couldn't quite guess Ren's temperament. He was so closed in, so contained, never letting anyone in. Could anybody love someone like that?

"I don't know," she finally told François truthfully. "It doesn't matter. He *is* my husband now."

"You truly are a different person here, Rosalie." François straightened his spine, seemingly understanding that they were clearly over.

"I am." She nodded, and in the process said goodbye to the carefree college student she had been for a few years. Now was the time to grow up. Take on her responsibilities to her family, to her pack. She firmly rubbed her bare thighs and tapped the heels of her sandals on the uneven ground.

"We could have been happy together," François said in one last appeal.

She gave him a regretful smile but didn't answer.

"I better go." He stood and brushed the dirt from his summer suit.

He was indeed handsome in a city way. She recalled seeing him rush into the hall in his scrubs, stethoscope at the neck, barking orders at the staff to save a young girl who had come in with a crushed spine from a car crash. He really would have made a fine life companion. And maybe she had loved him.

But she couldn't.

She cast a quick glance at the people enjoying the summer by the lagoon and felt the strong kinship run through her blood. She was giving François up for something important. Them. And she *would* fight for them.

"Yes, it would be best you leave." She stood to give him a light hug. "You take care of yourself out there, François."

"You, too." He returned her embrace before reluctantly letting her go to take the path in the forest back to the parking lot.

She was watching his silhouette disappear behind the pines when a scent of male strength mixed with clean aftershave diffused over to her.

"You okay?" Ren lay a palm at her shoulder, his strong bicep flexing below the T-shirt sleeve.

"Yes, that life is over." And though she knew she had chosen the right path, a piece of her was sad at the loss.

Loud music suddenly erupted from the bushes and they both turned to witness Charlie and his gang emerge in the clearing.

"Oh snap." She watched her enemy roll his wide shoulders as he approached the local crowd and started to shake a few hands, a broad smile plastered on his lips.

His cousin Hubert was dragging the noisy speaker on

the ground while Julien Lambert carried an oversize case of sodas. His cousin Tom rounded the rear with Danny Fortin.

"Rosie, did you hear?" Max's brother Don rushed to her side. "Charlie is taking over the corn shucking party this weekend."

"What?" She frowned with irritation at how her aggressors had assaulted her earlier and were now mingling with everyone as if nothing had happened.

Don had no time to answer before Charlie called her out. "Hey, little alpha!"

Her challenger stopped in front of her, coolly dressed in khaki dress slacks and a dark green polo shirt. He extended his hand to her with a pleased grin. "You must have heard. Bouchard, Inc is sponsoring our annual *épluchette* this year."

Ren rested back on his heels next to her with a closed-in look, silently studying her opponent.

"The *épluchette*? Why you?" The corn shucking party was always run by the *Cercle des Fermières*, a group of locals whose mission was to preserve their artistic and cultural way of life.

"You were right earlier." Charlie shrugged. "This town needs more from their leader than fighting. They also want a good time. My enterprise will bring them that. I hired a band and everything for the day. Tickets are all on me this year."

"Really?" she exclaimed. "That's a lot of money to spend, Charlie. This is a fundraiser to get a new roof for the senior center.

"Oh, don't you worry about that," he chuckled. "I just straight-up donated the money. My crew will take care of hiring the work."

"Isn't that generous of him?" Mrs. Lambert, the owner of the town's real estate agency, approached them, accepting a free can of soda from her rival. "I have misjudged you, Charlie. You truly did turn your life around."

"I did." With a serious look, he took in the locals standing nearby. "Clean living, healthy body, healthy mind. My business is thriving. I want to give back now."

Rosalie was stunned. There was no hint of the creep who had assaulted her this morning in the confident entrepreneur, except for the cold, calculated undercurrent that only *she* seemed to be able to perceive. And dammit, would he ever had thought of the *épluchette* if she hadn't mentioned it to him earlier?

"You wait and see, sweet pea. I have something for everyone!" A smug grin was plastered on his wide face as he presented her with a free drink. "Apart from the band, we'll have a biergarten and gambling tents, food trucks, vendors as well as a giant bouncy castle for the kiddies. I hired a firm to handle every detail. It's going to be a whole lot of fun for all!"

Her clamped jaw ached at the list of promised attractions. Charlie was now crossing into her territory.

She may not have his physical strength, but her power resided in her genuine care for the people here. She was good with them. And had counted on that to win their approval.

She tightened her fists with frustration. There was little she could do to counter money and a good time!

CHAPTER 8

*A*s soon as Caro opened the door of her cottage a
few hours later, Rosalie felt her restless heart settle.
She hadn't intended to visit so close to her wedding, but
the events of the last two days had her rattled and she
needed her girlfriend.

"Hey, Rosie." Caro hugged her against her willowy
body, a clank of silver bracelets accompanying each of her
graceful movements. Her fragrant scent of lavender and
sage was something Rosalie had missed dearly when she
was away.

Caro had stayed here after high school to study the
traditional healing craft under her *grand-maman*, the town's
elder, and was now the official *guériseuse* of the village.
They'd been tight since their first day of preschool.
"Where's your husband?"

"He's with Dad. Helping with the backlog at the
tavern." Her stomach, which had been churning with
anxiety since she'd met Charlie and his gang at the swimming hole, finally eased in the warm atmosphere of her
friend's home. "Your house is so cool compared to outside,
did you decide to get A/C installed?"

"No need." She winked at her. "It's all magic."

"For real?" She bent down to pat Moira, Caro's little black cat who was rubbing herself at her ankles.

"Hey, you learned how to reset bones and diagnose skin rash," she quipped. "We Merciers do it our way."

"Nice." Rosalie noticed the altar to Caro's ancestors in one corner of the living room. A multitude of lit candles flickered in the cool air. Bookshelves packed with ancient tomes lined the wall and a soothing harp melody chimed in the background. The small display of glimmering fairies dancing above the fireplace was something else. The tiny figures swirling amid cute little mushrooms and butterflies were definitely not from this world and held all the signs of an enchantment. She'd been aware of Caro's grandmother's healing talent, but this magic was entirely new. Rosalie admired Caro's skills.

"You've learned a lot since I last saw you."

"The Ice Witch visited a few times." Caro covered her smile with one hand, obviously pleased at the experience. "She taught me a few things."

"Ren's mother?" Rosalie hadn't been around Ren much, but she knew all about his background. His mother was a powerful immortal sorceress originally from somewhere in Europe.

"Yes. And Maisie Thibodeau, you know, the wife of Ren's brother Val, was here a few months ago."

"The White Holly High Priestess," she recalled. "Dad told me Justin St-Amand lost his vision in a fight and you two brought him back."

"Maisie did all the work. I've never met someone so dedicated to the craft. Poor Justin, Mom was beside herself."

"Oh right, she's the housekeeper at the big house." Chateau Briac had always been there at the top of the mountain. The pack lived in the village and the St-Amands owned part of the land outside Beaver Woods.

If she remembered her history correctly, it may have been how Ren had found himself being chased by a righteous mob into wolf territory hundreds of years ago.

The whole thing made her skull ache again and she pursed her lips with weariness. She absentmindedly picked up a small leatherbound book off an end table beside the couch and flipped through the pages. The compendium was filled with sketches of dragons. Each one was more stunning than the other, but did little to hold her attention, which was wrestling with uncertainties.

She dropped the book back on the side table. "Caro, I don't know how I'm going to pull this off. Being the alpha and all."

"Come into the kitchen, *fille*," Caro cooed. "I have some tea that may help your nerves. And you can tell me all about it."

Rosalie followed her friend padding barefoot in a light-colored gauzy dress toward the large kitchen at the back. The distinct smell of warm sweet pastry overpowered the subtle herbal and flowery air.

"Have a seat right there. I just baked." Caro turned on the kettle and selected a few dry flowers from her collection hanging from the ceiling.

She crushed various herbs under mortar and pestle while Rosalie's gaze settled on the stack of cupcakes layered on a tiered serving plate. They were adorably pretty, decorated with silver sugar balls and pastel icing.

"These look good," she told her friend.

Caro shrugged with modesty. "I was trying to figure out what to make for the *épluchette*. I know they like their beer and corn, but the kids, they might like something sweet."

"There's no *épluchette* this year." Rosalie plopped herself at the sturdy table in one of the wooden kitchen chairs by the window. She stared at Caro's vegetable garden through the lace curtains, feeling the fatigue seep into her bones.

"What do you mean?" Caro's head flinched back a notch.

"I mean that scum Charlie is sponsoring the night. Instead of a family bonfire, we're getting a band and gambling tables." She grimaced.

"Really?" Caro paused with her hand over the teapot.

"Yep." Her throat closed with frustration. "Look, I can win people over by making sure every single person is catered to, the charity social was one way to do that. It was good Aunt Camille could help when I was gone, since our family always collaborated with the *Fermières* to throw the event. Now Charlie is taking over. He's fighting on my turf."

"He truly wants to take on the leadership." Caro frowned with concentration as she poured boiling water into the teapot, casually mumbling a few foreign words in what sounded like a magical incantation.

"Dad calls him a dimwit but he's smarter than he looks." She gave Caro a pinched expression.

"When you left, he was just another drunk, dealing dodgy deals and barely hanging on to his father's business." Caro selected a few cupcakes and carried them to the table on a serving plate. "But since getting clean, it didn't take long for him to turn things around. He brokered one big deal last month that brought in a lot of cash."

"I saw the new truck." She shuddered at remembering the attack this morning.

"Oh, right, his pride and joy." Caro brought over the tray with mugs and the steaming teapot. "He paraded it into town for days after he bought it."

"And his gang, what's up with that? When did Julien

Lambert and Danny Fortin start hanging out with Charlie Bouchard? It's not like them."

"The gym. You know how these jocks are. When Charlie joined Gabe's gym and started mouthing off about Ren and his immortal brother, that was it. They're young wolves, Rosie, they don't like feeling inferior to the vampires."

"We're not inferior. Immortals don't see us this way."

"Oh, most people know this, but when the professor came down and beat Charlie up, it rattled quite a few of the younger ones," Caro informed her. "They never really minded Ren because he keeps to himself but Justin's a scholar, tweed, glasses, and all. It didn't look good for Charlie to be overpowered by him like that in front of the whole town."

"I see." Rosalie absentmindedly helped herself to a cupcake.

"Charlie couldn't accept that. He got clean and started to get followers."

"Dad never mentioned anything to me."

"Your dad wanted you to finish college without worrying about the locals for a few more months. You were so set on your program when you left."

"I was. It seemed easy then. I did it for the people here. I wanted to help. I know your family has always been our healers, but your grandma was getting old."

Caro nodded as she poured the tea. "We need traditional medicine here as much as we need the Merciers' gift. It's great that you're basically a doctor now."

"But I also have to be the alpha."

"Wasn't that always in the plan?" Caro reached out to touch her arm with empathy.

"Not really. I think we all vaguely assumed Liam would eventually take over."

"He's young," she acknowledged.

"Yes. He's a good kid, but he's all about video games and figuring out how things work. He hasn't had his first shift yet." Warmth expanded in her chest as a protective feeling for her little brother rose inside her. "Maybe when he hits puberty it will change, but right now, he dreams of working for NASA and going to space."

Caro blew over her steamy drink and nodded a few times with understanding.

"And Delphine, well," Rosalie continued, "not only is she also a girl but she's too young and doesn't have the temperament."

"She told me she wants to move to Montreal and be a fashion designer," Caro said.

"And she'll do that. I have no doubt," Rosalie attested. "She can be extra but there's a will of iron under that drama queen act."

"A family trait."

"Huh?"

"I've never met anyone more stubborn than you." A twinkle appeared in Caro's eye.

"You think I'm stubborn?" Rosalie tilted her head, somewhat baffled.

"Oh yes, so much so you forget your own well-being." She motioned toward the untouched cupcake and mug. "Drink my tea, it will settle you."

Rosalie dutifully took a sip, finding the piping-hot liquid strangely soothing. Caro was the only one she trusted to see her not fully in control of things. Maybe her friend was right—she *had* run herself down lately.

"Ever since your mother died, I've seen you take care of everyone else."

"I have to. They're too young." She closed her eyes for a second. Liam had still been an infant when her mother had been brutally killed. Rosalie had had no choice but to take over her responsibilities.

"And your dad?" Caro's features softened.

"He was heartbroken." She pursed her lips with sadness at recalling how her father had retreated behind a hard façade for months.

"But it was his job to take care of them, of you all," Caro insisted. "And if not him, you had your aunt Camille."

"She did her part. It was not easy for any of us then. Mom was so good at this, thinking of everyone else."

"Like you do," Caro maintained.

"Hey, you do the same." Rosalie smiled at her friend who, alongside her grandmother, had taken care of so many villagers since she was a teen.

"Maybe," Caro mulled over. "But I wouldn't marry a stranger for the sake of my family."

"Oh that…"

"It's the twenty-first century, Rosalie. Don't you think it was too much to ask of you?"

"I genuinely thought Dad was dying. It terrified me."

"You're not truly in love, right?" Caro asked. "I mean Ren's hot and all. And most people in town believe you two are head over heels for each other, but I'm not fooled by it.

"No," she conceded. "I don't love him. It was all Dad's idea."

"So, you did what he asked without question?" Caro slowly shook her head in disbelief.

"He asked me to marry Ren to protect me as I become the pack leader," Rosalie forcefully defended her father. "He knew I would get some opposition. And he was right, look at Charlie and his followers. He wants to fight me."

"To the death," Caro winced with sorrow.

Rosalie shrugged, attempting to be casual about it. "I don't know if he actually would do that."

"I heard he cornered you this morning." Concern

shadowed Caro's gaze and she reached for Rosalie's forearm again.

"How did you hear that?" Rosalie frowned, still shaken by the morning's attack. "We haven't told anyone."

"Danny Fortin told his sister, who told my mom." The corner of Caro's eyes softened. "My mother is furious. She says what happened to you is unforgivable."

Rosalie exhaled. "Ren was there in time."

"Good for him," she nodded her approval.

"Dad was right," Rosalie acknowledged.

"You do need protection," Caro pointed.

"I don't know. I mean, I know if I shift, I can hold my own." She took another deep breath and fiddled with the handle of her mug. "But fighting Charlie?"

"Yeah. That would be tough." Caro agreed with a slow dip of her chin. "What if you just let him take over?"

"What do you mean?" The pitch of her voice rose a notch.

"What if Charlie becomes alpha?"

"Yikes." She took a small sip of her tea while shuddering at the absurd idea. "Well, first, I would let my family down. Generations of Gauthiers."

"After all you did for your siblings and father, would it be so bad if someone else took over instead of you?"

Not Charlie for sure. Rosalie tried to imagine what would happen if Charlie and his creepy followers took over the town. How would her rival and his men treat her young brother?

"We obviously can't have Charlie in charge," she said, her upper lip stiff with resolve. "He would train all the young wolves to fight. Dad and Ren have kept the peace with the other packs, like the Val D'Or and that cagey Labrador pack up north. Charlie wouldn't be happy just leading our town, he would challenge Rémi Desmarais. I don't want my little brother to be forced to fight a war no one wants."

"You're right," Caro chimed in. "That man is obsessed with being popular."

"And he doesn't care. Look how he treats his old grandmother," Rosalie added. "Last I saw she's still living at the *Jardins du Domaine*. Charlie's family owns that seniors' residence. It's so run down;, it's a death trap. He wouldn't be taking care of this town like I will. I can do this job, Caro. I will do it well. It has to be me."

"But you can't fight him and win." Worry lined Caro's forehead.

"Maybe if I train more." If she faced him in combat, she would only battle him, not his whole gang like she had this morning. She had a chance to win. "Aunt Camille will help me."

"I have a better idea." Caro rearranged her cheery teal placemat on the table before narrowing her eyes at Rosalie. "Did you and Ren…"

"What?" Rosalie frowned.

"Last night. It was your wedding night."

"He slept on the couch." She huffed. A hint of sadness hit her out of nowhere.

"Oh."

"Look Caro, it truly *is* a fake marriage. We're just roommates," she cringed. "You should see his place. For someone who has lived for centuries, he hasn't collected anything of value. He's like one of those stoics. There's nothing there."

"Really?" Caro laughed. "I bet you rectified that quickly."

"No kidding. The place needs some comforts."

"And he let you," she chuckled some more. "I'm just picturing this now, the manly man Renaud St-Amand surrounded by quilts, furry pillows, and scented candles.

"Why not?" Rosalie shrugged with a smile, recognizing that she might have been overbearing with all her stuff. "He's actually really nice. He's trying to make it easier on both of us."

"Then maybe you should do it."

"What?"

"Sleep with him," Caro said. "Don't tell me you don't think he's hot. Every girl I know wants a taste of him. I know that's weird, but even my grandma eyed him in her days."

Her jaw slackened. The thought of *Grand-Maman* Mercier hankering for Ren was too strange for her.

Of course, the man was hot. But in her fear for her dad's health, his appeal hadn't really impacted her choice to marry him.

"Here's the thing, Rosie." Caro leaned closer in a co-conspiring tone. "I did a lot of research on this and consulted with *Grand-Maman* after Charlie threatened you on your wedding day."

Rosalie frowned at her friend, not liking where this seemed to be headed.

"If you sleep with him," Cara added, "you may actually imprint on him. You two would be fully mated."

"Mated?" She jerked her head back. "But that hasn't happened in a really long time."

Her Gauthier grandparents had been mated—a soulmate connection bestowed to wolf-shifter couples by their patron goddess Selene. With the influx of newcomers, the magical bond was now dying down and the blessed gift between younger wolves was rare.

And Ren was not one of them. Caro's idea was nonsense.

"I know how to make it more likely to happen. In fact, I made this for you, just in case." She stood and stepped to her kitchen counter before returning with a small silk sachet tied with red and purple ribbons. She pushed the charm below Rosalie's nose. "Put this under your pillow and get on with it, seduce him."

"Why on earth would I ever do that?" Shocked by her friend's suggestion, she carefully took the charm bag from Caro to examine it, the scent of dried roses rising to her nostrils. "I barely know him. And I don't think he's attracted to me. He married me to help my father. And why would I care if we could ever become soulmates?"

"Because once you're mated, your true alpha powers will come in. And that, *ma chère*, that's how you beat Charlie."

CHAPTER 9

*R*en watched Rosalie push through the door of the tavern in the middle of the afternoon. The place was quiet under the large whirling fans doing little to beat the heavy heat. Two towny kids were sipping cold wine coolers and playing pool. Old Simon nursed a frosty beer at the counter while Alcide leaned on the other side of the bar to hear stories from Old Simon's time in the Air Force.

She paused at the entrance, nodded curtly at him before walking to embrace her dad and gracefully take a seat on a stool beside the elderly postman. Her expression was pure empathy as she listened to him, patting his forearm as he went on.

Ren's heart expanded with appreciation. She was good for the people here. Her patience was endless. What would it have been like to have her by his side after he'd lost his friend Pierre to a mob of despicable humans?

As always, his gut tightened at the tragedy that had drawn him to live here.

He'd had Rosalie's ancestor to rescue him from the horror, his steady presence had brought Ren back, both physically and mentally. The burns all over his body had taken months to heal. His soul, though, that was something else. He would never forget the shock frozen upon Pierre's face as he was impaled by the pitchfork. Or the silent plea for Ren's help as he drew his final breath.

The cheers of their attackers still resonated in his mind two hundred years later.

He closed his fists tight to cast away the pain and focus on his bride.

Alcide had opened a cold soda bottle for her, and she was smiling at something Simon had said. The poor man was so lonely now since his wife had passed. He had no children to look after him. Where Ren had had Joseph-Marie Gauthier, Simon and the rest of the town now had Rosalie.

She was the rightful leader of this pack.

He wondered if he'd have been able to voice his torment to her as he'd recovered from the attack. Maybe. He'd always kept his emotions close to his chest, but here, there was a part of him that was drawn to her nurturing streak.

He groaned as her slim bra strap fell off her shoulder, dredging up all sorts of unfamiliar feelings inside him. He couldn't help but notice the swell of her breasts in the blue tank top matching her denim shorts.

She was his to protect and yet, his hands were tied.

He cursed under his breath. He should have drained Charlie on the spot when the bastard had ambushed her. The wolves would let it slide, wouldn't they? Charlie had attacked her, the heir of the Gauthier line.

Ren had assisted alphas since 1775 but had never been on one side of any sort of civil war. They'd skirmished with other packs for territory but never within their own.

He leisurely scanned the quiet premises again. He took in the brand-new mirror behind the bar and the polished counter, all replaced by Pelletier's construction company after the explosion that had nearly killed his brother a few months ago. The establishment was like a second home to him. He'd seen it grow from a trading post to the friendly neighborhood joint that it was now.

He had planned some days off from his usual place at the back of the establishment to get to know her and help her settle into their new life, but after she'd been rattled by her encounter with Charlie at the lake, he'd gently suggested that she pay a visit to her friend Caro. The healer might make her feel better. He'd said he'd swing by to check on the tavern and wait for her there.

His senses dulled with longing at watching her return the lacy bra strap over her shoulder. Not comfortable with emotions, he had no idea how to help work through the run-ins with Charlie.

He could maybe take her to *Bistro Laurie*, the only fancy restaurant in town. It was her honeymoon after all, and the wining and dining might make her forget her problems for the night and help them get to know each other, away from exes and rivals.

At least it would make people believe their union was real. He'd approach her with the suggestion when she was done with Old Simon.

He was reaching for his beer when a clash of glassware had him bolting from his seat.

Rosalie had dropped her drink and, white as a sheet, was staring into her phone.

Ren was at her side in a heartbeat. "You okay?"

"Dad!" Distressed, she shoved her screen under her father's nose.

Alcide stared at her device, his fists tensed. "Oh shit."

"What?" Ren frowned, his heart racing.

Tears welled in her eyes as she turned the phone toward him.

Fucking hell. His muscles quivered with mounting anger. It was a picture of her ex, the doctor, bound and blindfolded in what looked like someone's barn.

"Charlie," he spat.

"That punk." Alcide pushed the sleeves of his work shirt past his elbows, grabbed the baseball bat behind the bar, and walked around the counter. "You stay here, Rosalie. I'll go get your friend."

"Dad, you can't." Rosalie took a deep, controlled breath. "Your heart. No, he wants to meet me. He says so in his text."

"Oh hells, no!" Ren barked. "You two stay here. This is for me to deal with."

He watched her spine straighten and her lips purse as she stared at the picture of her captive boyfriend. There was a true feral undertone below that empathic, caring nature. She was entirely ready to confront her rival.

"What's going on, *ma p'tite.*" Old Simon had picked some of the broken glass from the floor and looked at them all with deep concern.

"Simon, it's Charlie," she told him, the distress in her tone unmistakable as she helped him clean the remaining glass shards. "He kidnapped one of my friends."

"That Bouchard kid is trouble, always been." Simon shook his head before grabbing a bar towel to mop the spill at their feet. "Someone should just walk him out of town."

Which was exactly what Ren intended to do. Not just walk him out, but so much worse.

"You can't get involved, Ren." Her brows knitted with resolve as she took the damp rag from Simon and passed it to her dad. "Charlie is clear on that. He wants me."

"What does he say?" His fangs prickled under his tongue. He was ready for action.

"He asked to talk with me," she said. "He's visiting his

grandma at the senior's residence and wants to meet me there. He said he'll let François go after we talk."

"That punk just wants to see you freak out," Alcide seethed, his features bunched in resentment as he hurled the towel into the bar sink.

"You're not going, are you?" Ren said.

"I have to." She gave him a pained look. "He'll hurt François if I don't."

Her distress pinged at his heart. She cared deeply for her city doctor.

"I'll go with you," Ren insisted. "It could be a trap."

"At the *Jardins*?" Alcide said with disbelief.

"He says if I bring any of you, Ren, Dad, or one of my cousins, they'll beat up François, break a couple of bones. That bastard's not thinking straight. How can he expect the pack to follow him after this?" She let out an uncontrollable moan and brought a fist to her mouth. "Oh my god, François must be so scared. He knows nothing about all of this."

Her anguish for her ex was obvious. Man, this business was a mess.

While she may be good for the town, the town was not good for her. She should have stayed in the city, married her doctor, and lived a life free of violence away from here.

Someone else had to take over from Alcide. Not Charlie, that son of a bitch. No, Ren had to drum some sense into her cousin Max. There was no reason why he shouldn't be their alpha.

Forget Alcide's wishes. As soon as they'd get the boyfriend back, he would have a talk to with her carefree cousin and have him take some responsibility for a change. All this was way too much for her.

He'd sign divorce papers and she'd be out of this mess. Back to the city with her Dr. Beaumont.

"I will go with you," he insisted, his tone measured.

With both hands gripping the side of the bar counter, her dad leaned in. "Take him with you."

"No, Dad," she maintained. "It won't look good if I need an immortal to visit an old lady at a nursing home. You trusted me to do this. I'll have to go alone."

"But he's your husband. That was the whole point of this marriage."

"And if Charlie wasn't challenging me, it would have been fine." She held on to her father's arm. "It was a good idea, Dad. But we got blindsided."

"Scumbag!" He slammed a fist on the bar.

"I'll go with you, *ma p'tite*."

They all looked at Old Simon, whose shoulders suddenly looked wider.

"The wolf in me still has a few fights," the elderly shifter said with a half-grin.

"That's not a bad plan," Rosalie agreed, looking at her father.

"Wait, no," Ren countered. "Sorry old man, but you're past your prime." He worried his old friend could get hurt.

Simon raised an ornery, bushy eyebrow. "Of all people, Renaud, you, here, know my skills."

They had fought side by side during the Wolf War twenty years ago and the veteran had been fearless. But he could barely make his postal rounds nowadays and was less than a year from retirement.

"I can at least watch out for her," Simon insisted. "Call you guys if something goes wrong."

"It's the only way if we are to come to an agreement," Rosalie added. "No one will blink if I bring an older gentleman with me to meet Charlie at the *Jardins du Domaine*."

"You're a good man, Simon," Ren relented.

"I'll take care of your little girl, Alcide." The old wolf

stood from his barstool as he reassured his alpha. "I swear I won't let anything happen under my watch."

Ren cracked a smile, knowing without a doubt that Rosalie would likely protect Simon instead of the other way around, but the idea of having him tag along was not a bad one.

No one would dare attack her with Old Simon there, the postman was the town's war hero. Everyone, even assholes like Tom and Hubert Bouchard, respected him. Charlie wouldn't risk that.

"Remember, your goal is to free your boyfriend," Ren insisted. "Forget your rivalry. Agree to any of his terms, just get him to release the doctor. I'll deal with Charlie later."

She nodded, the corner of her eyes tense, her amber pupils darkening by the minute. She looked both angry and anxious at once.

"The motherfucker," he snarled. "He won't get away with this."

She finally laid a steady palm on him, a resolute expression settling on her restless features. "I got this."

"And you, Simon," he addressed his old friend. "Don't go do something crazy. Charlie could very well kill the human if it serves him. He never cared much for them."

"You hear him, right, man?" Alcide added. "Don't you go think you still have your youth. You call us if anything goes wrong."

"Copy that, Alcide." The postman's spine was ramrod straight.

"Appreciate it, buddy." The taunt crevices of Alcide's brows relaxed.

The old man straightened his canvas jacket over his craggy frame. "Nothing will happen to you, *ma p'tite*. I promise."

"Thank you, Simon. I'm really afraid for François," Rosalie said. "I'm glad you'll be with me."

"You get some sense into that crazy Mrs. Bouchard," Alcide said. "Let that woman know her grandkid shouldn't be kidnapping innocent outsiders like this."

"I think she doesn't have much say in his life anymore," Rosalie informed him, "but it's worth trying."

"You be careful, kiddo," Alcide warned. His concerned tone told Ren that it wouldn't take a lot to convince him to let Rosalie live her life outside the pack. He probably knew by now that having her take over from him had been a wild plan from the beginning.

"I'll be at the top of the road. You call me." Ren laid his hand over Rosalie's bare arm, much too aware of the soft skin under the pad of his fingers. His heart raced at the idea that something could happen to her.

"It's the *Jardins*." She gave them both a grim expression. "How much trouble can we get into in a nursing home?"

CHAPTER 10

*R*en had no reason to believe Charlie would release the doctor, which was why this meeting at the *Jardins du Domaine* was the perfect diversion for him to act. After parking his truck up the road from Charlie's estate, he was now striding down the gravel path to the asshole's place with his brothers Cass and Griff by his side.

"Are you sure this is where they're holding him?" Cass cast a doubtful look at the compound spreading in front of them, the run-down bungalow flanked with various makeshift buildings, each one shabbier than the other.

"Yeah, sure. I think I recognized the old barn at the back," Ren informed him. "I was there a few times when his dad was in charge."

"And you needed us for this?" Cass chortled as they approached the barbed wire gate.

"Why? You have somewhere else you'd rather be?" Ren pushed the enclosure open as a mongrel dog tied to a pole in the front yard barked meekly at them.

"Not now. Hanging out with Griff is boring as hell. I miss Justin."

"He's not here. Plus, you talk too much," Griff snarked.

"What can I say? I like people." Cass casually shrugged.

"Then just go to Montreal for a bit."

"If I show my face there before the jazz fest, I'll be swarmed," Cass said.

"Where's your band?" Ren asked as he surveyed the perimeter. Despite the few vehicles parked on one side, the whole place was dead quiet, the summer breeze gently blowing the meager dry patches of grass around the property.

"With their families."

"Well, there you go, so are you." Griff chortled.

"They have girlfriends, wives," Cass countered. "Some even have kids."

"Yeah, we don't have those," Griff admitted.

"Mag sort of has a kid," Ren pointed out.

"That little Catalina? Nyssa's sister?"

"Mag would die for that teen." Ren shuddered at recalling how Cat had been kidnapped by daemons a few months past.

"He almost did," Cass reminded him, his tone turning wistful.

"And what, big star?" Griff snorted. "You want kids now? A picket fence?"

"See what I mean, Ren." Cass raised a knowing brow. "Griff is so bitter, he's no fun to be around."

Ren huffed. "Are you both here to help me, or bicker like two old women?"

"It's damn quiet here," Griff said, as Ren motioned them toward the cluster of outbuildings. "Why the backup, Ren?"

"If that doctor gets hurt while I try to rescue him, Rosalie will never forgive me."

"Is he her lover or something?"

"He was." He nodded, a ping at his heart. "Still might be."

"She cares more for a regular human than you," Cass said. "There's something wrong with that, bro."

"Nothing wrong with that," he said. "Why would she care about me? We barely know each other."

"Didn't you know her as a kid?" Griff asked. Despite being in the midst of the Bouchard's silent decrepit farm buildings, neither of Ren's brothers bothered to be quiet, too confident in their abilities to take down a few wolf-shifters if necessary.

"Not really," Ren said. Alcide kept his family away from his business. "I met her once or twice when she was in high school."

"Yet, you married her," Cass said. "This is truly a fake marriage."

"Yep." He pursed his lips as they peeked into an empty building filled with farm equipment.

"You're weird, you know that?" Cass said.

"Why?" Ren turned a puzzled frown to him.

"You're a freakin' immortal and you've lived with wolves since the eighteenth century," Cass replied.

"*Lived* is the key word here," Ren explained. "I wouldn't be alive now if it weren't for Joseph-Marie Gauthier. And I would forever honor my oath to him, to protect him and his line of descendants."

"Burned at the stake, like a damn witch." Cass shook his head, empathetic to what Ren had gone through. "I still can't get over that."

"You wouldn't have died, Ren," Griff said. "You can't kill an immortal with fire."

"Well, smartass, how would you know? Have you ever been burnt at the stake?" Ren argued. "Not pleasant, I tell you. They had to bury me deep into the earth to save me."

"You'd need angel blood to kill one of us," Cass said as they stepped into the next building, packed high with moldy bales of hay.

"Right." Griff scowled.

They were all well aware of that grim fact. Justin had nearly been killed with angel blood five months ago.

"I doubt Charlie and his gang have angel blood," Ren finally said. "The only sample I know of is the one we took from LeGall. It's in the vault at *Sanctuaire*."

Their friend Father Grégoire had taken the vial back to the nunnery where he spent his time rehabilitating the line of young vampires that had been sired by his brother's wife when she had been a soulless vampire herself.

"There's a whole lot more of the stuff," Griff said grimly.

"Where?"

"In a strongroom belonging to the LeGalls," Griff answered. Wrongly believing to be tasked by the Almighty himself to rid the world of supernaturals, the zealous European family of hunters were set on exterminating every single one of them.

"You've seen LeGalls?" Ren stopped in his tracks. Shocked by Griff's words, he almost forgot about Dr. Beaumont's rescue mission.

"In Budapest. Fought a few."

"And survived? Damn, Griff. That fucker nearly took both Emme and Justin. He could have been blinded for life."

"I had help."

"Help? *Baptême*, bro, did you meet other immortals like us?" Cass's jaw turned slack. He was as surprised as Ren. The revelation was astonishing.

Griff's lips were pursed. "I encountered Ambrus."

"What?" Ren and Cass both shouted at the same time, Dr. Beaumont now completely forgotten.

"Yeah. I was surrounded by a gang of hunters. He swooped in and took down all of them."

"You saw our *father*." Cass couldn't believe it.

"Our father was Papa Antoine," Ren corrected. But damn, he was shaken to the core. Griff had met their birth father.

"What is he like?"

Griff shrugged. "I don't know. He looked at me and said, 'The way you fight kid, you must be one of mine'."

"Just like that?"

"Yep."

"And then what?" Cass asked. "Did he explain what he did to Mom?"

Ambrus the Exiled had somehow seduced their mother centuries ago before she boarded the ship sailing to New France as a so-called King's Daughters—young women recruited by the French government to marry single male settlers and increase the population in the new colony.

Their adopted father Antoine St-Amand had fallen fast for the young woman despite her being pregnant by someone else. He had welcomed the sextuplet immortal babies as his own.

"Nah, he was casual, like, you know…" Griff replied. "Like he didn't care much. His aloofness reminded me of Mag. Told me he was my father, Ambrus the Exiled. And then he left."

"Damn."

"Yeah. It was a totally accidental meeting." Griff's jaw tightened and bitterness echoed in his tone. "I tried to find him after that but nothing."

"Doesn't make any difference to me." Ren proceeded toward a third building, a wide shed made of two-by-fours. "I don't really care for meeting him."

"Did you tell Mom?" Cass asked as he stepped behind him.

"No way. No one else knows. I'm telling you now."

"Shit, brother you could have said something earlier," Ren griped. "Not when I call you for a rescue party."

"It never came up before." Griff snorted.

"Right." Griff was always so goddammed unpredictable.

"Are we doing this, or what?" Cass asked.

"Focus, bros." Now weary of their banter despite the revelation about Ambrus, Ren wondered if he should have done this alone.

"How many vehicles were by the house?"

"I counted four," Griff replied.

"I recognize three," Ren said. "The rundown Blazer is Lambert's. The F-150 belongs to Hubert Bouchard and the green Kia is Fortin's car. I guess he's still under Charlie's thumb. That idiot."

"And that big new Wrangler?"

"Don't know," Ren said. "Not from around here."

"This place is dead as a doornail," Cass pointed. "You think they're all at the house?"

"Wait." Griff laid a hand on Ren's arm. He nodded toward the building at the far side. "I see someone's in front of that old red barn, must be guarding something."

"Black fatigues, T-shirt, submachine gun," Ren said. They retreated into the shed to examine the sentry further, still distant enough to be out of earshot. "Not someone I know."

"He looks like he's ready to protect a small kingdom or something," Cass snorted.

"He's hired muscle," Griff realized.

"Well," Ren sneered back, "that's how Bouchard sees himself right now. The would-be king. Not many people on his side yet, but they're warming up to him. If Rosalie backs down because they have the doctor, that's what this little village will turn into."

"What? An army?"

"Yeah. He'll start with wanting to lord over the Val D'Or pack. Then move to the Laurentian Timbers."

"You really know your pack's politics," Griff sneered.

"Hells, I've seen them rise and fall. Trust me, Alcide Gauthier is one of the best they've had."

"And his girl?"

He thought for a moment. "Better."

"My, so sure," Griff commented. "Damn, bro. You like her."

"She's a fine woman." His voice hardened, thinking of Rosalie's perfect mix of compassion and determination.

"No, I mean, you *like* her. That's why you're here, aren't you?" Cass noted. "That's why you called us."

"She doesn't need that punk Bouchard hurting her by taking someone she loves. The oath I took meant that I would protect her. I stand by that, nothing more."

"I don't buy this fake arrangement," Cass continued. "You're hot for her."

"Shut up."

"You think if you save the guy, she'll be grateful, she'll fall for you." Cass just wouldn't drop it.

Ren shot him a deadly look. "Cassiodore."

"Ok fine." His brother raised both palms in the air, finally backing down. "But I give it to you, it's not a bad plan. She *will* be appreciative for your help."

"Will you just let it go?" Ren warned.

"Hey guys," Griff interrupted. "I see some movement at the house."

Ren peeked out to survey the bungalow. "That's Tom Bouchard."

Charlie's lecherous cousin ambled to the bed of the F-150 truck to fetch a six-pack before hiking back up the shabby steps of the house. That creepy jerk. Ever since he'd grabbed Rosalie, Ren's fangs prickled with the strong need to pierce his flesh.

"I say we go see what's in the barn first." Ren was dying for action. "Looks like they're guarding someone, probably the doctor."

"Good plan," Griff agreed.

"What like, just barge in?" Cass asked.

"Let me check with Simon first." He took his cell out and pressed the postman's number.

The veteran answered on the first ring.

"Is Bouchard there?" Ren asked.

"He's on the porch with his grandmother," Simon replied. "We're about to meet with him."

"Ok, keep him there."

"Wait, why?" Alarm rose in the old man's tone. "What are you doing?"

"No time to explain. Just look after Rosalie, pal."

"Copy that, Ren."

He ended the call and slid his phone back into his pocket. "You're ready?"

Griff shrugged.

"This is fun." Cass's eyes lit with an inner glow. "Haven't had any action like this together since that time we helped Mag take down those mobsters after his club in the twenties."

"Come on, let's do this." Ren jutted his chin at his brothers, and they took off at lightning speed.

The military-looking guard had no chance. Ren had him in a quick choke hold before he could grab his weapon and he fell unconscious to the ground without a sound.

"Coyote," Ren spat, disgusted. Those damn coyote-shifters had no loyalty and hired themselves to anyone who could pay. They were the ones responsible for the unwarranted kill of Alcide's wife just days after peace had been reached between wolf-shifters.

"What do you think we'll find in here?" Cass slid the barn door open.

As his vampiric sight adjusted, he saw Hubert Lambert sitting on a dirty old recliner in front of a big TV screen. His short, stocky legs were stretched on an overturned crate, and he was playing a busy video game.

"Well, well, well," Ren sneered.

The moron seized, dropped his game controller to the dirt ground, and bolted to his feet.

Frozen with shock, he stared at them, his face pallid, the stench of cold fear unmistakable.

Ren slowly crossed his arms to consider Rosalie's assailant, his brothers on either side of him—Griff casting a dark look upon the son of a bitch, Cass's amused stare more feral than friendly.

"How did you get past the guard?" the idiot blurted out, his thick arms dangling uselessly at his side.

But Ren was no longer looking at Hubert. His gaze had been drawn to the captive in the back corner, surrounded by carcasses of dead animals in the hay. And it was not the good doctor he was staring at.

There in the dark, chained to a wall, with bloodshot eyes and gaunt limbs, was Jérôme LeGall—the former hunter turned into a cursed vampire by their own brother Justin.

CHAPTER 11

*W*hen Rosalie arrived at the *Jardins du Domaine*, she found Charlie sipping lemonade with his grandmother. It was just before dinnertime and cooking smells emerged from the nursing home. The pungent odor of heavy oil and onions lingered on the veranda despite the whirling blades of the two rickety fans creaking above them.

The whole building had seen better days, with its peeled paint and the missing boards from the deck were a real hazard. The front garden that had been the pride of the estate had turned into decrepit overgrowth since the Bouchards had acquired the place.

But with his brand-new pressed outfit and wide smile, Charlie could no doubt play the part of the upstanding citizen. And just like at the swimming hole this afternoon, there was no sign of her assailant in his appearance. He looked every bit the thriving business owner about to step into the political arena.

His dirt-brown eyes lit upon her as she stepped up the porch and, in an instant, his cold calculated gaze destroyed his professional image. He was still the same bastard.

Her fear for François brought on a surge of anger and she went on the offensive instantly. "Where is he?"

Old Simon was right next to her, his body tense and on the ready.

"Grandma, look who's here," Charlie sneered. "It's the little Gauthier girl."

"Which one?" his grandmother barked as she fumbled with the glasses that hung from a chain around her neck and attempted to peer through them. "The slutty nurse or the little tart?"

Ignoring the insult, Rosalie strode directly to them and looked down at him, shuddering with disgust at the thick fingers wrapped around the tall icy drink.

"Now, now, Doris," Old Simon said beside her. "Alcide's kids are fine children."

"Simon Tremblay, you crazy old fool," the woman snickered.

"Hello, Mrs. Bouchard." Rosalie had hoped to turn the old lady to her cause, but this was not boding well. She had forgotten that the woman could be a cantankerous old bat to anyone who was not her beloved only grandson.

"Charles tells me you think yourself good enough to be our alpha," the elder woman said with apparent indignation.

"Grandma, wait. Be nice. I'm sorry," Charlie drawled, his smile slimy. He gestured to a couple of rickety rusted lawn chairs facing them. "Please have a seat. Simon, good to see you, old man. How's the leg?"

Simon had none of it. "Better than yours if I had my way, punk."

Her composure regained, she patted Simon's shoulder a few times before sitting across from the Bouchard pair.

"Come on, Old Simon," Charlie said. "You know I turned my life around."

"I've seen you terrorize the town since you were a kid,

114

lad." Simon carefully folded his old bones into the chair beside her. "Seeing you beat up by Professor St-Amand after you assaulted his girlfriend was a whole lot of fun."

Charlie's features took on a ruddy tint. "That fucker."

Rosalie stared at Mrs. Bouchard to see how she'd react to the mention of the incident.

"Bloody vampires." The pink straw hat sitting crooked atop her stiff gray curls shifted with the shake of her head. "I'll be glad when my Charlie gets rid of all of them."

"Renaud St-Amand has been around my family for centuries, Mrs. Bouchard," Rosalie justified. "He's done a lot for our pack."

"Vampires don't mix with wolf-shifters and that's that." Her skeletal hands whitened as her grip tightened on her chair's plastic armrests.

"Your own son didn't think so, Doris," Simon said. "He fought side-by-side with St-Amand during the wolf war."

"Poor little Johnny, he was such a sad case. Weak blood, I tell you." She firmly readjusted her old hat. "Got it from my husband's family."

"Oh Grandma, don't be so hard on Dad," Charlie tried to mitigate her disappointment.

"Your dad," she griped. "Not a great role model, kid. Couldn't even keep his own wife from running away on him and got himself killed in that freak accident when you were eight years old. Such a disappointment. Thank goodness, you got good old Lambert blood, Charlie. My family is strong stock."

Rosalie thought of whiny little Julien Lambert tagging along with whoever would have him. That man had never had an idea of his own, even in school. But she was not here to discuss the Domaine-Lasalle pack families. She wanted François freed.

"Release Dr. Beaumont, Charlie." Her tone was icy. She was all for diplomacy, but kidnapping was not that.

"And why would I?" he cackled. "It got you rattled, didn't it?"

"Is that what you wanted?"

"Yep." A callous smile appeared on his lips.

Dammit, this would not be as easy as she'd expected. "Then yes, you got me. Now you can release him. He has nothing to do with you and me."

"He's human," Charlie scoffed. He leaned back in his chair, crossed one leg over the other, and took a sip of his lemonade through the plastic straw as if he had all the time in the world. "Pack members don't involve themselves with humans. Simon, tell me you get this, man?"

"Doris," Simon said. "Can you not get your grandson to back down?"

"I say he's doing the right thing." She raised a smug shoulder. "My grandson is exposing her for what she is. A human lover, heck, a *vampire* lover."

Rosalie flinched.

"Nothing wrong with mixing with humans," she corrected the old lady, her hands shaking with irritation. "The Merciers have been living among us for decades."

"Well, they have the magic gift, not the same," Doris Bouchard snickered. "I was told you left our town to shack up with some human doctor and came back to marry a rotten vampire. You're diluting our wolf-shifter bloodlines, girl. Why should we let you lead us?"

"Grandma is right, Rosalie." Charlie deposited his acrylic tumbler on the cracked glass table with a self-satisfied expression. "We can't trust you as our alpha. That's why I'm here."

"You're trying to convince me that your claim for alpha comes from the goodness of your heart?" She was flabbergasted. "That you care?"

"Of course, I care."

"Look at this place. Mrs. Bouchard," she insisted. "It

116

used to be lovely when my own grandfather lived here. Now that this building belongs to your grandson, he hasn't bothered with its upkeep. It's falling apart."

"Watch what you're saying, girlie." Mrs. Bouchard bent her gnarly frame forward with an accusatory finger in Rosalie's direction. "This is my home you're insulting."

"Nick's grandpa fell down the stairs last year." Fury was slowly rising inside her. "What about the fire escape on the third floor? It needs to be fixed. And the heat barely functions. Mrs. Savard's aunt was so cold this past winter, my dad had to move her to the old folks' home in *Bois-Franc Village*."

"Nonsense! Jo's a weakling." Mrs. Bouchard dismissed her arguments. "We just need to put on an extra sweater. Wolves have gotten so fragile in the last decade."

"We don't fight anymore," Charlie offered. "That's the problem."

"What?" She turned to her rival.

"Your father may have brought peace but now all the pack does is set traps for a few rodents." Charlie swung his shoulders around as if he was indeed ready to throw himself into a fight. "We're predators, we're meant to hunt and protect our territories with teeth and claws."

She rolled her eyes. "You don't get it."

"Really?" He leaned toward her in his chair and rested his thick forearms over his thighs. "You claim to be an alpha wolf-shifter and you're scared of fighting me. You should be ecstatic, looking forward to the kill."

"You're insane." She stared hard at him.

"No, I'm not." His zeal for battle was palatable and sent a cold shiver to her spine. "This is who we are, sweet pea. We fight, we die."

Horrified by his archaic attitude, she ground her teeth. Her mother had died because of the shifters' need for blood. And here was all Charlie wanted, more bloodshed.

He truly wanted to fight her. Kill her. It was obvious in his arrogant look upon her.

This was so much more than jealousy and a mere desire for elevated status. He wanted to kill someone and be celebrated for it.

She turned to his grandmother and saw the same exaltation on her face. She'd been shamed by his drunk behavior all these years and now he had transformed himself into not only a prosperous businessman, but a built-up wolf filled with the power to kill.

Dammit. She had really hoped to appeal to her. Mrs. Bouchard had been a fixture in town, house cleaning for a lot of Briac Falls' families, even for hers in the early days of her mom's passing, when Aunt Camille had too much on her plate with her own family.

Rosalie mistakenly thought she could count on Doris Bouchard's support. But the old woman was obviously taken with her grandson's mission.

Charlie had touched a nerve within his grandma. The same nerve that had rallied some of the younger wolves in the village.

She inhaled slowly and rubbed her bare thighs to settle her heart. She wasn't here to convince anyone to her side right now. She needed François back.

"What do you want from me, Charlie?" she finally said. "What will it take for you to release Dr. Beaumont?"

His unfriendly lips stretched, and he leaned back in his chair, his large body making the rusted metal creak. "Drop the claim or I kill him."

"Hey! You can't be in here." Hubert Bouchard wrinkled his mean bulldog face at Ren and his brothers as he stood in front of the old, busted armchair in the barn of Bouchard's compound.

In one swift move, Griff bolted to grab the bully by the neck and flung his barrel-chested body across the barn.

His head hit a wooden beam above them, and he fell into the hay, unconscious.

"Griff!" Cass protested at their brother's sudden action.

"He'll live," Griff huffed casually.

Ren stared back at LeGall. He tightened his fists and forced a slow exhale, unable to forget the creature's crimes.

The former hunter had bombed Alcide's Tavern right under his nose. And infected his brother with angel blood.

Had Maisie and Caro not intervened in time, Justin would have remained blind. And without Justin's keen intellect, the zealous bastard would have killed his wife Emmeline.

"Fucker," he muttered under his breath.

"You know who this is?" Griff stared at the wretch chained at the neck and stooped over himself in meager patches of filthy straw.

"Not one of Father Grégoire's cursed pupils I gather," Cass noted, detecting Ren's hatred for the fallen scumbag.

"It's LeGall."

"*The* LeGall?"

"Yep."

As LeGall raised demented, inflamed eyes at them, there was no mistaking his identity.

He was in poor shape but still wore his tattered coat with the insignia of the LeGall hunters.

"A goddammed *Chasseurs*," Griff said.

"Yeah," Ren croaked.

"And Justin turned him into one of us," Cass added.

"Good for him," Griff spat.

"Should we release him?" Cass asked.

"You're kidding, right?" Ren smirked.

"It doesn't seem decent, having him chained like that by wolves."

Ren shrugged. "It was Justin and Emme's decision to let him run free. Alcide and I were ready to execute him. If I recall, I made a promise to do just that if he hunts humans. Didn't I, *Jérôme*?"

LeGall hissed at him, any resemblance to a human—or even a sane vampire—completely gone, his consciousness replaced by insanity.

"He's turned feral," Griff noticed. "And he's gaunt. Doesn't look like he drank any human blood since his turning."

"All these dead animals…" Cass shook his head at the small furry carcasses on the ground. "That's kind of sick to leave him like this."

"He shot Max, tortured Emme…" Ren was still studying the shell of a vampire at their feet without a hint of sympathy. "Hells, he nearly killed Mrs. Mercier. I ain't getting involved."

LeGall didn't seem to hear them. He darted forward to quickly grab the remains of a rat and sunk his fangs into it to extract what was left of the dead animal's blood.

"I feel bad leaving him here." Cass raised a brow at his brothers.

"There's no gray area here, Cassiodore." Ren wrinkled his nose in disgust. "He was Justin and Emme's to judge. They voted to let him fend for himself and I will not intervene."

"It's always right or wrong for you, Ren, isn't it?" Cass insisted.

"It's not that hard. As far as I'm concerned, LeGall made his bed when he chose the life of a hunter of super-naturals. Hells, Emme said he killed his own wife."

"Damn." Cass jerked his head back.

"We're here for the doctor." Ren cast one last look at the former hunter. "Not this scumbag."

Griff seemed bored with the whole LeGall thing and was already bent over Hubert. He slapped the wolf-shifter a couple of times. "Come on, kid. Where's the doctor?"

Hubert blinked rapidly. He tried to push his hefty body up, but Griff held him down with a knee at his chest.

"Hubert Bouchard, come on," Ren called out, leaving LeGall behind to stride leisurely toward Charlie's cousin. "Don't be a fool."

Griff snapped open his jaw at the shifter, fangs fully out, while Hubert kicked his feet in a useless attempt to scramble away.

Griff always had that surprising effect on people. His nonchalant attitude quickly changing to that of a stone-cold killer the moment he meant business.

"Hubert," Ren warned. "I won't ask twice."

Griff bent down to his neck and growled in a sound so primal, Hubert trembled with fear. They couldn't control the mind of a wolf-shifter, but they could for sure scare him into telling them what they wanted to know.

"No need," Hubert croaked. "House… The doctor is in the house."

"Let's roll." Griff released his prey who stayed back in the hay, gulping with terror.

"Don't hurt him," Ren cautioned his brother.

Hubert was no threat. Ren had no desire to anger Rosalie further by maiming members of the pack. He was already going behind her back to get things done.

Cass found some steel wire and an old cloth from a corner of the barn. He passed it to Griff who bound and gagged Hubert and then dumped him back on his old couch before stepping outside to do the same to the coyote still unconscious by the barn door.

Ren dropped one last look at LeGall before leaving him to his fate as they took off for the house.

"What's the plan?" Cass asked as they reached the steps of the run-down bungalow that had seen better days when Johnny Bouchard was still alive.

"No plan," Ren answered. "There isn't time."

CHAPTER 12

*C*harlie's ultimatum didn't surprise Rosalie. He'd do anything to become alpha. Even if it meant killing a human.

"Why do you want to run the pack, Charlie?" she calmly asked.

"You don't have the making of a leader, punk," Old Simon said.

She looked at Simon, paused on Mrs. Bouchard's tight, righteous expression before turning a heavy gaze on Charlie. "Why?"

"Simon is wrong." He pursed his lips and raised his chin in defiance. "I can lead."

"Do you even know what that means?" she said.

"I'm the strongest here." His jaw was taut. "Stronger even than your cousins Max and Don. Both my ancestors, the Bouchards and Lamberts, were here since the beginning of this town. Just like yours. I have as much right as you do."

"The Gauthiers have always led the pack," she noted.

"Always males."

"Why does it matter?"

"Females can't be alphas," Mrs. Bouchard muttered under her breath.

Rosalie turned a surprised gaze at her. She could see Charlie thinking so, but her?

"All about hormones," she crowed with conviction. "You don't have the right kind, girl."

Rosalie let the comment slide and passed a weighty look on Charlie.

"Being alpha is more than fighting and protecting the pack from being attacked," she said quietly. "It's also about caring for them all. Knowing them, attending to their needs. Dad recognizes that."

"Your dad no longer knows what our needs are." Charlie's mouth twisted with derisiveness. "What about Tom? And Hubert? What about their need for battle?"

"The war is over, Charlie. We don't need the violence anymore."

"I need it. The young wolves need it," Charlie roared. "Look at your brother. He's a weak little sissy."

Her blood ran cold, and she shot him a deadly look. "Leave Liam out of this. He's a child."

"A child who should have already shifted by now."

"And what would you have him do?" Protective feelings welled inside her for her sibling who was growing up without a mother. "Fight another wolf? Become a heartless murderer before he's even old enough to shave?"

"It worked for our ancestors."

"No, it didn't." Simon's tone was stark. She knew he still had nightmares from some of his spell in the military.

"It's a different time, Charlie," she tried to soften her words. "We have to adapt. Hells, even Rémi from the Val-D'Or pack agrees with Dad."

"Old men," he grumbled. "This is not a time for old men."

"No, it's *our* time," she stated. "A time to stop fighting and thrive. Your idea of leadership will see us all killed."

"I don't negotiate. It's not in our nature."

"And what will happen when the Order of the Black Oak descent upon us if we violate our peace treaty with them?" she asked. "When Maisie Thibodeau and her coven come to stop you?"

"Fucking warlocks and witches."

"The pack will be destroyed," she insisted. "If those young men don't die, they'll rot in a Montreal city jail for murder. Our heritage decimated."

"Oh, talk about heritage. Look at you, marrying a freaking vamp." He wrinkled his wide nose in apparent disgust. "Next thing you know, our alpha won't even be a wolf-shifter."

Frustrated, she sighed. No need to continue this. He would never see her side.

"Tell your gang to release Dr. Beaumont," she ordered. "He's not part of this. Let him leave town."

"Not until you publicly renounce your claim." His lips stretched into a gloating smile. "I don't want to kill you. It's not the smart thing to do. Your father still has allies. I want you to drop the claim and get out of Briac Falls. I'm fine with your family staying here. I'll train your siblings properly. No more of that sissy stuff."

Her jaw dropped and her neck and cheeks burned with rage. How dare he even think about drafting Liam and Delphine as soldiers of war.

She was about to come back with a scathing retort when a cell phone rang.

Charlie reached into his suit pocket to answer it. "What?" His face flushed red with fury. "How the hell did they get in?" he sputtered into the phone, the vein in his neck pulsing madly. "What the fuck am I paying you for?"

He barked a few orders before jabbing his cell phone off. "You devious little bitch."

"What?" She frowned, confused.

"That fucker husband of yours is roaming on *my* property," he exploded, bolting to his feet. He stretched wide to his full height in a hostile pose.

"Oh, honey." Mrs. Bouchard fussed over her grandson. "That's not right."

"Wait, what's going on." Puzzled, Simon glanced around them all.

Rosalie tried to make sense of what Charlie was saying.

"I don't like you, Rosalie." He bent down to her, jabbing his finger into her face. "But I trusted your honor. That's low."

"What on earth happened?" She stood to meet him straight on.

"Your fucking vampire is trying to break your boyfriend free, you slut," he raged. "And I'm not going to let him get away with this."

No. That wasn't possible. Ren had promised he'd stay out of it.

"I was prepared to let your doctor go," Charlie added with wrath. "Let you both leave town unharmed. But no more. Our fight is on, bitch. And I'll enjoy gutting you."

REN KICKED the bungalow's door open to find Charlie's three dutiful followers playing cards at a rickety Formica kitchen table.

A beer bottle crashed to the linoleum floor as Bouchard, Lambert, and Fortin all stared at him in shock.

"Where is he?" Ren yelled, his brothers following behind, blocking any way in or out of the small house.

The counter was littered with pizza boxes and crushed

soda cans, the dishwasher door ripped from its hinges. The place reeked of unwashed bodies. For all his money, Charlie still lived in a slum.

Tom Bouchard, one arm heavily bandaged, dropped his cards on the table, while Lambert's hands started to tremble.

"I told you this was a bad idea." Danny Fortin was shaking his head with nervousness.

"Where is he?" Ren asked again.

"Bedroom." Fortin sheepishly hunched behind his cards as if he was trying to disappear.

"Shut up." Tom Bouchard had his hand flat on the table, staring at Fortin with loathing.

"Seriously, Tom," Fortin said with a hesitant nod at the door. "Do you really think we have a chance against these three? Getting your arm snapped by Rosalie wasn't enough?"

Ren glanced at Griff and Cass beside him. Both brothers had their fangs out, features lean and deadly, and ready to rip into anything coming their way. He could see Fortin's point.

"Cass, go get Rosalie's doctor," he instructed, sending his more civilized brother to approach the poor man while he guarded the wolves.

Griff stepped out of the house when shouts erupted outside. Hired muscles, no doubt, coming to the rescue. A few grunts followed before Griff strode back in.

"All clear, bro," he barked.

Moments later, Cass had Dr. Beaumont unconscious over his shoulder. "He was tied to the bed, but he's okay."

Tom Bouchard continued to smirk at Ren but didn't dare move a muscle.

Ren recalled the shifter's paw on Rosalie, and it took all he had not to beat him senseless. There'd be time for that on some other occasion. Right now, all he wanted was to get the doctor out of there.

"Let's go," Griff called.

"Wait for me outside." Ren was not willing to let Rosalie's assailants down so easily.

Fangs fully drawn-out, he stepped toward Tom Bouchard and grabbed him by the throat. He heard Lambert jump back in his chair while Fortin held onto the table with wide eyes, silently moaning a prayer under his breath.

Still gripping Bouchard's windpipe, he glared at them one by one with a lethal promise. "If you *ever* go near my wife, I will kill you." His deadly gaze rested on Fortin before turning to Lambert. "You understand me?"

They both agreed vigorously while Tom Bouchard grappled at Ren's clamp with his free hand.

"And I won't do it quick," he snarled. "I will eviscerate you first. Leave you alive with your guts hanging out from your belly. You'll be holding onto them hoping to die."

The two minions had turned white.

"You'll be so far gone that even Caro Mercier won't be able to bring you back," he continued in a chilled tone. "The last thing you will see is this face."

He bent his fangs down to Bouchard's neck and dug deep into his flesh to start draining him of his blood. Tom Bouchard stopped struggling as Ren whipped his head around to pin them all with a murderous stare, Bouchard's sour blood dripping along his chin.

He stretched his bloodied palm out at them with a snarl. "This hand will claw your eyes out until you're left in darkness, regretting the day you followed an idiot like Charlie Bouchard instead of your rightful alpha."

With their eyes like saucers, they gulped in unison, not daring to move. Julien Lambert let out a pitiful whimper.

"You hear me?"

Lambert and Fortin both nodded frantically again without a word.

Ren released Tom Bouchard and the shifter dropped unconscious on the floor, bleeding from the two puncture wounds at his neck.

"Tell your boss to leave Rosalie alone." Ren narrowed his eyes at them before wiping the blood on his face with his sleeve. "And leave Charlie Bouchard to fend for himself. Otherwise, I will come for all of you."

Terrified, these two looked as if they soiled themselves. Pathetic. "I fought with your grandfathers," Ren snapped. "They'd be ashamed to see you now."

Julien Lambert let out another whiny mewl while Fortin crossed himself, holding his breath.

On his words, Ren strode out of the house, pleased to have enacted justice by half-draining the scumbag who had dared touch his wife.

It didn't matter that Rosalie had told him to stand down, he was bound to protect his alpha, and nothing would make him renege his lifetime oath.

CHAPTER 13

*S*he had been calling and texting Ren non-stop since they'd left the *Jardins du Domaine*, filled with both rage and worries as she'd followed after Charlie.

Her hand seized on the steering wheel of her jeep while she searched the country road leading to the Bouchard compound. No trace of Ren's truck anywhere. What if François got hurt? What if *Ren* got hurt?

And what if he did succeed in breaking François out. She'd have to explain everything to the doctor.

Her claim to the pack's leadership had gotten a whole lot more complicated. Charlie was beyond furious. There was no backing out of the combat now.

Her heart palpitated hard against her rib cage. First, she'd have to make sure they were all okay.

As she narrowed her eyes at the road, she saw nothing but a few crows skittering across the hot pavement, still cracked from last winter. Charlie's powerful Silverado had left her small jeep a good mile behind.

"Do you see him?" she asked Simon, who sat looking grim on the passenger seat of her vehicle.

Simon shook his head no, his cell phone to his ear. "He's not picking up from me either."

"Dammit."

"We should call your dad."

"No!" This one she had to handle herself. They couldn't run to her father each time something bad happened.

"Your husband should have consulted with you on this," the postman said, not wrong one bit.

"I know," she agreed between clenched teeth.

She was barreling down the road when a familiar black vehicle appeared on the other side, racing toward town. *Finally*.

"It's Ren's truck!" Simon called out.

"Yep." The black Ram barreled past her. Ren hadn't recognized her jeep.

She applied the brake and took a three-point turn to chase down after him.

"It's only him in the cabin," Simon said. "I saw no sign of your friend."

Damn. Her heart fell. François was still captive.

She honked her horn angrily to catch Ren's attention.

He caught her eyes in his rearview mirror and eventually slowed his vehicle along the curb.

He lazily got out of the truck and strode up to hers, his plaid shirt loose over his white tee, his swagger underscoring his strength. He was an imposing man, all right, but she couldn't get past her fearful anger to appreciate his appeal.

She shoved her door open, and stepped out onto the gravel, ready to unleash hell on him.

He raised a hand to stop her.

"I took care of it, no need to worry." His tone was meant to be reassuring but came out low and dangerous.

"What do you mean?" She stared at him coolly, leaning back on the heels of her sneakers.

"We should probably get out of here before Charlie finds out, though." He tossed his head at the empty road.

"What happened?" she asked cautiously, not knowing what to think. "Where's François?"

"It's fine, I told you. I went in with my brothers." He leaned back on his heels and hooked his thumbs into his jeans pocket. "Got your doctor out."

"Well done, pal." Simon came out from around the front of the jeep and shook Ren's hand. "I knew you could get him back easily."

"You did?" She frowned. "Where is he?"

"I compelled him to forget everything and sent him with Cass to retrieve his car from the swimming hole's parking lot. He'll be on his way back to Toronto shortly, not remembering a thing about his abduction."

"Compel, what do you mean compel?" She was not convinced.

He did a funny wiggle of his hand at eye level. "Compel, you know, that thing we vampires do."

"Mind alteration," Simon added.

"You altered his mind?" Her jaw went slack.

"Not really, just made him forget his whole experience here." A slow, satisfied smile curled his lip.

"And me, too?"

"Well, yes a bit, sorry." He raked his hair back. "Made it so that he'll think he took a drive in the country. Stayed overnight to the B&B and drove back."

"You did what?" She was utterly confused. One minute she had feared for his and her ex's lives, and now he was casually telling her he'd erased the whole ordeal.

"I called Mrs. Beaulieu," he added. "They'll send his stuff over once you give her his address."

She was still staring at him stunned. Who on earth gave

him the right to mess with someone's mind like that? And not just anyone, *her boyfriend*!

She took a deep breath and closed her eyes. François was not her boyfriend anymore. She had to sort that one out once and for all. They'd all been referring to him as such, but he wasn't. That was done.

"Oh, and I'm pretty sure Lambert and Fortin have decided to stop following Charlie." Ren chuckled, looking pleased with himself. "You should have seen the look on their faces after I threatened them."

"Good on you, Renaud," Simon interjected. "That's the way to do it!"

"Not so sure about Tom Bouchard, though," Ren mused. "But I'll get him on the next round."

"Next round?" She zeroed in onto his last words, her heart skipping a beat. "Did you hurt him?"

He shrugged. "Just roughed him up a little."

"So, while I was trying to negotiate with Charlie, you went behind my back and roughed up his gang?" Her limbs tingled with a deep rush of epinephrine. Her nostrils flared as she blinked with frustration. "Enough to get them all pissed at us?"

She wasn't sure who was upsetting her the most at the moment. Her enemies, or the husband who had decided to take matters into his own hands without consulting her.

"Your boyfriend is safe." He looked at her puzzled.

"He's not my boyfriend," she spat.

"Well, your friend then." All traces of Ren's amusement were gone. "The good doctor. He's out of here, unharmed. He still knows nothing about shifters, or anything. Isn't that a good thing?"

"You messed with his mind," she muttered under her breath.

"It was the only way, Rosalie." His jaw was clenched with irritation. "I couldn't bring him to you after that. He'd been captured by a group of shifters on the war path. They even have hired guns."

"Mercenaries?" Simon asked.

"Looks like it." His tone turned somber. "Coyotes. They're probably the ones who snatched the doctor while we were all at the swimming hole."

"Those fuckers!" Simon no doubt remembered Rosalie's mother.

She didn't care about the hired guns right now. Even coyotes. She was still wrapping her head around the consequences of Ren's actions.

"You went behind my back," she accused. If they were to become partners, this wouldn't do.

"There was no other way," he countered. "Would you have agreed to a rescue?"

"No," she scowled. "You and François could have been hurt. You said it yourself, they have backup."

"You worried about me?" The lazy smile returned as he raised a surprised brow at her.

"You're not invincible," she pointed out.

"Almost," his expression eased further. "But I did have both my brothers with me, Cass and Griffon."

"Oh. "

"The wolves had no chance," he explained. "Fortin and that little Lambert whiner were already on the fence about you, so I got you some new followers."

"Because they're scared of you." She felt her racing heart settle.

"Well, yeah."

"That's not the way to do it," she protested.

Simon wisely remained silent, staying out of the fire.

"It's the only way," he insisted. "Why do you think they follow Charlie?"

"Not because they fear him." She leaned back on her jeep. "They like him."

"Are you sure about that?" He took a step forward.

"Oh yes, I'm sure," she smirked. "He's bringing them some kind of war fantasy where those wolves get to play heroes. They want that."

It had taken one conversation with Mrs. Bouchard to understand what she was truly against.

"Now they will want to fight you, Ren. You just made it worse." She deepened her frown with her accusation.

"I don't think so." He drew himself to his full height above her. "He kidnapped your boyf—, your friend. A human doctor. That's crossing the line. The wolves may like fighting, but they have a strong sense of right or wrong. Attacking Dr. Beaumont was wrong."

"I thought your job was to do as I say." She knew it was the wrong thing to tell him as soon as the words left her lips, but she felt underpowered, trying to get a grip at some control.

Simon sucked in a sharp breath.

"I'm not your minion, Rosalie." His tone turned dead cold.

"What are you then?" She jutted her chin at him, her spine straight.

"Your protector," he growled.

"I don't need a protector." She desperately wanted to tell him about Charlie's last threat to her. That the combat was on. But raw determination took over. She was soon to become the Domaine-Lassalle alpha. She could no longer show weakness. Not to Simon, not her father, or to her aunt Camille.

And certainly not to Ren.

It suddenly occurred to her that she was on her own here.

He stared down at her, his gaze unreadable, while she held her own equally steady.

"I never needed a husband." She motioned for Simon

to get into the idling jeep. "You shouldn't have married me."

She jumped into her vehicle and forced herself not to look back at him as she took off toward town. There was no backing out of anything now.

The alpha path was a lone one and duty had made it her destiny.

CHAPTER 14

*H*e hadn't even called. Rosalie sighed, trailing her hand along the curve of the brand-new reception desk of Briac Falls Medic.

Still seething from her fight with Ren the previous evening, she had stayed the night in her old room at her father's and decided to use the afternoon to check on the progress of her new clinic.

Her heart heavy, she wistfully took in the large bay window of the waiting room, empty of furniture and half painted in a neat cheery green taint.

The workers were outside, packing their tools at the end of their workday after putting the last touches on her dream of providing her town with the latest in modern medical care.

But the dream was all kinds of wrong now. It was not supposed to be this way. She had sacrificed a possible life in a thriving hospital with her doctor boyfriend to return here where she thought she could make a difference to her people.

She would help them at the clinic during the day, consulting with her best friend Caro for the ideal health plan for each of her patients. She had hired Mrs. Savard as her receptionist. The widow loved people and had been so lonely since the passing of her husband last year.

Rosalie had been excited to start her business, but now she couldn't stop the lump mounting at the bottom of her throat and the incredible weariness taking hold of her.

She was destined to become the leader of the town, advising each and every one, just as her father and grandfather had done before. Representing the pack at the summer parlays, going to the human county's council to make sure they left the wolf-shifter village alone and in peace.

But Charlie, he didn't want peace. She cringed to think of having him meet the witches and warlocks instead of Dad, or herself.

She'd heard of the Order of the Black Oak warlocks who'd recently allied with their pack. Diesel Stanford, their mighty leader, had magical abilities matched only by Maisie Thibodeau, high priestess of the White Holly Coven, and Charlotte Callan, the Ice Witch and Ren's mother. Underneath their civil façade, the spellcasters held a power that was much stronger than anything the Mercier healers had been able to achieve.

They were all united now—warlocks, witches, shifters, vampires. But Charlie would put a stop to that.

And what about the wolf-shifters outside of their pack, aside from their Val D'or neighbors? The Laurentians Timbers pack in the mountains, the Labrador wolves way up north, and the Great Lake Boreal south of the province.

They had finally made peace before her mother's death, but that would all be over if Charlie Bouchard took over. Rémi Desmarais would be his first target. And Charlie being younger, he could likely win. Kill the middle-aged alpha.

Rémi had three sons and two daughters. They would surely retaliate. War would start again.

Dammit. She stared again at the small construction crew across the window. Jacob Pelletier was laughing at something Ed Beaulieu had said. They both chugged water bottles as they waved goodbye to Noah Landry, the teenager she hired to paint. She pressed her lips together with determination. She had to protect their peaceful way of life.

But it was just her, now. She stood alone in this. She had the diplomacy to keep the peace, she knew it. She would not offend the warlocks. She'd barter with the witches and strengthen their alliances with all shifters.

She knew she was good at it because she truly believed compromise was best for everyone. For Delphine and Liam, for the Merciers, and even for that thick-headed Bouchard. His business would crumble if he led the pack in an all-out war. Human authorities would get involved and he could kiss goodbye to the golf club he wanted to establish on their land.

Just the thought of how life was before the peace treaty made her shudder. She would never be able to scrub the memory of the night her father had told her Mom had been killed. She'd been devastated, unable to wrap her mind around it. The tears in his eyes had broken her. In an instant, her life had been obliterated.

Her siblings remembered none of those violent times. But with Charlie at the helm, they'd suffer through it with Delphine being the first enlisted.

Her sister could fight as well as Rosalie could but if the teen's heart wasn't in it, would she even survive? How fair would it be on her when her head was filled with patterns of clothes and dreams of the big city.

And little Liam, they would force him to chuck his

video games and model rockets. Have him fight the other boys to toughen him up like they did in the old days.

She wouldn't put it past Charlie to do just that to spite their family. Dad wouldn't survive the heartache of seeing his kids used this way.

And where did Ren fit in all that? Here he had gone and rallied his brothers to help her. Was that what the pack would be now with her as alpha? Indebted to all the St-Amand immortal brothers? Because that was how it looked at the moment.

Unless she did something.

But what?

The answer was right in front of her. She *had* to fight Charlie.

But how would she defeat him? She had skills but so did he. She'd almost taken down creepy Tom, but freakin' big, bad Charlie? He'd fight dirty, for sure.

She would need to ask Aunt Camille to help her train again. With her wolf-style of Kung-Fu and general street smarts, she had tricks on how a smaller female wolf could overtake a large wolf-shifter like Charlie.

Rosalie attempted to purposefully ignore the suggestion Caro had made about mating with Ren. But the thought was too overwhelming and turned her weak at the knee.

She didn't know Ren well. She couldn't possibly just *sleep* with him. Have his powerful hands seize her waist, his enticing lips taking hers, trailing down her throat, right in the valley between her breasts.

Her heart picked up speed. No way. She wouldn't go there. Right now, she hated him for having put her in an impossible situation.

She tightened her fists. She had to convince the town that she was the better choice for alpha. Have them see it her way. With the coronation during the full moon in nine days, the combat was not imminent.

If she could win everyone's favor before that, she might not have to fight. The *épluchette* social was a few days away. Charlie was involved but that didn't mean she had to avoid the event. It would be the perfect venue to plead her case to her people.

Jacob Pelletier opened the front door, jolting her from her grim thoughts. Ed Beaulieu was right behind him to pick up one last toolbox before heading out. "You like the color, Rosalie?"

"Looks great," she told Nick's uncle.

"This clinic will be really handy," Jacob added. "Our mom has to go into town for her treatments. It's an hour each way."

"And my little sister," Ed said, "with the baby coming. You can deliver, right Rosalie?"

"Yes, I certainly will. I'm not technically a doctor but nurse practitioners can do a lot. And I have Dr. Fillion from *Bois-Franc Village* on call for emergencies."

"It's great to have you back," Jacob said. "When Alcide told us you had just graduated college, we all thought you'd stay in Toronto."

"With his heart attack, I *had* to come back," she said.

"He's fit as a fiddle though," Ed commented. "I just saw him at the tavern last night. Not sure why he's stepping down as alpha."

"Yeah, that sucks," Jacob said with a wince.

"I'll do good by him." Rosalie tried to put as much certainty into her words as she could. "Don't you worry. You know I will."

"Sorry, girl," Ed gave her a slow shake of his head, "but it's hard to believe you can actually take over."

A silence fell over the two workers as she considered them, a crease at her brow. Not them, too.

"What?" she finally countered. "You don't think I can do the job?"

Jacob shrugged with a small smile. "You're a nice girl, Rosalie."

"And smart, too," Ed added eagerly.

"What's the problem?" She stared at one then the other.

"With the clinic, you'll be busy," Jacob explained. "Being in charge of the pack is a lot of work."

"Dad did it." She pursed her lips, her body turning rigid.

"And you're married, too," Ed remarked.

"Is this about my husband being an immortal?" she probed. "I didn't know you were a bigot, Ed."

"No, I don't mind that. St-Amand's a good guy," Ed replied, holding up his hands. "But you're a married woman, and our doctor now. How can you have the time to protect us as well?"

"Protect you? Ed, you're a big shifter," she pointed out, her tone lightening. "What are you actually scared of?"

"I'm not scared but I heard rumors." Ed was dead serious.

"What kind of rumors?" This didn't sound good at all.

"Val D'Or is coming down to take over," Ed said. "To assimilate our pack."

"What? That's not true," she protested, shocked at the gossip. "Dad was just talking to Rémi Desmarais. They seem fine."

"Ed's right," Jacob said. "I heard that once they were told a woman was stepping into Alcide's place, they decided to take over."

"Who said that?" She couldn't believe this.

"Tom Bouchard," Jacob told her.

"Oh, and you trust him?" She flushed with irritation. That creepy little bastard was spreading lies.

"Why would he make this up?" Jacob countered.

"I got it directly from Charlie," Ed informed her.

"That's nonsense," she disputed. "Rémi's mom led their pack when he was a child. They have no problem with female leaders."

"Well, you do have to admit," Jacob said, "if we have to fight another pack, Charlie would be a good replacement for your dad. He was a drunk when you left, but he really turned his life around. His business is thriving. He just bought the old shoe factory outside town to turn into condos for the ski trade."

"Yeah. And you should see what he can bench now," Ed added. "Impressive."

She looked stunned at the two men she had known since she was a child. "You truly would support Charlie's claim because he can bench heavy at the gym?"

"No, it's not that, Rosalie." Ed shifted his weight with caution. "You're way nicer and we know you care—hells, this new clinic shows it. But we don't think you can do it all. Charlie's business is running fine, he's single. And he *is* stronger. That still means something."

He had said *we*. Who else besides Jacob could also be thinking this? She rolled her stiff shoulders back. She couldn't believe it.

"Are you both feeling that way?" The revelation that more people supported her opponent did not bode well.

"Pretty much," Ed said. "I know you fell for St-Amand, and good for you both, but many people here think you should have married a wolf."

"Like Charlie," Jacob said. "It'd be easier if you'd married him."

"What?" A tide of revulsion washed over her.

"Yeah, that's too bad you didn't," Ed added. "I mean, it would have been perfect. Your brains and his strength. The pack would thrive."

"Good grief, are you kidding?" she spat. "He wants to *kill* me. The guy's a creep. He tried to assault me with his gang yesterday morning and he kidnapped my friend from the city."

"I'm so sorry. Heard he let the doctor go, though," Jacob said. "That it was just a little joke."

A joke! She'd been sick with worry at what could have happened to her ex. And they totally dismissed the part about how he attacked her.

Her anger at Ren vanished all at once. It didn't matter who had rescued François, apparently the odds were already stacked against her.

"How many others feel like you do?" She needed to know just how deep the divide had grown. "That Charlie should take over?"

"Oh, I don't know. No one really wants to see you fight him." Jacob nodded at her. "They like you a lot."

"But not enough to accept me as their alpha," she said, her tone frostier now.

"At first, we all did," Ed assured her. "We know you have the best interest of the town at heart. But ever since the threat of the other pack…"

"Which is a lie," she pointed out.

"It's always possible." Ed shrugged, an uncomfortable expression on his features.

"We started to think we do need someone physically stronger," Jacob explained. "No offense, but you're just a little thing."

"And your husband, well…" Ed winced.

"We need a wolf leader," Jacob said. "Not an immortal. St-Amand has always been here and we're okay with that, but he can't be our leader by default."

"So how many are against my claim?" She had to know.

"Well, the Bouchards and Lamberts for sure. The Fortins are divided."

"The Merciers are strongly in your camp though. And

Mrs. Savard, of course." Jacob nodded at the reception desk. "She's grateful for the job here."

"You two?" she insisted.

"I'm sorry, Rosalie. Please don't fight him." Ed wouldn't meet her eyes.

"Maybe we could put it to a vote," Jacob suggested.

"A vote?" She narrowed her gaze at him.

"Yes, a town vote. Like when we decided to ally ourselves with the supernatural council down in New England last year, remember?"

"Aye," Ed said. "People would like that much better than seeing you get hurt."

Dammit, did they really need a vote? She took a deep breath.

On the night of her wedding—and despite what her dad feared—she had thought everyone had her back except for a handful of cronies like Tom Bouchard. But now, with Charlie spreading crazy rumors about a fake takeover from the Val D'Or pack, she wasn't so sure.

She stared uneasily at the two construction workers as they gathered the last of their tools. The town could maybe be convinced to hold a vote instead of a fight. That was an improvement over combat. But she still ran into the same problem. Charlie was much savvier than she'd originally given him credit. And he wouldn't be above rigging or buying off votes, either.

She rubbed the back of her neck with anxiety while Jacob and Ed pushed open the glass door of her clinic, casting an awkward glance at her on their way out.

Charlie was winning the town over with potent charisma, literally beating her at her own strength. Spreading lies, pretending he cared. The vote could totally go in his favor. And then what?

She wouldn't be run out of town, but the pack would get caught up in Charlie's ambitions. Liam would still be drafted to fight before he finished high school. Delphine's only chance would be to leave her home.

Rosalie couldn't let that happen.

Her warm medical center suddenly looked cold and clinical. She'd always prided herself in setting goals and following through with them, meeting the needs of those she cared about. Always knowing what to do—duty and responsibility being her guide. A simple, rightful path.

But right now, she had no idea how she would stake her family's leadership claim and protect her town. Voting would be too much of a risk. She actually did have to defeat Charlie in one-on-one combat.

She seized the edge of her shiny-new reception counter in her grip and lifted her chin with newfound resolve.

She'd have to give Aunt Camille a call.

CHAPTER 15

*A*lcide's Tavern was packed tonight, and Ren had been busy. A scuffle had started between two young wolves at the dart board. Ti-Jo Leclerc had drunk too much and needed a ride home.

Suzie Savard from the hair salon had come in mad as hell before jumping onto Dick Fortin, the local accountant, accusing him of cooking her books in his favor. The pint-sized woman was fierce, and it had taken some time to calm her down.

Ren was now sitting at his usual table at the back, next to the old-fashioned jukebox playing classic rock, while checking the patrons, making sure no more chaos erupted. Things seemed different now that he'd married Alcide's daughter and Charlie had challenged her.

People looked at him with slightly more hesitancy than normal. A few with some sort of dare in their eyes. The town was talking, alliances were shifting, and certain locals were starting to rally behind Charlie's way of thinking.

They had been civilized for a while now, but they were still shifters. The wolf in them was always present.

Even in someone like Rosalie.

He had seen it in her gaze when she had mentioned he'd had the doctor compelled. Her light amber pupils had flickered a shade of pristine blue for a brief second, just like her alpha father. They would remain that way forever once her coronation was completed.

She was their queen alright. But was she still supposed to be his wife?

The memory of her shape barely concealed by her summer nightgown flashed before his eyes and he gulped to quench the desire making him suddenly feverish.

It had been just over twenty-four hours since they'd had that fight on the side of the road. She had chosen to stay at her dad's overnight and maybe it was all for the best. She affected him in ways that disturbed his usual no-nonsense attitude.

He took a slug of beer and dug the heels of his boots on the flagstone floor as he watched Léa Pelletier sliding between tables with her waitstaff apron and serving tray.

Alcide had been in his hospital bed when he'd asked Ren to wed his daughter. *She needs your protection, old friend*, he had pleaded.

He tightened his fists to stop the slight shaking of his hands at the emotions emerging inside him. The urgent need obvious on his friend's face had reminded him of that other time when a friend had needed him, but he'd failed.

Pierre's expression had that similar imploring look as he lay bleeding on the ground, the pitchfork embedded in his chest, while Ren—a supposably invincible immortal— had been tied to a tree trunk and set ablaze by the mob.

He shuddered as, even a century later, the unbearable scorching heat melting off his flesh still left a phantom sensation along his limbs. His throat closed in on the trauma, the sharp memory quickly repressed and buried deep into his subconscious.

He'd never failed a friend after that. He'd seen all of

his alphas die of old age. Never in battle or by some secret execution by another pack, but always fading peacefully in their own beds surrounded by their family.

Rose-Aimée Gauthier, Rosalie's mother, had fallen when he was away visiting his siblings in Montreal just after the announcement of the wolf peace pact. Her death had filled him with bitterness, making him even more entrenched in his loyalty to the pack.

Seeing Alcide hit with a heart attack ten years later had rattled him to the core. And now he found himself married to his daughter, a sexy she-wolf—with her life in the balance due to complex wolf politics—and disturbing his need for an uncomplicated life.

The idea that Charlie should fight Rosalie to the death to claim the pack's leadership was as insane as bringing back kidnapping as a way to choose their life mate.

But here they were, and it was obvious that the notion was appealing to the younger crowd who had never seen combat.

And here Ren sat, feeling helpless.

Because it truly was not his place to interfere with the shifters' affairs.

He drew a sharp breath in frustration. Even if he had now married into the Gauthier family and was responsible for guarding Rosalie.

His simple rules were useless in completing his task of protecting his alpha. He had decided to get involved by helping her save her ex, and she was now mad at him and staying away from his home.

How she explained that to Alcide, he had no idea, but his alpha hadn't said a word when he'd seen Ren at his usual post.

They were married, *calvaire*. Ren clenched his jaw with annoyance. She couldn't stay away from him long if they wanted to keep this pretense up to the locals.

Was their marriage truly a sham? There was no denying that the physical attraction was there. For him, anyway.

The lust he experienced every time she was near was nothing like he had felt for anyone before. Hitting him like a potent summer thunderstorm, a heavy but soothing downpour that washed all bad memories away. It caught his breath and made him hard with desire every single time he rested his gaze on her.

He'd heard of the concept of wolf-shifters soulmates—two partners connecting at the primal level. He'd seen it in action decades ago, but it hadn't happened in the pack since Alcide's parents. Rosaire Gauthier had explained something very much like this when he'd described falling for Adalie, the youngest daughter of the Beaulieu's clan.

There was no way something like this could apply to Ren, though. He was not a wolf.

Yet as soon as she'd walked toward him in her wedding dress, as he drank in the curve of her throat and graceful waist, he'd been hit with a mind-blowing longing that could only be explained by some mystical force at play.

It had grown even deeper once her fresh scent had folded over him while the priest had recited the ceremony bonding them together. And here he was, in incredible lust for the woman he'd married in appearances only, bound to protect her at all costs.

His own oath urged him to go find Charlie and rip out his throat.

But *she* would not want him to.

And maybe she was right.

But it didn't mean he was okay with it.

He looked up as the heavy double doors opened and realized that the woman who occupied his constant thoughts was now walking into her father's tavern.

Tidy denim shorts with a cute lacy cotton top and her

hair in a high ponytail, she looked fresh despite the heat that affected everyone.

He bit the inside of his mouth to douse the craving hitting him again. What he wouldn't give to trail his palms up those shapely, tanned thighs and see them part for him. Draw his fingers along her wet center, feel her shiver under his touch.

He let out a slow breath as she walked farther into the bar. She knew he would be here tonight and for a second, he hoped that she had meant to come see him. But his wishes were quickly crushed when she took a seat with Ed Beaulieu and his pals and caught the waitress' eye to order the men another round.

She chatted with them with animation, smiling and listening, doing what she did best, while he watched her from afar wondering if she would ever come sit with him.

She stood and patted Beaulieu's shoulder before moving to another group. Suzie and the other hairstylists this time. Again, she called the bar for more drinks and settled with the cluster of trendy-looking girls to chitchat.

Léa appeared at their table with a tray of colorful shots and the girls all downed them with laughter, Rosalie included. She tilted her head back with a rich, throaty laugh and the tip of her ponytail swayed attractively below her bare shoulders.

He finally understood what she was doing. She was trying to gain support for her cause. While she had a lot of the older folks on her side, she needed to schmooze the younger ones, who were as likely to go for Charlie as for her.

But in doing so, she was ignoring her own need to clear the air with him. She had to have calmed down about the secret rescue by now, seeing that his freeing the doctor had been the best course of action. She had to be ready to return to his place.

His heart raced to have her in his home again. He'd stay with her this time, not run away to his brothers. Talk over drinks into the night, make her breakfast the next day.

The domestic scene made him smile.

As she downed one more shot of liquor with the stylists, her gaze finally locked with his for a moment.

Goddamn. He wasn't prepared for the intense hit of hunger that crashed into him.

Their connection was unmistakable. He *had* to have her.

A strand of her hair had been caught along her dewy bottom lip and he couldn't tear his eyes away from that delicious mouth. Everything in him pined for scooping her up, carrying her to his home, and taking her.

Bury himself in all that she was, feel her warm breath on his neck, her smooth body in his embrace, slide in and out of her until she cried out her desire for him.

Hells, she was his wife! He wanted to drink her blood and draw her over the edge with ecstasy.

He craved to have her arms around him, feel her soft touch, and experience the compassion that she gave to everyone finally directed toward him.

But *calvaire*, he couldn't forget her livid face when she had shouted at him that she never needed a husband. She despised him.

He truly should stay put and let her come to him. But instead, possessed by an insane yearning, he slowly stood from his chair.

As soon as he unfolded his frame to his full height, he felt the look of the bar's patrons fall on him. They knew that whenever he got up from his spot, things were about to get serious.

He strode to her table as she lowered the shot glass under his penetrating appraisal.

"Hi, *honey*..." As he trailed his gaze down her throat and to her chest, she flushed at his scrutiny.

The gaggle of laughing women at the table ogled him with coy smiles.

"Ren, oh my," Suzie teased. "We're a bit loud. Are you here to *arrest* me again?"

"Or take *me* outside," her friend Myriam Lambert said. "You can toss me over your shoulder all you want, *mon beau*."

The other, Marie-Pier Landry, was speechless but wouldn't stop gawking at him.

Rosalie had quickly recovered her spunk. She raised a silent brow at him.

Turmoil rolled inside him recalling how mad she was with him, but he kept his gaze steady.

"Not tonight ladies," he smiled lazily at everyone.

"Another time then?" Myriam teased with a hope-filled grin.

"I'm a married man." He shrugged at her, still trying to calm the longings for his fake wife.

"That you are," she huffed.

"Rosalie," Suzie said. "You shouldn't let this beefcake go out at night, girl. Isn't this your honeymoon?"

Rosalie glanced at him, and her nervousness returned. "Sort of."

"Suzie's right, *hon*," he said. "Shouldn't we go home?"

She wouldn't contradict him now in front of the crowd. She had to play the part of the satisfied wedded woman if she was to gain everyone's trust.

"I suppose so." A worried frown crossed her forehead. She obviously had more on her mind than playing up their pretend marriage for the crowd.

"She's lucky," Myriam stated. "If I was married to someone that hot, I would never let him out of my bed."

"Is that so?" He chuckled.

155

"I came to see how you were doing." Rosalie craned her neck to look at him.

"All good." He shrugged. "The place is pretty tame now."

"Right." She pursed her lips for a moment, absent-mindedly twirling her wedding ring set around her finger.

His heart expanded and without thinking, he offered her his hand. He knew she'd prefer to stay and mingle but he couldn't help himself. He legitimately just wanted to leave with her, take her home and start over.

"Let's go then," he said.

"Fine." She stood, and he gently took her by the elbow.

He was dying to slide his arm along her slim waist, just above the curve of her hip but he didn't dare.

"Have fun, Rosalie," Suzie said with a knowing smile.

"Uh-huh," she said.

He sensed her quiver at his side as they headed toward the doors. He wasn't sure if it was from anger or desire. He was praying for desire, but knew she was likely still mad at his interference with Dr. Beaumont's mind.

How on earth did she not feel this sensual connection between them? He was at a total loss to explain it.

He waved at Alcide behind the bar and led her outside. As soon as they were alone, she swiveled under his arm and her gaze shot daggers at him.

"What the hell was that!" she exclaimed, desperation obvious in her tone. "You *know* I need to rally them all."

"Oh. Is that what you were doing?" He hadn't been blind to her endeavor but was still upset that she had chosen to stay the night at her dad's instead of returning to his cabin.

"Well yeah." A strain of tiredness tainted the anger in her voice. "You were watching me the whole time, didn't you notice?"

"You knew I was watching?" He raised a surprised brow.

"Of course, I did." She crossed her arms at her chest, leaning away from him.

"You didn't even say hi."

She shook her head with pressed lips. "I'm still mad at you."

"You didn't come back home last night."

She started to say something then bit her lips. A shadow of guilt tainted her amber pupils.

"I thought we were trying to make this work." His features eased as he attempted to give in a little.

"Our marriage?" There was a sharp edge to her tone.

"Yes, you wanted to do couple things," he noted. "Make it look like we're truly together."

"That was before."

"Before?"

"Before you went behind my back to rescue François and messed with his mind," she grumbled.

How could she not see he was helping her, not going against her?

"Charlie was never going to let him go," he insisted.

"I know," she finally relented. "He said he would release him only if I left town."

"Would you leave town for Dr. Beaumont?" he asked, his heart not wanting to know.

"Ren, I'm in an impossible dilemma. I can't leave the leadership to Charlie. He's war hungry. He'll lead the pack to destruction, take Delphine and Liam down with him. Dad, too."

"I see." He had never realized that her siblings would also be impacted.

"You just made it worse." She no longer looked angry, but tired, her shoulders stooped with sadness. "Now he really wants to kill me."

"No one has done that since the eighteen hundreds."

"It doesn't matter. Some of the young ones want it." She gave a slow, grim shake of her head.

"Which is why you're here tonight."

"Yes." Rosalie looked down at her hand for a moment and twirled her diamond set. She lifted a troubled gaze at him. "It's a very pretty ring. I never thanked you properly for it."

"I thought it might suit you."

"You chose it yourself?" She pulled her head back with surprise.

"I did. The shine of it reminded me of the Falls." He shot her a small, depreciating smile. "I live simply, but I do have means. I never need to spend money on anything. This seemed a good reason to."

"It was not supposed to be this way," she exhaled the words.

"In what way exactly?"

"Everything. Me coming back, taking over Dad's responsibility, our marriage."

"And what did you expect?" He genuinely wanted to know.

"I'm not sure but something different. We'd be friends, grow to like each other. My family always respected you. In a way, I respected you, as well."

"And you don't anymore?"

Her brow pinched as if confused, struggling with how to put what she meant into words. "I have no idea. You're so...real."

"Real?" he chortled.

"You have your own ideas about things."

"And you truly thought I'd be a silent knight to his queen?" he said, half-amused, half-slighted. "Do your bidding without question?"

He wasn't mad, just startled that she hadn't put more thought into this. She seemed so sensible.

"I didn't expect you to run straight to Charlie's compound," she clarified, "and take back François."

"I'm a man of action, Rosalie. I do things."

"You did. He's safe now," she reluctantly admitted.

"I'm not reckless, however," he asserted. "I knew I would easily rescue your doctor safely if I brought my brothers along."

"He's no longer my doctor."

"No, he's not." He wondered if she truly meant it or if a part of her still pined for the polished ex-boyfriend.

"You made sure of that," she smirked.

"I did not interfere with his memory of you." He cleared his throat, unexpectedly doubtful of his actions. How was he, a man of a few words, suddenly keen on explaining himself. "I removed any thoughts of his abduction trauma and him coming here, but nothing before that. He still remembers your time together."

"Oh."

"I wouldn't do that to you," he insisted.

"I thought…" A shadow of hesitation creased her forehead.

"You didn't ask," he added.

"No, I didn't." She remained silent before finally considering him with a trustful look that took him by surprise. "Ren, I don't know what to do."

"What do you mean?"

"The guys doing up my clinic think that we can persuade the town to do a vote instead of the combat."

"I see." His shoulders relaxed with unexpected relief. "Not a bad idea. They used to do things that way for a while."

"It sounds like a good idea, but what if he wins?" She wrinkled her brows with worry.

"The vote? No way," he reassured her. "The locals love your family. And you."

"But they fear you and your brothers will take over. Ed Beaulieu and Jacob Pelletier, they say they like me but would vote for Charlie as our leader. Charlie is spreading lies about other packs wanting to take us over and they believe him."

"Really?" He hadn't expected it from those two. They were sensible guys.

"Which is why I'm here tonight."

"To secure votes." He mulled over the extent of Charlie's influence.

"Yes," she said. "But even then, I'm still not sure voting is the right way to do this. What if he *does* win. I'll have no more recourse."

"Don't tell me you *want* to fight?" He leaned in closer, as if to protect her from harm. It took all his resolve to hold himself back from wrapping his arms around her.

"Maybe." She chewed on her bottom lip.

"No offense, *fille*. But you *will* lose." He quickly dismissed her idea. "No, it's easy, I told you. I will fight. It's been done before. Isn't that how Nicole Desmarais took over the Val D'Or pack when Rémi was just a pup?"

"Her champion was her brother," she stated. "This case is very different. You're not a wolf."

"And you're not strong enough."

"I just started training with Aunt Camille again." She pointed to a large bruise on the outside of her thigh. He winced, wondering how he hadn't noticed it tonight. He spotted more faint marks on her forearms.

"She used to fight with my mother," she added with a wistful tone. "I wish Mom was here. She would know what to do."

"I'm sorry." His heart thawed at her distress, his

craving for her replaced by an intense desire to take her burden away.

He reached for her and gently stroked her shoulder. She had so much grief in her. Her mom died when she was barely a teen.

"That's why I don't want Charlie to take over," she stressed. "I don't want war. Delphine and Liam…"

He acknowledged the enormity of her dilemma. "Then let Max take your place."

"It's too late. Charlie's already bent on fighting me," she fretted. "And Max is family. Charlie's followers now want someone who's not a Gauthier to take over."

"Nick Pelletier then, anyone but you."

"Charlie is looking forward to taking me down in front of everyone." She shivered under his touch. "He never got over your brother's thrashing and he's taking it out on me."

"Son of a bitch," Ren spat, furious that his family's actions were spilling over her.

"Charlie's always been jealous of Dad," she said. "His grandmother probably has a lot to do with it. She took over when his mom abandoned him and his father when he was little, and these Lamberts have always been bitter. I saw Charlie grow colder and more calculating each year. Your brother was just the last straw."

"So, what do we do now?" He grasped her arm a little tighter, trying to reassure her that they were in this together.

"I don't know." She wrapped her arms around herself in defeat as he reluctantly let her go. "I need to get back in there, though."

"To canvas for votes?" His tension relaxed. He had no doubts she would win the votes. He had seen nothing but smiles for her tonight. They were a few that doubted her, but most would rally behind her in the end.

"Yes," she replied with a tiny but more hopeful smile.

"They all think you went back for a night of hot sex with me." He chuckled, trying to lighten her mood.

"Yeah, well." Amusement lit her face. "We'll need to sort *us* at some point."

"Not now," he said, more seriously. "You have a town to win over."

"I'll go back in." Her expression had taken on that determined look again, her doubts completely vanished. "Buy a few more drinks."

A small ping drummed his heart. He realized that she had just trusted him enough to let him peek behind the sunny façade.

"I'll leave you to it," he said, his sense of loyalty renewed. "It's worse for your cause when I'm around."

"Not always."

Her smile brought hope that they could indeed become friends, and maybe more.

"I never said thank you," she said. "You know... I *am* grateful."

"For the ring?"

"For saving François." The genuine look she gave him hit him straight in his soul and left his emotions a jumble of confusion.

"No problem."

"It was a nice thing to do." She reached for his cheek. A touch so light he barely felt it. But her feminine scent was all over him.

Dammit. He repressed a growl filled with raging needs.

"It *is* my duty," he murmured under his breath.

"Still, I'm thankful you did. It was the right call," she acknowledged. "I'll stay at my dad's for a couple of days. Delphine and her friends are helping me with flyers for the *épluchette*. It'll make things easier for now. I know people will talk, but I'll find some excuse."

"Okay," he croaked.

"We have our family barbecue tomorrow night, you'll be there, right?"

"You want me there?" When he'd said yes to the marriage, he hadn't realized family gatherings were part of the deal.

"Of course," she said with enthusiasm. "You're my husband, you have to be there."

"Alright," he agreed, pleasantly curious and happy to be included. His own family dinners, when their mother dared to show, were formal, gloomy affairs that always made his skin itch. "A barbecue it is then."

He watched her walk with purpose toward the bar, a small figure trying to save her town. Her shapely hips sashayed in the cutoffs, the bruises on her body more visible under the harsh spotlight of the parking lot.

His heart as heavy as the stifling summer heat, he stayed there observing the doors close on her, underscoring the differences keeping them apart—he an immortal, legacy-born vampire and her the future leader of a small-town wolf-pack.

CHAPTER 16

*R*osalie repressed a smile as she stood behind the screened patio door of her childhood home. She stared at the picnic table laid out for dinner in the backyard where Ren sat with her sibling. They were all waiting for her dad to finish cooking burgers while Aunt Camille regaled him with the latest gossip from town. Max and Don had skipped their weekly dinner, more interested in going into town to tour the clubs to celebrate Gabe Beaulieu's birthday.

There was nothing normal in tonight's family barbecue. But as she watched Ren patiently talk to her little brother who was explaining his current video game quest, she couldn't help but feel her heart melt. This handsome man was her husband.

He was patient with Liam, talked to Delphine like she was a person whose opinion mattered and not some silly teenager. And, of course, he got along well with Dad.

Her dad, who she'd been so worried about since her mom died, had an ease about him with Ren around.

The immortal had been a vague figure when she was a child. He'd never come inside their house and only parked in his truck across the street if some threat had been looming. Dad had always kept that part of his life separate from them.

Ren had to have been there at her mom's funeral, but the service had been a blur. Rosalie had been too busy looking after Liam and Delphine—keeping the façade of the responsible daughter—to remember who had attended.

Ren patted Liam warmly on the shoulder before unfolding his tall frame from the bench and stepping to the cooler to help himself to some cider. He filled two red plastic cups and headed to the smoking barbecue pit to pass the drinks to Dad and Aunt Camille.

The age contrast was significant. He was centuries old but looked somewhere in his late twenties while Dad was twice that with his grayish temples and a salt-and-pepper beard, and Aunt Camille had a mature appearance despite her slim and powerful body.

While he talked to her father and aunt as the sun set behind the pine trees of the Domaine-Lassalle forest, Rosalie couldn't tear her gaze from the enticing curve of his firm backside.

If she wasn't constantly worried about Charlie, she would be exploring ways to make the physical side of their marriage real. What would it be like to have him take her to his bed?

She absentmindedly rubbed her bare arms, still sore from the day's training, while remembering how he had seized her shoulder the day before in the parking lot of the tavern.

Despite her troubles, she'd been hit with a desire that had shocked her and she'd decided right there and then, that she did not have the strength to spend the night at his cabin.

He laughed at something her aunt had said and Rosalie admired the lines of his sculpted jaw. His face was perfection, all sharp planes without looking harsh. With full lips that she would welcome taking hers in a slow, seductive kiss.

She warmed uncomfortably at the thought, and she reached for the rings on her finger.

As she twirled the bands, she recalled the heated looks Myriam and Marie-Pier had for him at the tavern. Some men here may resent him, but the women liked him alright.

And he was hers.

How easy it would be to have him hold her so she could rest her weary head on his well-defined chest.

She'd feel safe.

He would hold her, stroke her back, and tell her that he'd take away all her problems.

Beat up her contender, run him out of town, so she could lead in peace.

But there would always be another Charlie.

She huffed. Had her father truly expected Ren to confront everyone who challenged her? She wouldn't be much of an alpha if she couldn't fight her own battles.

In that, her rival was right. She might disagree with him on the need for war, but a leader fought their own fights.

"You like him, don't you?" Delphine had stopped taking selfies in their well-lit dining area and put her phone down to charge it on the kitchen counter.

"Who?" She dug her hands into the pocket of her denim shorts and turned to her sister, trying to compose herself.

"Your husband, silly."

"Of course, I do." She smiled. "We just got married."

"Oh, come on," Delphine shot her a no-nonsense look. "I know you married him because Dad asked."

"You know, huh?" Rosalie relaxed against the door frame.

"Dad tells me stuff now."

"I'm sorry." She tilted her head to the side, admiring the new summer dress her sister had sewed just this afternoon. The simple lines complemented her sister's youthful curves, the color bringing out the amber in the teen's eyes, so like her own.

Delphine frowned. "What are you sorry about?"

"I don't know." She shrugged. "All this drama we've experienced because our family is the one leading the pack."

"I'm not the one who's being challenged to be alpha," Delphine retorted with honesty.

"True," Rosalie said. "I'm making sure all this doesn't touch you. I want you to be able to chase your dreams."

Her sister's features eased. "You've been taking care of us your whole life."

"Since Mom died," Rosalie said. "Do you remember her?"

"A little. I was five. I remember you more." Delphine flattened some imaginary crease from the skirt of her dress.

"It was hard on Dad," Rosalie reminisced.

"And on you?" She lifted her chin at her, the child still visible in the roundness of her cheeks. Delphine was turning into a fine teen, but she still needed to be protected.

"Yes. Why do you ask?"

"I don't know, you were younger than I am now when she died. I've been wondering about what that'd be like. Taking care of us and all."

"It was not easy." Rosalie recalled how the busyness had prevented her from thinking too much about her loss. "I still miss her. She would have loved who you have become."

Delphine nodded to herself. "You must have been so tired all the time. No space for friends or anything."

"You do what you have to do, sis," she said. "Dad needed me. And Liam was such a sweet baby. You were easy, too."

"Still."

"I had Aunt Camille," she reassured her sister.

Their aunt had been a huge help. Arriving at their home every morning with her own boys before they all headed to school together, taking care of the baby during the day, staying until Rosalie had had a chance to do her homework and help settle baby Liam for the night. It was probably why Rosalie was so tight with Max and Don, they'd been raised together.

"But you had school."

"We made it work. Look at you both," Rosalie added with pride. "Grown-up, kind and smart."

"Yeah, that's us." She chortled, glancing at their little brother back on his handheld gaming device.

"On a good day." She picked a loose thread off the sleeve of Delphine's new dress.

"You truly married a stranger just to carry on the family legacy?" Delphine asked with a genuine desire to know more.

"In a way," Rosalie offered. "But not entirely."

"How so?" Delphine paused before giving her sibling a wide grin. "Oh, I know… You were always hot for him."

She turned her gaze back upon Ren, now fully invested in the chitchat with Dad and Aunt Camille. He was part of their family now.

And he was indeed enticing, with the strapping shoulders under the plaid shirt and that easy-going twinkle in his eyes when among friends.

"He's attractive, no doubt," Rosalie conceded with a half-smile. "And don't forget, he's a legacy vampire who's been alive for some three hundred years. But he's no stranger to our family. Dad has known him forever."

"Still," Delphine frowned as she studied the immortal. "If you'd decided to stay in Toronto, it could have been me in your shoes in a few years."

Oh god. The idea of her little sister saddled with her worries was unthinkable. Not only would the responsibilities derail her dreams in fashion, she'd also not have a chance to find herself as a person, live outside their community and experience the world beyond their village. And she was simply not old enough or skilled enough to take on Charlie. Despite everything going on, Rosalie was glad she'd returned home to shoulder this task.

"Don't you have a boyfriend?" she asked her sister to lighten the mood.

Delphine blushed. "No. But Noah Landry apparently has a crush on me."

"He asked you out for the *épluchette*?"

"No, not yet." Her eyes sparkled with excitement. "But I made this killer outfit for the night. I spent weeks on it."

"If he doesn't, you ask him," Rosalie pressed with affection. "Take charge."

"You didn't tell me the reason why you agreed to marry Ren."

"It was Dad," Rosalie conceded. "The heart attack scared me to death."

Her throat closed in as she remembered that night in vivid detail. The dire phone call from Aunt Camille. Her frantic five-hour drive to the Montreal hospital in the dead of night, the rain pummeling down on the canvas top of her Jeep. Her father hooked up everywhere with tubes and patient monitors, his pallid face just visible under the serviceable blankets. She vowed to do whatever it took to alleviate his suffering.

"It scared me, too," Delphine admitted quietly.

"See, so now, you're less scared." She gave her sister a comforting pat on the shoulder before opening the screen door to lead her to the picnic table. "Dad recovered and I will be in charge of all those responsibilities. It was too much for him."

"But now I'm scared for you." Delphine sighed as she took her seat at the table next to her brother in front of the summer spread of fresh salads and condiments.

"Because of Charlie," Rosalie acknowledged, sitting across from her.

"Everyone from school is talking about it," she said. "We were all at the swimming hole today and they kept probing me for information."

"Really?" Rosalie hadn't expected that. They were all so young. She didn't remember worrying about pack politics at that age.

"Yeah." Delphine pinched her lips together with worry before glancing at their brother still engrossed in his video game.

"What does your crowd say about Charlie?" Rosalie was curious now.

"That he's a pig," her sister spat.

"You think?"

"He's gross, don't you agree? Maika told me his grandma is crazy."

"That she is." The old woman had no problem with François's abduction. "I wish you and your friends were old enough to vote for me."

"You won't be fighting him, right?"

"I won't need to." She didn't want Delphine to worry about her. And as she canvased the tavern last night, most patrons had agreed that a vote instead of combat would be sensible. Some liked Charlie, but no one wanted him to fight her.

"Oh good." Relieved, Delphine helped herself to a handful of potato chips. "I've been really worried."

Rosalie peered over at Aunt Camille. The kung fu master had been training her hard at the dojo for the last two days. Just in case.

Every muscle in her body ached, but she couldn't tell her sister.

"Rosalie won't get hurt, Delphine." A rich and sensual voice said above her. "I give you my word."

Ren laid a hand upon her shoulder and an unexpected wave of desire flooded low in her belly. She swallowed to subdue the craving prickling at the edge of her skin but couldn't repress the intense effect he had on her as he sat on the bench beside her, his powerful thigh gently pressed against her.

She was suddenly overtaken by a strong need to place her hand on that muscular thigh in a propriety gesture. She inhaled deep to stop herself and reached for some chips.

"You promise?" Delphine asked him, her tone dead serious.

"I do." He smiled at Rosalie as she placed a small piece of salty chip on her tongue, wildly wondering what his skin would taste like instead. "If there's a combat, I am the one who will take it."

"There won't be any fight." She shook her head at Delphine, bringing her mind to her current problems. The coronation was in over a week. The fight was set a couple days before. There was still time. "Many people last night said they will vote for me. And I have the *épluchette* to win over more people."

She was still disturbingly conscious of his body heat next to her. There might be this myth about vampires being cold but that was absolutely not true of Ren.

Her heart fluttered once more with longing. This

yearning truly seemed to be coming out of nowhere. Were her shifter hormones about to complicate things?

She glanced up to the evening sky and noticed the waxing moon. It was at first quarter. As a wolf-shifter, she usually kept track of its cycle, but the latest events had taken the forefront of her concerns.

She-wolves could get a little antsy past the new moon. If they didn't share a bed with anyone, such as all underage teens here, they got rid of that restless feeling by running the woods as wolves with a group of females from the pack every month. She'd had many runs with her friends in her days, just like Delphine was likely doing now.

Rosalie had François in the last year in Toronto but that was over.

And now that she was married, the ceremony seemed to have channeled those hormones to be desiring her husband.

No. That would be crazy. They didn't love each other.

Her needs for him were just a by-product of her exhaustion and the dread of having to deal with Charlie.

Ren tilted his head at her as their eyes connected. Had he noticed her hesitation to have him sit so close?

For mercy's sake. She swallowed again as his lips curled into a half-smile while he trailed his gaze over her cleavage down the exposed valley between her breasts.

"Dad," she cleared her voice as she called to her father. "Everything here is ready. How are those burgers coming?"

"Just about," Dad replied.

"You kids hungry?" Aunt Camille asked.

"Starving." Ren flashed a predatory look on Rosalie. His expression was filled with lust. No, she had to be reading him wrong. He couldn't be affected by her shifter's hormones, could he? He was not a wolf.

"Yeah, Dad. Hurry," Delphine urged. "I'm going to Maika's later."

"You girls are running the woodland tonight?" Dad proceeded to the picnic table with a large plate piled high with cooked meat. "Careful of those young pups out there, kiddo."

"Oh, they're fine, Alcide," Aunt Camille assured as she followed behind him. "Maika's mom and I will be with them."

"I should go with you, too," Rosalie said, feeling a sudden itch to be far away from Ren and his disturbing appeal.

"If you want to," Delphine shrugged. "The more the merrier."

"No need, Rosie," Dad cast her a benevolent look. "Cam will be with them. You go on back to Ren's. And I'll be fine here with Liam. Right, son?"

"Huh?" Liam finally looked up from his handheld game.

"Put that thing down and get yourself some dinner," Dad castigated in a warm tone. "Want to catch a movie with me tonight when your sister is out?"

Liam was still too young for midnight runs under the moon.

"Horror?" Her brother's eyes lit up.

"Sure," her dad chuckled. "Not too gory, though."

"No Dad, I promise." Now excited, Liam proceeded to pile his plate tall with potato chips and slices of corn bread.

"You two will be back at the cabin, right?" Her dad was not asking. He was worried about appearances.

Ren shot Rosalie a half-smile and she suddenly was no longer hungry for food. A strong need sat deep within her core.

Dammit, was she actually experiencing serious lust for her fake husband? She absolutely could not go back to the cabin in that state.

But she sensed she had little choice.

With their plates filled, her family dug into their dinner, the table devolving into familiar chitchat, discussing the best horror movies appropriate for a ten-year-old.

She took a few bites, but her mind was elsewhere.

She was taking a sip of cider when she noticed Ren had leaned in closer.

"I'll be glad to have you back at my place," he whispered at her side, his features unreadable. If he felt her lust, he hid it well. "It is your home now."

"Is it?"

"Yes," he said seriously. "I made a promise under the Almighty. It was no joke to me."

"We *are* married," she said, mostly for herself.

"We are." His deep voice purred in her ear.

She swallowed, hesitantly peeking at the rest of her family still engrossed in their conversation and not paying attention to them. "You intended to go with…everything?"

"At first, yes."

"I thought you said we should divorce." She turned her eyes on him.

"That was after I met your doctor," he continued. "I didn't want to get in the way."

"He's gone now." She looked down at her hands, again resting her gaze on the new rings as if they didn't belong to her.

"Are you still upset at me about that?" She sensed some frustration in his tone. "I thought we had that cleared last night."

"I'm not mad at all." She lifted her gaze to him. "You did the right thing. It must have been awful for him."

"I'm sure it was, Rosalie." Concern suddenly creased his forehead. "And I have to warn you, I didn't want to say anything to your dad, but Charlie *is* dangerous. He has LeGall chained in his barn."

"LeGall?" She didn't follow.

"The hunter that attacked Max in the spring."

"The one your brother sired into a vampire?" She hadn't been there when the hunter had descended upon their town, but the way Dad told it, this hunter was a real threat to them, and Ren's brother had stopped him by turning the slayer into a cursed vampire.

"Exactly," Ren replied.

"Chained?" She winced.

"Like some feral pet."

"That's despicable," she said. "Shouldn't we do something?"

"Do something? Like what?" He frowned, puzzled. "You didn't want me to rescue your ex, but you want to go free some fucked-up vampire?"

"It seems wrong somehow. Charlie can be cruel."

"Maybe." Ren's lips were a thin line. "But that psychopath chose to attack my brother and his wife. And don't forget he bombed Alcide's Tavern. I just want you to remember what Charlie is capable of."

"You're a hard man," she said, feeling the weight of his gaze on her.

"Because I won't save that scumbag?" Ren grumbled. "LeGall is dealing with the consequences of his choices."

"Is he not redeemable?"

"Not everyone is, Rosalie." His expression on her softened.

"Yeah, maybe." She looked down at her plate. Liam was talking with his sister. Dad had gotten up to get more drinks, and Aunt Camille was fetching something from the kitchen. Fireflies danced at the edge of the forest behind their house.

"The *épluchette* is in three days," he said. "You should be focusing on charming the town. Not think of that bastard."

"Charming the town?" she asked. "Is that what you think I do?"

"A little," he grinned.

"I haven't charmed you," she said, not knowing where that came from.

He reached for her shoulder to slowly rearrange the strap of her tank top, his burning touch making her quake inside. "I wouldn't say that."

There was heat in his gaze. It was real and it was fierce.

That was when it hit her. Despite not being a shifter, he could actually sense her desire.

He hooked his finger into the band of her top and softly pulled her in his direction. He bent his head to the crook of her neck, and she felt his warm breath against her skin.

"You should come back to the cabin with me, Rosalie." A low growl emerged from his throat. "I *am* your husband, after all."

Oh, have mercy. Shivers descended all the way to her toes.

It would be so easy. Go with him. Let her lust take over.

And if her friend Caro was right, the goddess Selene could grace them with a soulmate connection that would provide her with super strength. If he did feel her hormones, could there not be a chance that they would also bond?

"Come," he rasped. The tip of his fangs grazed her skin as he traced the back of her spine with his palm.

Oh damn, he would surely bite her, too. She had heard that the sensation could be incredible if done between lovers.

"Rosalie," her sister interrupted. "Remember that movie where the babysitter is being chased by some lunatic throughout a boathouse by the sea? You think Liam is old enough for it?"

"What?" Rosalie shook herself from her trance to look at Delphine.

Ren pulled back slightly but still kept his hand at her back, his close masculine scent driving her senseless.

"Um, I don't know," she finally answered her sister, "it's pretty scary."

She glanced at Ren and saw his eyes had taken a fiery touch. Oh god. She would fall into his pull in no time if she followed him to the cabin.

"Hey, Delphine," she suddenly asked her sister, glancing up at the sliver of waxing moon taunting her. "Where exactly are you all running tonight?"

"Just up the Beaver Woods hills."

Her heart was in turmoil, her mind telling her to stay well away from him. Getting close would only add to her troubles.

"I'm sorry, Ren." She avoided connecting with his captivating gaze. "It's been too long since I ran with my sister. I really need to be with the girls tonight."

CHAPTER 17

*C*alvaire, they'd been so close to getting together after her family barbecue. Ren couldn't let the thought go as he strode with his brother Griff onto the town commons in the late afternoon for the *épluchette*. The vast grassy area at the edge of town behind the community hall hosting the yearly corn shucking party was packed with locals, young and old.

She could have been in his bed that very night. He'd been so sure he had sensed her desire for him.

But no, he'd been mistaken. She had chosen to run the woods with her sister instead.

It had been three nights now!

She had found other excuses not to return to his home, various night events she told him she needed to attend to convince more people to vote in her favor. There had been the late meeting with the ladies at the *Cercle des Fermières*, and then the evening book club at the library. And she'd had to oversee the last touches to her clinic during the day.

He'd caught sight of her little jeep in town once and had later seen her walk the street with her sister, with fliers in hands as they canvased the local stores.

He hadn't tried to talk to her, though, leaving her the space to do things on her own. Working on expanding his cabin while he waited, thinking of her and their future—if they had any.

But tonight was it. He would see her.

Griff's attitude remained cool as he walked alongside Ren as they both entered the venue bustling with the residents in their best summer clothes.

The place was dotted with beer tents and long tables packed with vats of boiling water filled with fresh corn. Huge canvas bags were stacked on the ground with stalks ready to be shucked.

Food trucks were everywhere, as well as offerings from the community. A colorful bouncy castle could be seen at the edge of the forest, right beside a massive stage that was currently empty. Loud classic rock resonated through the crowd from the huge speakers erected for the concert that was scheduled for when the sun would start to set on the sweltering evening.

"Seems busier than before," Griff noticed with a detached, half-smile.

"It's Charlie," Ren grumbled. "He put on a big splash. Even got a band."

"Really?" Griff raised a brow. "Anyone Cass knows?"

"No idea." Ren shrugged. "Where *is* Cass?"

"Montreal. He was bored and said you'd handle it without him. Guess he couldn't stay too long away from his adoring fans."

"Uh," Ren huffed. He could have used the support. "And you?"

"Here for the entertainment." His brother snorted.

"Thanks." Ren rolled his eyes but knew deep inside that Griff's bantering was just a façade. His brother had his back. He'd been away for decades but their bond was still strong.

"Honestly, I don't like you being rattled like this," Griff added as they neared a beer table manned by Alcide's staff. "I've never seen you so emotional before. It's that she-wolf."

"My wife," Ren stated.

"You're hot for her," Griff insisted.

Ren muttered. "I don't get rattled by women."

"It's her pheromones. You've been around wolves long enough." Griff accepted a plastic cup filled with foamy beer from a cheery Léa Pelletier. "You should know that."

"Huh?"

"You're physically attracted to her, right?" Griff passed him the beer and took another one from Alcide's waitress. "When you married, you triggered the mating process."

"But that's for shifters." Ren nodded absentmindedly at Léa and turned toward the stage. "I'm an immortal."

They strolled through the tents, avoiding a pair of children zooming past them.

"Maybe the goddess Selene has decided that you are now part of the pack," Griff offered.

"You're kidding!" Ren stopped mid-stride. This was impossible.

"Hey, I've seen things I can't explain in my travels." Griff's dark expression gave Ren a chill.

"We're mated?" He just couldn't believe this. He'd spent over a century with wolves, but he'd truly never been one of them. "Dammit!"

"Not quite yet. I assume you still sleep on the couch?"

"She hasn't slept at the cabin since our wedding night."

"Damn, bro." Griff frowned. "That's rough."

"Yeah."

"Well, at some point, you two won't be able to resist each other, and you'll bond." Griff's look on him was now dead serious. "You'll be mated for life, brother. For her life, anyway."

"Hells, now I really do have to divorce her." Ren shook his head in frustration.

"I thought you liked her?" Griff remarked.

"Yes, I do, but for life?" This whole thing made his brain hurt. And possibly his heart.

"Sorry, bro. But did you not think when you proposed?"

"I did not propose," he winced. "Alcide asked and I said fine."

"How did you not know about the shifters' mating bond?" Griff's brow wrinkled.

Ren shrugged and resumed their walk. "It doesn't happen *that* often anymore. I know Alcide's father was bonded with his wife, but I'm not a shifter. How would I know it could affect me."

"Well, there you go." Griff shook his head with sympathy. "Better get that divorce quick before it gets worse."

"I'll be dammed." Ren couldn't believe this. The desire he had felt was not real. It was all orchestrated from the beyond. Just because he had married a female wolf-shifter.

Damn, this was all too complicated for a simple guy like him.

"What now?" He prided himself in always knowing right from wrong. But now he remained conflicted.

Was the right thing to do to sleep with her and be mated for good as the pack traditions demanded? Or instead, divorce and return her freedom? If he did stay, it would only be a generation to him, nothing really. But for her? It was her whole life.

"Does she feel it, too?" he asked Griff, who strangely was more informed about shifter customs than he was.

"What?" Griff was distracted by a street performer juggling a series of colorful bottles for a row of kids watching in awe.

"You know. These hormones," Ren snapped at him.

"Hormones, yes probably." Griff turned his focus back on him before taking a healthy swig of his beer.

"She doesn't really show it." Ren remembered how she'd been at the barbecue. Uncomfortable maybe but... could she have been lusting for him, though?

"Sorry, bro."

"Nothing to be sorry about." Ren tried to take the news in stride. "Divorcing now might be for the best."

"Yeah, probably," Griff agreed as they passed a stall selling cotton candy. "Mixing vamps and shifters is not good. You always insisted to live among them but—"

"She's got her hands full right now." Ren interrupted as he caught sight of her chestnut ponytail in the crowd.

Damn, she was hot. Neat denim shorts with a fitted bright pink tank top. Long, shapely legs propelling her decisive strides across the grass. She was passing flyers and talking to the locals.

He took a sip of his beer to cool down his rising desire and tumbling heart.

"These people want a vote, not combat," he told his brother.

"I said it before," Griff advised. "You should just go kill the bastard. Slip quietly into the night. Done."

"Maybe. But she'll lose their trust. They'll think she ordered the hit."

"And what is wrong with that?" Griff protested. "Plenty of leaders have started their reign with a little bloodshed."

"Not her. She's got too much integrity." The idea of her committing any kind of unprovoked violence was completely wrong.

"And you like that about her, don't you?"

"I do." There was no doubt in his mind. He had it in for her.

"Maybe it's more than hormones," Griff noticed.

"Could be." And perhaps it was. Her sense of justice, just as her father possessed, was appealing.

She wanted to meet the needs of everyone here. He'd heard the rumors. Since she'd been back, she had helped cheer up Mrs. Savard who had lost her husband last year and had arranged to get the elementary school's plumbing fixed.

And it was his tormented soul that yearned for her. The flashes of his scorching agony and the gnawing guilt over Pierre's murder receded when he was around her. She brought him peace.

"Then don't divorce her," Griff was saying.

She finally caught his gaze for a second before turning back to Mrs. Pelletier and a shot of devotion pierced him straight through his heart.

"I won't." There was determination behind his declaration. "I'll stick by her."

And suddenly the possibility of living a mortal lifespan at her side seemed amazing. Be in her presence for decades, share her lifetime. He couldn't see it any other way.

Was he falling in love?

"It will have to be her decision," he grumbled.

He'd heard that the voting had been set for the next day, right after the church service. And she would win, no doubt about that. As long as Alcide made sure Charlie didn't rig it.

As he watched her smile at the locals, he knew she was esteemed by all here.

Once she won the vote, he would be there for her if Charlie retaliated. And take the bastard down if needed. This time the town would be on her side. Yeah, that was a good plan.

They'd make a life in his cabin by the water. Explore this bond that had been created between them.

Wow. The whole prospect made his chest expand with hope.

"Well, well, the fiend has arrived," Griff warned. "And he brought his pet with him."

Ren followed his brother's gaze to Charlie and his gang, with LeGall in chains led by Hubert behind them. Seemed that Fortin had stopped following them, but the other three minions hadn't heeded the St-Amand warning and stuck with their hero. Two hired guns were with him, sporting fatigues and tactical vests.

Coyotes, most likely.

"Oh shit."

Rosalie hadn't seen her opponent yet and was talking with the Landrys.

The crowd gawked and thickened around Charlie and his followers. LeGall was a mess. Emaciated to the bone, eyes bulging out of his sockets. His mind appearing to be completely gone as he tried to keep up with barrel-chested Hubert Bouchard yanking on his collar.

The sun had disappeared behind the mountains and, had they arrived earlier, the former vampire hunter would have been burnt to a crisp.

The villagers couldn't tear their eyes from LeGall, whispering at each other in shock.

Ren had a hard time feeling pity for the psychopath who had nearly killed his brother Justin, but this went beyond the limits of decency.

He hastened his steps toward Bouchard, followed closely by Griff. By the time he neared the crowd, Rosalie had noticed the scene and was walking toward them.

"What's this?" Outraged but poised, she spoke loud enough for everyone to hear.

"This, little lady, is *my* vampire." Bouchard sneered and rolled his overblown shoulders. "You got yours, I got mine."

"That's a vampire?" she asked.

"Yes, it is." He grabbed LeGall's chain from his cousin and yanked it hard. "Show your pretty fangs, pet."

LeGall fell on the ground and hissed, his cheeks hollow and elongated incisors fully out.

The crowd gasped.

Mrs. Mercier, Justin's housekeeper, was looking at her former torturer with shock, her hand trembling on her daughter's arm. Caro slid an arm around her mother in support as people shook their heads in disgust, not knowing what to think.

"This is sick, Charlie," Rosalie said. "Return this beast to the immortals."

"Oh, so they can release him again?" Bouchard boasted with defiance.

"Miss Emme chose to let him go," Mrs. Mercier proclaimed. The sturdy woman was now standing her ground in her pressed jeans and tidy *Cercle des Fermières* white tee. "We, at Briac Falls, honor our promises."

"Emme Dubois, that slut vamp!" Bouchard narrowed his small eyes at the housekeeper. "Is your family a vampire lover now, old woman?"

"Miss Emme saved my life, which is more than you've ever done for us, kid," she spat, filled with spunk.

Ren tuned out the debate to study LeGall.

The fallen creature had been a fearless supernatural hunter and now was nothing. His coat hung around emaciated features, his family's insignia half ripped off the canvas fabric.

After Ren's brother and his wife Emme had survived the zealous predator, Justin had enacted what Ren believed was justice, by turning the sociopath into what LeGall hated the most, a vampire. He'd been given the choice of going down to the *Sanctuaire des Truants* to learn to live with his bloodthirst or be set free to the wilderness, as long as he avoided any human contact.

And by the looks of it, LeGall had kept his side of the bargain and stuck to animal blood.

Ren didn't know how long he'd been in captivity, but Bouchard had obviously enjoyed torturing him. LeGall was dying.

"Should we do something?" Griff asked Ren under his breath.

Ren shook his head, remembering his brother Justin blinded by the angel blood LeGall had poisoned him with. Without Caro Mercier and Maisie Thibodeau, Justin would have remained blind forever.

Emme and Justin had sealed the hunter's fate. And what happened after that was out of Ren's hands.

Rosalie took a step forward. She bent down to LeGall who was still on his knees and touched the steel collar around his neck. Ren held his breath in fear for her. LeGall had once been a vicious killer.

"This is pure cruelty," Rosalie protested as Ren silently moved in closer to her. "Whatever he did, he's a living creature. You have to let him go. Send him to Montreal to the cursed vampire shelter."

"No chance, sweet pea. He's way too much fun." Charlie cackled and he yanked LeGall back on his feet with glee. He addressed the crowd. "This, people, *this*, is what we do to vampires. We keep them in chains, not in our bed."

"Aye," a few voices erupted from the onlookers.

Griff side-eyed Ren as he let the insult slide with a shrug. This small group of dissenters didn't matter. He knew most were grateful for all he had done to keep the peace over the centuries.

"He's dying, you asshole." Rosalie slowly stood to face

her challenger, exhaustion palpable in her voice, breaking Ren's heart. She'd been working herself too hard.

He yearned to wrap an arm around her but didn't want to diminish her in front of her foe. But, dammit, he'd give anything to just rip that smug look off Bouchard's self-important features and be done with it.

Shit, he hated all this. The whole politics thing. If he intervened now, he could ruin everything for her.

So he stayed back and let her handle it. But *calvaire*, he didn't have to like it.

He remained on alert. He wasn't worried about Lambert and the Bouchard cousins, but the hired guns could mean trouble. He wouldn't forget that it was their kind who had murdered Rosalie's mother.

"What, girlie?" Charlie spat. "You want this one in your bed, too?"

His circle erupted in laughter while the rest of the town looked nervously at her.

She pursed her lips, her fist tightening over the stack of flyers in her left hand, and silently stared at her rival with hatred. Then she turned on her heels and stomped off.

"That chick just can't take the heat." Charlie laughed again.

Ren took in a deep breath to force himself not to tear the scumbag apart. He cast one last look at LeGall before taking off after Rosalie, leaving his brother behind.

She was grumbling as she paced the grounds. "Freakin' bastard."

"Want me to kill him for you?" He tried to make light of the moment to diffuse her strain.

"No!" She stopped to level him with an annoyed look. "You should free that poor creature, though. Why didn't you?"

Ren frowned. "Because he's a monster?"

"Didn't look like a monster to me. What Charlie is doing is cruel." Her knuckles were white with tension.

"Oh, trust me, LeGall *is* a monster. Didn't your friend Caro tell you what he did to her mother?"

"No, she didn't."

"She was seconds from being electrocuted when Emme rescued her. That poor woman had been tied to a sink filling with water, live wires dangling over it. I can't imagine how scared she must have been." Ren let out a heavy sigh. "That bastard comes from a family that enjoys torturing supernatural beings and those who coexist with us."

"Still…" Her lips were tight.

"You think Bouchard is bad. LeGall is much worse."

"No one is worse than Charlie," she protested.

"Believe me, he is."

She crossed her arms at her chest. "So, you won't rescue him?"

"Rescue LeGall?" He reeled back. "Oh, hells no!"

"It's not easy to look at." Her expression turned crestfallen.

"Then don't look." His tone softened. She had such a good heart. She thought everyone could be saved.

"Are you always so hard?" Her features wrinkled as she tried to read him.

"For the likes of LeGall, yeah sure." He shrugged. He just couldn't explain his simple but unyielding personal code.

"I don't care what he did. They can't treat a live creature like this. Doesn't he deserve redemption?"

"No," Ren said, more forcefully than he'd wished. "He doesn't. The son of a bitch nearly blinded my brother for eternity. And Emme, dammit, he tortured her for hours."

Emme's torment, from what he'd heard, had been

close to his own when he'd been burnt alive by the mob of settlers. After removing her daylight ring, that fucker had restrained her to Justin's bed and exposed her to the sun, opening and closing the curtains, scorching her over and over to keep the torture lasting.

"LeGall shot Max with a silver arrow and blew up your dad's tavern," Ren added. "It took months to rebuild it. They just got the custom mirror installed last week."

"I know," she relented.

"You're blind to LeGall's crimes because Charlie challenges your claim."

"Not you, too?"

"What?" He looked at her bewildered.

"You're taking his side."

"No, wait." He placed his hand on her arm. "I'm not on his side."

"Then you should snatch LeGall from him." She just wouldn't let it go. "My father will know what to do with the creature."

Ren let out a slow breath, knowing very well that this had nothing to do with LeGall and all to do with the trauma Bouchard was putting her through.

"LeGall has already been judged," he said gently. "By the elders, your dad, and Father Grégoire. He was offered redemption at the *Sanctuaire des Truands*. He refused. His fate was ultimately decided by Emme."

"She didn't know he'd be captured by Charlie to be some sort of slave," she insisted.

"That's the point," Ren explained. "Emme didn't care what happened to him. She just let karma do the job."

"Can karma be that cruel?" She frowned at him, her distress breaking his heart.

"He's receiving what he dished out. It's justice."

"I can't have that." Her resolve returned and she lifted her chin at him. "Not in our pack."

"Then you have to win the claim. Force Bouchard to let LeGall go when you're the leader."

Clutching the fliers to her chest, she took a deep breath, deepening the strain visible at the corner of her eyes. Ren could hear Bouchard laugh with his pals behind him.

If only he could just whisk her to his cabin, away from all this. Take her into his arms. Melt the tension from her body.

Her misguided compassion was thawing his heart.

Oh fuck, maybe he should just go and rescue the damn psychopath to make her feel better.

It had always been easy. Right or wrong. No shades of gray. But she saw things differently than he did.

"Fine." She pursed her lips tight, her expression unreadable. "I'll do this myself."

He released her arm to open his palm at her. "These fliers," he said. "I can help pass them around."

She shook her head quietly, a stubborn gleam lighting her gaze. "No. It's my claim. I got this."

Not leaving him time to reply, she took off to join a nearby group of *Fermières*. She plastered a bright smile on her face and started to chat with them with a joy he knew she didn't experience—while he looked from afar, feeling absolutely useless.

"What the hell are you even doing here with these wolves, brother?" Griff had returned to his side. Sensing his unrest, his sibling laid a strong hand at his shoulder. "This is not our home. You should come back to Montreal."

A few days ago, Ren would have had a quick response for his brother. But everything had changed since Rosalie had come back to Briac Falls and married him. His place in the pack seemed lost.

He stared at his bride surrounded by the villagers and

suddenly felt like a complete outsider to the town he had called his home for over a century.

"I'm not sure, Griff," he told his brother. "I really don't know anymore."

CHAPTER 18

"*I*sn't that horrible, the way Charlie is yanking that creature around?" Rosalie joined the small group of locals who had organized the tents filled with homemade goodies for the *épluchette*.

"Oh, I don't know, *ma chère*." Mrs. Beaulieu, the B&B owner, had a serious look on her neat features. "That hunter was meant to kill all of us. Fabienne told me all about her kidnapping. She almost died."

"Yes, that's what LeGall deserves," the grocer, Mr. Fortin added.

"But you're right, Rosalie," Mrs. Beaulieu corrected herself as she tugged on her *Cercle des Fermières* T-shirt. "Dragging him like this on the field is too much. It's frightening the little ones."

"Yeah," Mrs. Fortin looped an arm under her husband's. "It's not just that the creature is a supernatural hunter, but now he's also a vampire! No offense, Rosalie."

"Offense?" Rosalie frowned at Danny Fortin's mom.

"Well, you married one, didn't you?" She fixed her eyes on Rosalie.

"I thought you all liked Ren." Rosalie browsed the crowd around her with a puzzled look.

"Oh sure, he's great," Mrs. Leclerc acknowledged.

"Didn't you have a thing for him when you were seventeen, Louise?" Mrs. Fortin teased with a grin.

"Of course, I did. Everyone did." Mrs. Leclerc chuckled as she fluffed up her sleek silver bob. "That was before Ti-Jo asked me out. St-Amand has always been a handsome devil."

"And mysterious, you know." Mrs. Fortin rose an appreciative brow at her friend. "That bad boy thing going on."

"He's more like a warrior." Jérémie Landry, the collectible shop owner, pulled his husband Thomas within his embrace as he gave Rosalie a dreamy look. "You know, the knight protecting the princess."

"And now he does have his princess," Thomas concurred.

She glanced back at the small, bearded man in the pristine white shorts and tattersall button-down. "I'm no princess."

"Well, you are a little bit. Daughter of our alpha," Jérémie said. "Married to his bodyguard."

"You'll be queen." Thomas nodded.

"I'm not here to be some queen, surely you all know this. I'm here to sort things out. Deal with the Val D'Or pack, the land fight with *Bois-Franc Village*. That's what an alpha does."

"That's what you see from your end, dear," Mrs. Leclerc said. "Because you're close to your dad. You see the day-to-day. But you miss the other things."

"What other things?"

"Your father is also a symbol to us. The Mighty Wolf."

Baffled, Rosalie frowned at her.

"Yes," Mrs. Fortin chimed in. "Oh, Alcide was really

something in his prime. Strong, handsome, no one could beat him. And with that, a true heart for our pack, just like your grandfather."

"Just like you, child," Mrs. Beaulieu added.

"Then why is everyone challenging my claim?" Rosalie wasn't following what the *Fermières* were saying. Were they not all on her side? "Is it because I'm female?"

"Not everyone is against you. I'll vote for you, *ma belle*," Jérémie said, reaching out to pat her forearm. "I know you're better for us than Charlie. But he's clever. Yanking that despicable hunter around like that, parading him about, it gives some pack members that symbol of strength your dad has been for us. It's nothing to do with you being female."

"Sorry Rosalie," Thomas agreed with his spouse. "I think your father made a mistake marrying you to his bodyguard."

"Because he's an immortal?" She couldn't believe this.

"I'm afraid so," Louise Leclerc said. "Oh, we do like St-Amand, no doubt. But we like him in the shadows. And now, he's walking at the forefront as some rightful heir, next to you."

"He's not like that," Rosalie protested. "He doesn't interfere."

"Maybe he should," Mr. Fortin proclaimed, firmly adjusting his denim shirt over the red tee advertising his grocery store.

"He should take down Charlie," his wife agreed.

"But then people will say I can't lead," Rosalie griped at their mixed opinions of the situation.

"Look dear, there's no way you can defeat Charlie at combat."

Oh mercy, they all still had that fight in mind. "I'm training with Aunt Camille," Rosalie revealed.

"Doesn't matter," Mr. Fortin said. "That kid is not only strong, he's sneaky. He fights dirty."

"But everyone agreed to the vote," Rosalie countered. Her father had acknowledged that voting was a good idea and had used his authority to ensure it would be a fair one tomorrow at the church.

"Of course, if most people go your way, you won't have to fight him," Jérémie agreed. "But then what? Charlie is not likely to back down."

"You have to let St-Amand do what he does best," Mrs. Beaulieu said. "Get rid of Charlie."

"What? Kill him?" Rosalie opened her eyes wide in disbelief.

"Maybe not," Mrs. Beaulieu clarified. "Maim him or something. Run him out of town."

"And what about his cousins?" Rosalie asked. "And Julien Lambert?"

"That weasel," Mrs. Leclerc snorted. "Yes, those three as well."

"I'm glad Danny finally steered clear of that lot." Mr. Fortin huffed while his wife nodded with pursed lips.

Rosalie blew out a frustrated breath as she looked up at her group of supporters. "He's got those hired guns."

"St-Amand has his brother here, right?" Jérémie threw a hand in the direction of Ren and Griff who were talking with the tavern's staff. "And you could rally the boys, Max, Don, and Nick. That's what leaders do."

"A civil war." She shook her head with dismay. Everything she hated.

"Maybe," Mr. Fortin stated.

"I can't start my leadership with a civil war." She'd rather step down than see her beloved town divided and at each other's throats. But what of her siblings if Charlie took over. The thought was unbearable.

"*Fille*, you have no choice. Look." Thomas pointed at a

small group of younger men laughing as Charlie made LeGall jump up and down with the yank of his chain. "Is that what we want here?"

From the corner of her eye, she saw her sister and her flock of girlfriends pass by Charlie's crowd. Delphine looked a vision of glamour in the brand-new dress she had spent days working on for the evening.

The men whistled at the girls.

"Hey cutie," Charlie barked. "Want to play with my new toy?"

"Oh, fuck you, Charles!" her sister snapped back with disgust. Her two friends looked warily at the group of crude men ogling them.

"Such nasty language for such a pretty thing." He gave LeGall's leash to one of his cousins and marched toward Delphine. His gang following right behind him.

Rosalie's fists tightened. "Sorry, folks, I better check on Delphine." She excused herself to the villagers as she raced to the scene.

"I'll talk to you the way I want to, asshole!" Her sister may still favor teenage drama but didn't lack spunk when confronted. She stood facing Charlie, a picture of right-eousness in her well-cut white-on-white summer dress.

"Oh, come on cutie, don't you want a real wolf by your side? I can show you things." Charlie crudely grabbed his crotch and thrust his groin in a pretend hump.

"Eww," her sister exclaimed. Maika and Élise, her two girlfriends, stared at Charlie with revulsion. Ren and his brother had also approached the crowd.

But Charlie wasn't backing down. He narrowed the distance between him and Delphine.

Everything Rosalie had repressed since her wedding, her outrage and resentment, came rushing back.

"Charlie!" she ordered. "Leave my sister alone!"

With his broken arm still in a sling, Tom Bouchard

leered at the other girls. "I think they all just want to have a good time."

That freakin' pig! Rosalie's nostrils flared with anger.

All she feared if Charlie took over the pack was right there in front of her eyes. Those fuckers would have no problem assaulting the teens. And then where would it end? If he became leader, he'd expect no less than subjugation and conquest during his reign. Like hell would she let that happen.

The wolf in her bristled with wrath.

"You're a pretty little thing, aren't you?" Charlie continued to advance toward Delphine, ogling her with a creepy leer. "All those sweet outfits, just like a girl should be. Not like your stuck-up sister."

"Back off, you prick." Delphine had her palm out, standing her ground.

"Guess what, *bébé*," he said. "When I beat your sister, I'll take you as my bride. I bet you'd like that."

He slammed his grip at her wrist.

Delphine screamed. As she tried to escape him, the delicate gauze sleeve of her brand-new dress tore open.

"Get the fuck away from my sister!" Rosalie roared and raced forward, her epinephrine overriding her body.

But Charlie was not paying her any attention, his eyes filled with lecherous urges.

"Come on, man," his cousin Tom urged him on. "Get that little slut!"

"It's your lucky day, cutie." Right there, in front of everyone, he yanked Delphine to his chest and hauled her dress up from behind to grab her crotch.

Delphine shrieked and ducked down to escape him, loudly ripping the skirt of the dress in her attempt.

Rosalie's shift to wolf form took less than a second.

Her shorts and tank top shredded at her feet, her

animal teeth and claws out, she snarled wildly at the bastard assaulting her sister.

"Rose!" Ren shouted after her, but she ignored him. Charlie had crossed a line and she would make him pay.

Fully changed into her gray wolf form, she pounced straight for his throat.

"What the—" He released her sister as Rosalie pinned him on the ground, her claws digging into his chest, her tail flipping madly.

He grabbed her by the scruff of the neck with one hand, his other at her flank, and shoved her off him.

She growled at him as he stood facing her, a satisfied smile plastering his face.

"So here we are, sweet pea," he snarled. "Ready to fight, huh?"

Low thunder echoed from deep in the pit of her chest as she gnashed her teeth. Her jaw ached to maul that smug smile off that human face of his.

And that's when he shifted.

CHAPTER 19

Oh shit! Ren bolted to stand between Rosalie and Charlie, but his minions were faster and blocked his way.

Tom Bouchard blustered at him. "Stop it there, vamp."

The two coyote mercenaries eyed him coldly, their military weapons at the ready.

Griff slammed his palm at his shoulder. "Brother, wait."

"What?" he snapped, his heart pulsing with the urge to punch someone.

"You can't get involved," Griff reasoned, his tone shockingly calm.

"The hell I can't." Ren took another step.

The two fully-formed gray wolves circled each other, one burly and much darker in shade and the other—Rosalie—smaller but agile.

Natural wolf-shifters—as in those born into it like the Domaine-Lassalle pack—had three forms, human, wolf and somewhere in between where they stood on two legs while sporting a snout, claws, and tail. His brother had taken down Charlie in his humanoid form, but this time the scumbag had gone for the full shift to face Rosalie.

The big gray wolf was impressive as he yowled at the smaller female. But Rosalie was not boasting when she said she was ready to take him.

She growled at her opponent as she paced back and forth on nimble paws in front of him, stopping only to show razor-sharp teeth in a menacing snarl.

"Damn, Rosalie's ready to fight Charlie!" someone shouted. Locals had noticed and started to gather in a wide circle around them.

"Sis. No!" Delphine had gotten to her feet and held her soiled, tattered dress with both hands, her shocked girl-friends surrounding her.

"Oh fuck." Ren vamped out, fangs out, disgusted by the whole situation.

"Don't even think about it, vampire," Tom hollered at him again. The two mercenaries stepped forward to block him with blank looks, fingers ready for the trigger of their submachine guns.

Ren could overcome them as they did when rescuing the doctor, but he couldn't risk stray bullets. And in truth, the only thing stopping him from jumping Charlie right now was his brother's steady grip on his shoulder.

Rosalie howled at the big wolf. His heart hammered with repressed adrenaline, and he cursed her desire to handle this on her own.

He'd seen plenty of wolf-shifter fights before. Aside from the wolf war, patrons at the tavern would often get angry, shift, and take it outside for a quick brawl that ended in scrapes and maybe a broken limb or two.

But this was different. This was a fight for dominance. To claim the rank of alpha.

Something that had not been done for at least a

hundred years when Rosalie's ancestor had battled young contenders in the ring to prove his worth.

Ren held his breath as Charlie lunged at her with a snap of his jaw.

She skidded to the side with a fast bite to his flank and the crowd cheered.

"You get him, Rosalie, come on!"

Her sister and her friends were huddled together in alarm as Alcide approached them and quickly gauged the situation. He silently wrapped an arm around his youngest daughter, his features set in a mix of pride and apprehension as he watched the fight of his eldest.

And boy, Rosalie *was* fast. Ren's tensed knuckles eased. She knew what she was doing. Running back and forth to stay out of Charlie's way, looking for an opening to attack.

Where Charlie had mass and strength, she obviously had speed on her side.

Alert on her paws, she was circling Charlie again, her ears perked up and tail straight up. She kept the big beast in her sight, while he crouched low, baring menacing teeth. His jowls dripped with saliva as he tried to isolate her location in order to strike.

She sprung forward to nip at him again—her fangs sinking into the flesh of his hind leg—before taking a quick retreat.

He lunged at her but again she swerved and ran out of bound.

After she gained some distance from him, she unpredictably turned and rammed right into him, hitting him square in the flank, her momentum flipping the wolf onto his back.

The audience gasped as Ren repressed a cheer.

She aimed her jaw at Charlie's throat, but he was faster. He bit straight into her neck and overturned her to sink his teeth deep into her flesh. With her in his grip, he managed to shake her entire body side to side with all his might.

Fuck! Ren's throat seized.

Griff finally let go of him and Ren lunged in her direction. This was not the time to let her fight alone, no matter what she believed.

"Ren, no!" Alcide's call thundered over the crowd, his leadership unmistakable.

Ren stopped mid-step, looking back and forth at his leader and the she-wolf that was desperately trying to escape her assailant. "What the hell?"

"She *has* to do this." Alcide's pain was obvious in his features, but his tone was unwavering.

"He's killing her." This was crazy. How could he allow his daughter to be thrashed about like that?

"He won't," Alcide stated. "She's spry. She can win."

"The hell she can, man." Ren was having none of it.

"Ren…" Alcide warned.

And right there, in that very moment, Ren knew that the rigid rules of the wolf pack life no longer served him. He was not some puppet to be ordered by anyone let alone the alpha who would let his daughter be slaughtered by a raging monster.

"She *can* fight him, Renaud," Alcide said, more quietly. "Look."

Ren saw that she had indeed succeeded in escaping Charlie's deadly grip. Blood poured from her silver mane and Ren could sense her anger.

But also her exhaustion. If her own father couldn't see it, he was blind.

She snarled and growled, tail flicking as she ran back and forth in front of Charlie who was as bloody as she was.

And that's when Charlie, who had been using very little energy so far, exploded into action and barged straight into her.

In a flash, she was flipped onto her back, Charlie's bulk pinning her down.

He dug into her throat and shook her hard.

"Charlie! Stop this. Now!" Alcide finally stepped in, this time the fear obvious in the alpha's voice.

Charlie was oblivious to the command and jerked Rosalie as if she was a mere rag doll.

There was no coming back from this. Her neck would be breaking in no time.

Ren leaped into action.

He caught Charlie by the flank and drilled his fangs into the large wolf's carotid.

The animal squealed and released Rosalie.

With a heart-breaking whimper, she curled herself on the ground into a tight furry ball.

Ren swung his grip and secured the big wolf at the crook of his elbow in a powerful choke hold. Charlie reverted to human form under his arm, all bloody naked skin and bulging muscles.

"Do I kill him?" Ren was asking Griff.

He had no place for wolves in his life. His change of heart had been instant. Alcide's willingness to sacrifice the daughter Ren cared for had been too much. The only opinion he'd consider would be that of his kin.

"Don't," Alcide said.

But Ren, still filled with righteous wrath at the situation, was only looking at his brother.

Griff shook his head quietly.

Yanking further on Charlie's throat, he narrowed his eyes upon Alcide. "He would have killed your daughter."

Alcide crouched beside Rosalie's defeated form. "Is that true, Charlie?"

But Ren didn't care to hear the answer. With angst for her fate, he was finally daring to look at Rosalie who had also just shifted back to human.

His heart shattered to see her naked body, lacerated and bleeding on the ground, her father covering her with his denim shirt. He wanted to run to her but didn't trust Charlie not to finish her.

Caro emerged from the crowd of onlookers to dash to her friend's side. She mumbled incomprehensible incantations as she laid her hands on Rosalie's broken limbs.

"Let Charlie go, vamp," someone heckled. Everyone else looked at the scene in silent shock.

The bloody combat was more violence than most had seen in decades. A complete contrast to the earlier cheerful festivities.

Ren wanted to hear from her. What did *she* want him to do?

But she wasn't saying anything. She was coiled in on herself in the grass, completely overpowered, and with her father, sister, and Caro grimly tending to her. No one had truly understood what she'd been fighting against.

He caught Griff's dark look on him and, angry as hell, choked Charlie some more.

Caro shot him a pleading look. "Ren, we need to move her."

Fuck. He shoved Charlie to the ground and quickly snatched Rosalie from the field and into his arms.

"She'll be at my cabin," he barked, enraged at the entire crowd of stunned villagers.

With her in his embrace, and at vamp speed, he whisked her away from that mad place and from the damned locals who would allow one of their best people be killed by a fucking bully.

CHAPTER 20

"Where's Ren?' Rosalie blinked awake and took in the cabin's bedroom.

She searched for him past her friend Caro who was solicitously bent over her, patting a cool cloth over her forehead. She was filled with a deep need to feel his arms around her again.

The recollection of the last few hours where a blur. She'd been hurt, in atrocious pain, and then experienced a blessed feeling of warmth and safety as he'd wrapped her in his embrace.

She recalled his soothing words as he'd tucked her into his bed, not letting go of her until she'd fallen into a peaceful slumber.

"Your family barged in earlier. They were so loud, I kicked them all outside," Caro mumbled with a shake of her head. "Renaud left with them. They're all on the porch, I think."

The combat with Charlie suddenly came back to her in a powerful rush of nasty memories.

"Oh mercy, Caro, he was really going to kill me."

The reality that she could have died hit her full force.

Her body throbbed and a sharp twinge at her side made her wince as Caro propped her up against the pillows.

"And he might have, had Ren not intervened in time." Her friend passed her a steamy mug filled with a foul smell. Medicinal potion no doubt. "Charlie didn't stop when your dad ordered him to."

Rosalie blew on her tea to cool it down and closed her eyes, trying to remember. "I was out of it by then, I think."

"Broken clavicle and two ribs. You're lucky he didn't snap your neck." Caro's grim expression underscored the seriousness of it all. "Thank goodness I was there and able to mend you in time. Even with your fast healing, your injuries could have crippled you for life."

"Thank you for being there." Thinking on how she'd barely escaped that fate, Rosalie dropped her head back on the pillow in defeat. "What are people saying?"

"What do you expect? Charlie's smarter than we thought." Caro straightened the coverlet around Rosalie. "He knew you were winning the people's votes. He *wanted* that fight. Now a lot say you can't defend them on your own and the voting is off."

"Bastard. He assaulted Delphine on purpose."

"Probably. Although he *is* a pig." She wrinkled her nose in disgust and pushed her long chestnut hair out of the way. "You still have a few on your side, though. Jérémie and Thomas. The Leclerc and the gals at the salon. My mom is beside herself, running around town trying to have everyone admit that Charlie's a bully."

"I love your mother." Rosalie gave Caro a small smile, fondly imagining the plucky housekeeper setting everybody straight. "Not enough people like her."

"Even with my and *Grand-Maman's* healing gift, we're still considered human here. It won't help with the wolves." Caro huffed. "And what was your dad thinking, letting you fight like that."

"My dad?" Rosalie frowned. "He was there?"

"He could have nipped this in the bud. Renaud's been griping that Alcide should have stopped the fight."

"Dad knew I had no choice." She shook her head, not willing to blame her father. Gauthiers had always led the pack. She *did* have to prove her worth. And the scumbag had assaulted her *sister*. Dad would have done the same.

"What were *you* thinking?" Caro protested.

"I lost it, Caro," she admitted. "And I'm exhausted. I can't tell anyone, but I'm drained. Coming back here, the fear from my dad's heart attack. Then there's the fake marriage, my new clinic and all that. Seeing Charlie assault Delphine was the last straw. My instinct took over."

"Some instinct," Caro groused.

"I had to protect her," Rosalie explained. "I *am* the future alpha of this pack. Protecting comes before my own needs."

"It's no good if it gets you killed."

"How's Delphine?" All her thoughts zeroed in on her sister. Being sexually assaulted like this. And her new dress, dammit.

Her blood boiled again at recalling it all.

"She's better now that she knows you're fine. She was so upset when Renaud whisked you away that she jumped straight at Charlie, screaming about you. Your dad had to rip her off him. Everyone was shouting at each other, taking sides. This whole thing is not good for the village."

And so, Rosalie's fears were founded. They were at the cusp of a civil war. Charlie was destroying the peace of the town.

Soon they would split into two clear factions, with the more war-hungry shifters wanting to take over, pushing away the few human families that had been living peacefully among the pack.

Rosalie couldn't let Charlie win.

Mercy, she'd been so close. The vote had been planned for tomorrow. If she had just beaten him tonight. It would all be over.

"I have to finish the fight." It was the only way to ensure the peace and harmony of Briac Falls.

"What? Are you insane? Fight him in this state? You're a nurse, you know better."

Caro wasn't wrong. Rosalie ached all over as she attempted to down her healing tea.

"No way," Caro continued. "You will have to let Renaud end him."

"It has to be me. You say the villagers need to see physical strength. I have no choice."

She tried to put on a brave front, but Caro was right. Was she truly willing to die for this?

Ren had scooped in to save her tonight. Could she survive another fight?

She mulled over the moves she used to take Charlie down. "I did use his weaknesses," she told Caro. "It worked for a while, at least. Didn't you watch the combat?"

"Watch? Oh *fille*, no. It was too hard. I was praying to Selene with all I had to keep you safe."

"Honey..." Warmth spread through her at how much her kind-hearted friend cared for her.

She couldn't have good people like Caro being overseen by the likes of Charlie. What would happen to Caro's family if Rosalie walked away from it all.

Would he chase all humans out of town? And take his gang up the mountain to fight the immortals? Would the pack even have a chance if all six St-Amand brothers came back with their allies to defend their land? And where would Ren stand in this?

The wolves had lived in quiet peace with the St-Amand for over two hundred years. Would a Bouchard reign end it all?

People would die. She couldn't let that happen.

"I'm fast, there is no doubt about it," she said, as much for Caro as for herself. She needed to believe that she could beat Charlie if she put her mind to it. "And I still have the skills."

"He's bigger and stronger," Caro objected.

"I just made one tiny mistake." She'd been too confident. But wouldn't be next time.

"And that was you. Done," Caro countered. "You were near death."

"I just have to be smarter than him."

"What you need, is more physical strength." Caro took the empty cup back from Rosalie. "And you know the one way you can get it."

Rosalie sunk back into the bed, not sure she liked where her friend was going with that.

"You still have the charm I gave you?" Caro asked.

"You want me to mate." Rosalie eyed her with reluctance. *That* was still not an option.

"Yes, I do."

"It's in my jeep." Rosalie sighed. If, and that was a big if, she could go through with spending the night with Ren, there were no guarantees they would tie the soulmate bond needed to make her stronger.

"Did you tell Ren about this?" she asked Caro.

"No."

She drew the cover up to her chest, still wincing with the stiffness brought on by each of her movements. "I can't believe I need to mate with a male to lead. That just sucks."

"Why?"

"I should be able to do this alone."

"Your father didn't. He had your mom."

"This is the twenty-first century," Rosalie groaned. "I should be able to lead without having a mate by my side."

"It's got nothing to do with what century we live in," Caro said matter-of-factly. "Don't be silly. It's about support. You've always wanted to take care of others without any help from anyone."

"No. I haven't." She chewed her bottom lip, thinking through Caro's words. "I go to Aunt Camille sometimes. I have Dad."

"Sorry but your dad has been leaning on you. He'd been counting on *your* strength to assist him. Who keeps the *Fermières* and the younger crowd satisfied? You always ask for their opinion and report to your dad."

"Maybe." She began to acknowledge that Caro had a point. Rosalie had been helping her father a lot before she left for college.

"And who do *you* lean on?"

"You?" She gave Caro a small laugh.

She rolled her eyes and nodded at Rosalie's bandaged torso. "Only as a last resort."

"You're a good friend, Caroline. I mean it. You've always been there for me."

"Then you should listen to me. I made more than one enchantment for you." She opened her velvet satchel and pulled out another charm. She sat the little bag on the night table. "You and Renaud need to mate."

"It seems so…antiquated."

"Sounds more like sexy times to me." Caro cocked an amused brow.

"But I barely know the man." Yeah sure, Ren was hot, and she'd felt so safe in his arms earlier, but she was still not convinced. Sex was a huge, intimate step.

"He cares about you," Caro insisted. "The only reason he didn't jump in the fray before the fight started was because you told him not to."

"Maybe. But sleeping with him… I mean. That's a big ask."

"Is it? Aren't you physically attracted to him? You should be. The wedding should have triggered something."

Rosalie had no choice but to confess her desire.

"Yes, it did," she admitted with a tiny shrug. "On my side, anyway."

"There you go." Caro was now grinning at her.

"How do I even ask him something like that?"

"In my experience, if someone asks a man for sex, they rarely say no."

Rosalie chortled, while remaining unconvinced that this was a good idea. "Ren is not just any man. He's an immortal."

"He's your husband," Caro pointed out. "He knew what he was getting into."

She mulled things over, trying not to let her emotions guide her. If she was stronger, she would for sure beat Charlie. She would take over the town, protect Delphine and Liam. Ensure that Caro and her family, as well as the other humans living in Briac Falls, remained free and respected. It would be just as she'd first imagined it when her dad had told her she was to fill his shoes.

But she had one big step to cross to get there. She'd have to have that conversation she'd been avoiding since the wedding. She would have to ask Ren to sleep with her.

And then, oh god, actually *do* the deed.

An image of his flexing bare torso reemerged into her subconscious, triggering a surge of desire. Her entire body heated at the idea, and she moaned involuntarily.

"Many here would love being in your place," Caro urged. "He *is* a very attractive man."

"Uhm." Rosalie was still conflicted. What if she fell in love with him?

What if being mated to Ren meant she would be overtaken by an all-consuming *need* of him?

She met other people's needs. Not the other way

around. She did *not* want to have to need someone. Especially if that someone was stronger and more worldly than she was. Would she lose herself in that union?

Could she be the true alpha of their pack if she fell in love with her vampire mate? He intended to divorce her. She would be left devastated by the loss.

"You have no choice, Rosalie," Caro insisted as if she could read her mind.

Her brows knitted in a deep frown. "Charlie can't be our alpha."

"No," Caro agreed with her. "Max could, maybe. But Max would not be as strong as you would be if you mate with an immortal."

"How do you know that?" Lost at what to do, she turned to Caro for answers.

"I know." Caro's elfin features held a certainty that made her look almost otherworldly.

Rosalie stared at her willowy friend with sudden respect, noticing the silver triquetra at the healer's neck and the large onyx ring on her finger.

Caro dwelled in planes Rosalie didn't even know existed.

Yeah, her witch friend knew.

Rosalie finally nodded. Then she raked her throat. "So mated, then."

"It can't be that bad," Caro asserted.

"No. It won't be." She winced, worried that her heart would not sustain being broken if she let herself fall for her fake husband. "And that's the problem right there."

CHAPTER 21

*I*t was the early hours before daybreak and Ren was pacing the length of his front veranda while Alcide and his two children sat silent and glum on the bench under the bleak porch light. They'd all been so worried not knowing just how severe her injuries had been.

Her heartbeat had been so slow when he'd carried her from his truck into the cabin. The whole time petrified that she wouldn't pull through, he had contemplated how devastated he would be to lose her.

When the slender figure of Caro Mercier came out of the house through the screen door, Ren stopped in his tracks.

"She'll be fine," the healer said.

Relief flooded him at seeing Caro's reassuring expression.

"Thank the Almighty." Alcide jumped from his seat and raked his silver mane back with trembling fingers. "I should never have put her at risk like that."

No shit. Ren had raked Alcide over the coals for not intervening sooner and not recognizing that Charlie was no longer loyal to the pack alpha. His delay could have cost Rosalie her life.

"Yeah, Dad. That was dumb." Delphine, with a borrowed, oversized leather jacket covering her ripped dress, stood beside him.

"She's okay. She's a strong woman," Caro said. "She wants to see Renaud."

"Me?" Ren's heart skipped a beat, surprised to take precedence over her family.

"Yep, handsome," Caro said. "She has something she needs to talk to you about."

The marriage. His mood dropped. She wanted out now. *Calvaire.*

He stared at Caro with hesitation.

"Go on," Alcide said awkwardly, still obviously riddled with guilt.

"It will take a while," Caro told Rosalie's family as Ren swung the screen door open. "I suggest we all leave them in peace for now."

"Let's go, Dad," Delphine said, taking charge. She motioned at Liam who stood without a word and pocketed his electronic device. "You heard Caro. Rosalie is fine."

"Have her call me when she's better," Alcide pleaded. "We'll come back."

"Yes. Please, Ren," Delphine asked, wrapping her arm around her little brother.

"Will do." Ren nodded at the Gauthier family as they took the steps down to Alcide's Chevy.

"It will be okay." Caro gave his shoulder a quick reassuring squeeze before following them to the driveway.

But Ren knew everything would not be fine.

Sadness crept in him as he stepped inside. She should have been the alpha, with him at her side. But the plan was crumbling and Alcide would have to stay on a little longer. At least long enough to convince Max or Don to take over.

He wondered if Rosalie would remain in town. He thought of her medical clinic which looked so welcoming now, with the Opening Soon sign on the front window. Would she still want to run it and remain here after all that happened?

Or would she return to the city? Maybe rekindle the relationship with her Dr. Beaumont.

He detected her scent as he neared his bedroom, its freshness sending shards of desire running down below his belt. He had never felt such a strong pull for someone, and he yearned to take her in his arms again. Kiss the heated skin at the crook of her neck. Sample all of her.

At over three-hundred years old, he had his fair share of women. He'd never married any, like Justin had done in the seventeen hundreds, or played the field, like Mag and Cass.

He'd courted a little in his youth. And now and then while with the wolves. More recently, he'd gone for quiet dates out of town, away from prying eyes. There'd been Gabrielle, a Mercier woman, Caro's great-great-grandma. She knew what he was, and they'd parted friends after their short fling. The last one was Martine Costa, a researcher of the occult from the university who had come to Briac Falls in the nineties. She was all about the thrill of dating a vampire.

They had been fun, his emotions not overly involved. Nothing wild.

But this, with Rosalie, was something else entirely.

Guarding his heart, he tightened his fists before entering the room, but couldn't stop his soul from melting at the sight of her in his bed—a small figure in a sleeveless cotton pajama top, with her dark hair cascading down her bare shoulders.

She was sipping some tea in one of his mismatched

mugs—this one a freebie from the local gas station—and the idea that she would leave him was hard to bear.

He swallowed. "You asked for me?"

"I did." She shyly smiled. "Please sit. You're so tall."

"Am I?" He couldn't stop from cocking his eyebrow, trying his best to sound casual.

"Yes. And you know it," she retorted lightly as he took seat at her bedside.

"Do you need anything? Extra pillows?" He fretted with the coverlet of the bed. "Water?"

"I'm fine. Caro said this brew should help." She took the last sip and placed the mug on the night table. "I'm a fast healer, you know."

"Shifter," he commented with a short, knowing dip of his chin.

"Yep." She lifted her top to expose the bandages on her torso. Caro had cleaned her up as best as she could with a sponge bath. "I had a broken collarbone and snapped two ribs. Caro healed most of the damage."

"That son of a bitch shook you pretty hard." He couldn't believe he had let it get that far before intervening. "I was too late."

"I shouldn't have let him take hold of me like that." Her face sported a determined look.

"You fought well," he commented. "You're very sprightly."

"My mother's daughter." She grinned.

"What was your plan when you attacked him?"

"I had no plan," she explained. "He assaulted Delphine. What was I supposed to do?"

"Caregiver to the end."

"Just like someone I know," she noted. "I heard they had to restrain you from jumping in at the start."

"It was not right." He was still mad at himself for staying on the sideline. "You fighting that thug like that."

"Why? Because I'm smaller?"

"No," he stated. "Because I care about you."

The words had come out of nowhere. But if they were to end the marriage, she at least had the right to know how he felt.

"You do?" Her eyes widened in disbelief.

"I do," he insisted, infusing warmth in his tone. "You're the most persistent and kind person I know."

"It almost got me killed," she countered.

"You'll be safer in the city." He gave her a benevolent expression, meaning to reassure her.

"What do you mean?" She frowned, her features sharpening with that resolved look again. "I'm not leaving."

"You still intend to open your clinic here?" he said, surprised. "Even after all this?"

Her spine straightened against the pillow. "Not only am I opening my clinic, I plan to keep my challenge to Charlie."

"What?" He couldn't help but be impressed by her tenacity to fulfill her duty to her father. "The voting won't fly now. He beat you."

"The voting may be off, but the combat is still on. I have two days."

"Wait a minute." He leaned in closer to the bed, not sure he followed. "You don't plan to actually fight him again?"

"I do." She pursed her lips with certainty.

"If I hadn't peeled him off you, you'd be dead." His tone came out harsher than he'd meant. Though his point was absolute truth.

"I know," she admitted. Her heavy sigh broke his heart.

"You want me to be your champion?" He eased back with relief. He'd beat that punk, no problem.

She bit her bottom lip with hesitation before answering. "Sort of."

"Sort of?" He wasn't following.

"What do you know about shifters' soulmates?" she asked.

"You mean the moon bond? Is that still an actual thing?" Despite what Griff had told him, he still didn't believe they could be supernaturally bonded.

"It is. My grandparents had it."

"I thought so. But what does this have to do with your rivalry with Charlie?"

"When a couple is joined as soulmates under the goddess Selene, especially for alphas, they become stronger."

"Okay…" he said slowly, nodding for her to continue.

"I'm fast and skilled at combat, but not as physically strong as Charlie."

"You need to mate to another shifter," he stated. He was starting to see what she was implying.

"Not another shifter. You."

"Me?" he answered with a jolt. Now, he hadn't expected that.

"We're married," she continued. "When we signed the register and became joined in the eyes of the Almighty, it triggered our bond."

"Huh?" In a mix of jumbled thoughts and emotions, he stared at her trying to see if this was some sort of joke. But he saw nothing in her amber pupils but gravity.

"I feel this physical pull toward you. I have since the wedding. It's getting stronger. I never knew it was a thing, until it actually happened to me."

"Oh shit," he exclaimed.

"Yeah, sorry." She winced, looking down at her wringing hands. "I never meant for this to happen."

So, she felt it too. That same pull he felt when he saw

her walk down the aisle, that same desire that consumed him in this very moment. The craving he had to seize the back of her neck and kiss her senselessly. The intense need he felt to climb in his bed, wrap her in his arms again, and sample her tantalizing curves.

As he inhaled her sweet scent, he stabbed his nails into his palms to control his body and dowse his hunger for her.

"Did your dad put you in this situation on purpose?" he asked her.

"I'm not sure. I don't think Dad calculated any of it. He just wanted me to be safe with you. Honest. But being bonded together is what would be best for the pack." She nodded, her face suddenly flushing.

"You are *attracted* to me?" he said it out loud to let it sink in.

She hesitated. Her eyes failed to meet his. "Physically, yes."

"Damn."

"I'm so sorry, Ren. I never meant to trap you into this. But now I need you."

He stared at her in shock. Her hair in disarray and the bruise on her jaw from the fight made his heart melt. There was more than just physical attraction going on there. He *cared* for her. Deeply.

"You mean you need me to…" he started.

She swallowed. "Yes."

"So you can get stronger."

"And beat Charlie."

He digested the news for a moment. A mix of feelings tugged at his soul. Not sure if he should be angry that Alcide may have conspired to make him Rosalie's soulmate or if such a thing was even possible.

"I'm an immortal," he told her. "I can't be soulmate to a shifter. That makes no sense."

"Caro thinks it's happening. She does know these things."

"Well, I'll be damned." He raked a hand through his hair. "Soulmates."

"I'm so sorry." She cringed. "We only have to do it once."

"Wait." He shook his head, focusing on what was actually happening right now. "Are you just asking me to have sex with you?"

"Basically yes."

His lips stretched into a slow smile. "This is awkward."

"Hey…" She narrowed her eyes at him with a hurt look.

"Sorry, *ma belle*, but this whole thing is wild."

"But *this* is real." She pointed to her bandages. "Charlie wants to kill me."

"Yeah." He remembered the fear he felt at seeing her near dead on the field. "It is."

"It's the only way for the pack to thrive," she insisted.

"Why do you even want to be alpha?" Sleeping with her was not a problem, obviously. He wanted nothing else. But for her?

Was it fair to her if she didn't have any feelings toward him? She had such a short life compared to his endless one, she couldn't waste it with him.

"At first it was to relieve my dad of all that stress, you know," she explained. "But now that I've seen what Charlie could do to the pack, it's for them all."

"You're sacrificing yourself for the whole pack," he told her. She was obviously trying to make him understand that she was not trapping him into this on purpose.

"And for my siblings. I can't have Liam fighting other wolves at this age. Not now. He wants to go to space. Learn to pilot jets. Not stay here and turn into one of Charlie's minions. It will kill his spirit."

"Uhm, I see your point."

"So, you'll do it." Her eyes brightened.

"Sleep with you, you mean?" He couldn't help but raise an amused brow at her. This was the most unconventional situation he'd ever been in.

"Yeah." She dipped her chin in a single nod.

"I've had worse assignments," he teased.

"Just once, it should be all we need." She took a small green sachet from the night table and flipped her palm open to show him. From the tiny stars stitched into the fabric, he recognized it as a Mercier enchantment. "With this under the mattress, it will ensure that it actually works."

"Just once," he asked.

"Yes, I promise."

"What if I want more?" He reached for a curl of her hair and slid his thumb along the silky strand as he gazed at her with insistence.

"More?"

"More than once," he pressed.

"Why would you?"

"Here's something no one had told you yet, honey." He dropped the strand of hair. "That pull you feel, I feel it, too."

"What?"

"From the moment I laid eyes on you in your wedding dress." He forced in a breath.

Puzzled, she sunk into the mattress. "What do you mean?"

"I've been hot for you since our wedding," he admitted. "Now I know why."

"But you're a vampire."

"Doesn't mean I don't feel." He reached out to place his hand on her fingers, tightly wound on her thin blanket.

"You feel *what* exactly?"

"For days, I've had a need to touch you, to be with you." He took another deep inhale. "I want you, Rose."

"You do?" She let go of the blanket and allowed him to take her hand in his.

"Uh-huh. I couldn't explain it." He captured her hand within both palms and gave it a warm squeeze. "I thought it was because I liked you, which I do. But now I know it goes further."

"We're fated."

"Looks like it. Regardless of whether he planned it or not, your dad set us on that path."

"Oh mercy, Ren. Can I ever apologize enough?" She turned a bleak gaze upon him. "Dad had no right to put you in that situation."

"No need to be sorry. It's not a bad thing." His need for her strengthened, his body hardening, and he suddenly felt deeply possessive. She might turn out to be his alpha, his queen, but right now all he wanted was to have her. "But as I said, I may not want to stop after that one time."

He was obviously not thinking straight. His hormones and that damn wolf soulmate curse had taken over any sensible side of him. He would never push himself on a woman, but she *had* asked.

"When?" he croaked.

"What?"

"When are we supposed to do this…mating?" The heat from within him was unbearable. He dropped her hand and stood to pace the length of his room.

"Oh, I don't know," she said. "The timing doesn't really matter."

"So, like…now?" He paused to look at her battered limbs, noticing for the first time a large yellow and purple bruise on her shoulder. She was in no shape to have sex.

"Now," she uttered.

He was surprised to see the desire in her eyes. "You're

hurt," he said. His cock hardened further, ready to take her right there and then.

"You can be careful." The way she pleaded and stared at him with slightly parted lips blocked any rational thought he'd ever had.

He wanted her. Now. Damned the consequences or the fact that he didn't know if there were any feelings between them aside from pure lust.

He dashed to her side and reached for the back of her head to capture her mouth.

She eagerly responded to his kiss and a rush of pleasure swelled over his entire body at sampling her taste.

She yelped as his elbow bumped into her torso.

"Sorry." He released her, suddenly brought back to the reality of her injuries. "You're not healed yet. We should wait."

"No." She pulled him in closer and wrapped her hand around the back of his head, digging her fingers in his hair, the tender gesture staking his soul.

Ren leaned down to her, much gentler this time. He dropped another kiss on her parted mouth before grazing the sensitive skin behind her ear and brushing the crook of her neck with his lips.

With a low moan, she drew him down onto the bed and he plopped an elbow at her side to hold his weight beside her.

"You taste like sunshine." He pulled back for a second to capture her gaze within his. Her irises were shades of glacier blue, the sign of the alpha. Her expression was haunted with desire.

She offered him a heated smile. "Don't stop."

"I don't think I can, *ma belle*." He dipped down to the curve of her shoulder and, being extra careful of the nasty bruises Charlie had given her, tasted her skin with his lips and the tip of his tongue. Her womanly scent mixed with the fragrant herbs from Caro's poultice folded over him. He was losing himself in her essence.

He wanted this woman. More than anything. He had wanted her bad for an entire week. And here she was, warm and willing.

Hells, she actually needed him to mate with her so she could complete her task.

His body had no care for the whys this was happening between them. The beast in him sought only one thing, to possess her, make her his. Leaning on his side beside her, he grated his fangs along her skin, and she let out a throaty sigh.

He had bedded she-wolves in his times—Marie-Christine, a Pelletier ancestor who had been relentless in chasing him, and also Chantal, the Aubry widow, a few times before she took her entire family away from town twenty years ago—but this, here with Rosalie, was different. The passion in him was almost unbearable.

He forced himself to recall that she had just been beaten to a pulp by her enemy. He pulled back to consider her as he brushed a gentle touch at the bandage above her stomach. "Does it still hurt?"

"A little." She dug her fingers deeper in his hair and drew him to her.

"We shouldn't do this now, Rose." He tenderly laid his forehead against hers. "We should wait until you're better."

"No need. I really want you, Ren." She cupped the side of his head with her palm. "I really do."

"*Calvaire.*" He closed his eyes for a second. He knew the pull between them was caused by unnatural sources, but it felt so goddammed real to him. So what if she wanted this for the sake of her beloved pack. And not truly for him. She *was* willing. "You're all bruised."

"I feel better," she purred. She slipped a hand down his back to lift up his T-shirt. He bristled under her hungry touch along his bare scarred side, as if, with merely her fingers she could erase centuries of agony.

Damn, he was hard as hell. But that little voice in the back of his mind also reminded him that they needed to wait. A little romancing maybe, and a few more days for her to heal fully. She still had two days before that damn combat.

But she was having none of it.

"Ren, we have to do this." She urged him on, pulling at his belt.

He wasn't sure if it was her need to beat her opponent or her lust talking. And he didn't know if he actually cared.

"Where's that damned charm?" he croaked.

"Here." She reached beside her on the bed for the small enchantment.

He caught the shimmering silk bag by its long straps. "This little thing will make you a stronger alpha?"

She shook her head. "It will make us soulmates," she said, her tone taking on a significance it did not have earlier.

"For life?"

"For *my* life," she said. And the fact that her life would end much sooner than his hit him painfully hard.

A wild thought suddenly passed through him. It might not be such a bad idea to have her as a companion for his eternal life. Her caring, nurturing presence by his side would make it all a lot less drab. Could that even be possible? Could she, too, be immortal after their mating?

"Okay." He was ready to go along with her request.

"You will do this for the pack?" She stared at him eagerly.

"I will." He no longer had the pack in mind. "Not for them, but for you."

"It goes under the mattress," she instructed him.

He nodded and slid the charm beneath them.

"Then what?"

"Then this." She threaded both hands at the back of his head and pulled him to her.

With his body filled with repressed desire, he inhaled her enticing scent again before pulling off his belt.

As her touch slid down his back and below the waistband of his jeans, he trailed his fingers down along her neck and nuzzled the curve of her shoulder again.

He was sliding down the thin strap of her loose pajama top with his teeth when a loud, repetitive bang at his door made them both jump.

"Hey, Rosaliiiiiie, are you in there?" A nasal voice echoed spitefully from the porch.

"Charlie." Ren's heart skipped a beat. He bolted straight up out of bed to shield Rosalie, fangs at the ready.

"Oh god." Rosalie stiffly sat up, her face pallid with horror.

"Roooosalie! I know you're theeere." The banging sounded angrily once more as Charlie chanted on the other side of the door. "I have a gift for you!"

Nasty laughter accompanied him. *Calvaire*, his gang was there, too.

"Come and seeeeee, Rosaliiiiiie," Charlie trolled again.

Ren and Rosalie remained frozen. Ren's pulse was quick with fury.

He clutched her shoulder as he urged her to stay calm with a silent look. She tugged the bedsheet to her chest, not daring to move a single muscle.

If the scumbag barged in with his minions, Ren wasn't sure he could take them all while also protecting Rosalie.

With his stomach clenched, he strained to hear and caught them taking down the steps of his porch in loud voices and snickers. Then heard sounds of engines turning over and car doors being shut.

Then nothing.

"Are they gone?" Rosalie's voice was a quivering whisper.

He stressed his hearing and found nothing but the chant of the river, the bristling of the wind, and the chirping of the birds awakening to a new day.

"I think so."

She let go of the bedsheet and passed him an anxious look, a deep furrow lining her forehead.

She'd been passionate a minute earlier, but Charlie's taunts were taking their toll on her. Her eyes were dull, her features showing pure exhaustion.

"What's this about a gift," she asked.

"I don't know but it can't be good. You stay here."

Ren strode out of the bedroom to cross the main room. The screen door was closed but the cabin had been opened to the elements. Dammit, Charlie and his jerk gang could have walked right in here.

He'd never thought of his own safety before, but this, now, was different.

Rosalie had not listened to his plea and instead followed behind him, padding across the wood floor barefoot in her cotton tank top and loose shorts.

"Go back to bed, Rose. It's not safe." He motioned for her to move away. His protective instincts on full alert.

"What's this?" she inquired with hesitation, ignoring his caution.

He followed her gaze past the door to a dark form slumped across the porch.

"Oh shit." He stormed outside to what looked like someone's dead body wrapped in scorched black canvas.

A charred arm had fallen from the incinerated bundle, the scaled, calcinated flesh revealing a protruding singed elbow bone.

The scent rising from the remains, both sweet and putrid at once, brought back a slew of memories buried deep within him centuries ago. He swallowed with revulsion.

Fuck.

"God." Rosalie repressed a whine.

He bent down to open the bundle, his heartbeat thumping in his ribcage as he prayed with all his might that this was not someone they knew.

That was when he saw the insignia on the long coat. A geometric sigil surrounded by a flaming heart.

"It's LeGall," he said, somewhat relieved. "He's been torched by fire, poor bastard."

His stomach suddenly dropped, he shuddered at remembering the feel of the flames licking his own body. He bit the inside of his cheek to douse the atrocity of his past and stared back at Rosalie. "Charlie put the coat on afterward, so we know who he killed."

But she wasn't looking at him. Trembling, she was staring at the doorframe where a note had been tacked.

Her horror-filled gaze returned to the scorched flesh of the late LeGall.

"This says you're next, Ren."

Her eyes suddenly turned white. The blood drained from her face and right there, before he had a chance to catch her, she fainted dead on the porch.

CHAPTER 22

She opened her eyes with a gasp. "What happened?"

Her insides twisted from a swift bout of nausea. The vision of the charred vampire, its jaw frozen in a burnt rictus of death, was imprinted on her mind. She couldn't get rid of it.

"Here, *mon coeur*. Drink this." He was beside her, kneeling by the couch where she lay and offering her a glass of water.

"I don't want anything." She swiveled to sit upright, her body surging with a hit of adrenaline. That bastard Charlie would not start killing the people she cared about like he did to LeGall. No!

That poor creature could have been her dad, or Ren. Oh mercy.

She rose to her feet, ignoring Ren calling after her and pushed through the screen door to look at the corpse laid across the porch. The canvas wrap was agape to a sickening sight. Burnt limbs barely covered with singed fabric, the vampire's blackened skull partly exposed at one side.

She closed her eyes with disgusted outrage. She knew

what this dead hunter had put people through, but this was all kinds of wrong.

"Rose," Ren said more firmly, joining her on the deck. "Come inside and sit down. I'll deal with this."

"Charlie had no rights to torture that poor thing." She turned a desperate look on him.

"He was a psycho. Don't think of it, please." He wrapped his arm around her shoulder, his strong presence soothing but failing to bring her full comfort—she would never escape Charlie. "Come back inside."

She snatched the note nailed to the doorframe and read the crude handwriting again. "It says you're next."

Ren grabbed it from her hand and crushed it angrily within his grip.

"I don't care about some goddamned message. I care about your health." Before she could react, he threw the paper into the bushes below and scooped her in his arms. He kicked the screen door open and carried her to the bedroom.

"Let me down," she protested. "I have to confront Charlie."

"You're not going anywhere." He dropped her onto the bed and tucked her under the bedsheets.

"I can't have him terrorize me like this," she pleaded.

"You stay here," he ordered with a finger down at her. Then his features relented. "Please."

The urgency that had fueled her suddenly eased. She sat on the mattress and gathered her knees to her chest. "Fine."

"There's a burnt vampire corpse on our porch and you just passed out." His expression was strained. "We can't just go to Charlie with you in this state."

"I know. But Ren, I have to stop him." With her rational side restored, she knew she had to find a way.

Charlie had always been a bully, but he was now turning into a sociopath.

"And you will. But not this minute. *Ma belle*, you need to take care of yourself first."

But she was adamant. "We have to mate." She reached for his wrist.

His lips stretched into an amused smile. "Yes. But not now and not like this."

"What do you mean?"

"Sweetheart, slow down." His voice was a low purr that hit its mark, soothing her frayed nerves for the first time since she'd seen LeGall's corpse at their doorstep.

"Oh god, Ren. I need to stop him. He already kidnapped my ex. And now this hunter creature..." She shoved both hands through her hair. "You can defend yourself but what if he does something to my sister, or my little brother."

"Don't worry, I alerted people to watch out for them."

"You have?"

"Yes. Your cousins and their squad—Matt, Nick, and the others—they've all been on alert ever since Dr. Beaumont was taken. I went straight to them, and asked they take turn keeping an eye on your siblings. You just jumped in faster than they could to protect Delphine at the *épluchette*.

"Oh goodness." She felt a weight lift off her shoulders. She wasn't alone in this. "Thank you."

"We'll deal with Charlie and his gang together," Ren continued as he sat on the bed next to her. "His numbers are dwindling. Fortin had already left him after I rescued Dr. Beaumont. And Lambert might be next, that weasel. Bouchard's only true followers are his cousins Tom and Hubert. And a few of the younger wolves who rely on his business contracts. With the hired coyotes."

"What do we do about those?" she asked, rubbing her

shins with clammy palms. The local families were one thing, but the mercenaries were a serious threat.

"Not sure yet." His expression turned pensive.

"We can't have a full-blown internal war, Ren. That's why I have to meet him in combat." She had never been more certain. She had to get physical, for her siblings, for her town. For those whose fighting past was way behind them.

But she was weary. Still dizzy from the faint, massive fatigue smothered her. She took a deep, slow inhale and closed her eyes.

"When have you last had a good night's sleep?" He swept a strand of hair from her forehead. Genuine concern wrinkled his brow.

"I don't know." She shook her head. "Before Dad's heart attack, probably."

"You're exhausted. You take care of everyone, but you don't let anyone take care of you."

"I have Caro." Her best friend was a bedrock.

"A few potions? That's not the same as plain, sound sleep. Especially after what he did to you last night." He seethed with clenched teeth. "You've been carrying the weight of this town on your shoulders with your dad ever since your mom died.

"Yeah," she croaked. "Maybe."

The gnawing pain of her mother's absence in her life hit her like a freight train. Mom had died when Rosalie was sixteen. Sometimes she felt that when she took over her mom's duties, it was like she was still there with her.

Ren reached for the side of her head and slid his palm along her hair. "It's okay to pause, *mon coeur*. Catch a breath, take time to rest."

"I can't, I…" She stopped herself at the depth of his gaze on her. "We were about to be mated."

"Were we?" His smile on her was kind as he cocked his eyebrow at her.

"Yes. You said you would." Her mind was a buzz of confusing threads. The last thing she wanted was to fight Charlie again. She'd acted on pure adrenaline at seeing him assault Delphine. But now, with exhaustion weighing her down, she was scared. The only way to beat him was to become stronger. She didn't want to fight again but she had to. It was her destiny.

And there was no denying that she was extremely attracted to the man who would help her become stronger. It was impossible to ignore his solid body beside her, his strapping shoulders and strong, defined jaw.

He was urging her to take care of herself and seeing to keeping her siblings safe. Aside from Caro, she never had anyone worry about her well-being before. Not even Dad. Oh, she did love her father, but he'd had so much on his plate that there was little left for her. He was never the same after Mom's death. When she'd taken the role of main caregiver, she had noticed the deep relief in him.

But here was Ren. The quiet man who could see right through her. He knew this rivalry was affecting her health.

"We *will* mate, Rose." He patted her hand and stretched out beside her. "But first you need to sleep this off."

"There is no time, Ren." She couldn't believe she was still asking him to sleep with her. Right now. But the urgency of Charlie's menace just wouldn't be silent.

"There is time." He traced her cheek with gentleness, his touch quieting her anxiety. "Your siblings are fine. Charlie will not dare hurt anyone else if he wants to win more favors in the village. The actual fight is not until the day after tomorrow."

"You think?" There was something wonderful about

relying on someone else for once. Someone strong and sturdy who she could lean on.

"You're going to take time to sleep," he said with a small smile, "even if I have to hold you here until you do."

"You'd do this?" The tension that had her so wound tight released. "You'd force me?"

"I am." He wrapped his arm around her and led her head to rest against his chest, his masculine scent both intoxicating and reassuring.

She finally allowed herself to fully relax and filled with a strong sense of safety, she closed her eyes. The horrific images of the dead hunter and angry script on the note receded as her pent-up strain eased.

He continued to softly stroke her hair. "You will sleep. And I will watch over you, sweetheart. For as long as it takes. Your family is safe. You're safe. You can rest."

As she drifted slowly into much-welcomed slumber, her heart swelled with gratitude that Ren knew exactly what she needed.

"What about our soulmate bond?" She buried her cheek farther in his chest, the soft cotton of his T-shirt pressing against her nose. "I still need to beat him."

"Shush…" he said with his lips on her temple. "Don't worry, *mon coeur*. Once you get your strength back, I'll do everything in my power to help you take down that scum."

CHAPTER 23

*R*en watched her sleep. Her dark auburn curls were spilled across the pillows and quilts he had brought outside for the night, her skin dewy under the warm breeze in the glow of the moonlight and array of lit torches around them. A basket filled with a light fare of fruit, cheese, and crackers, along with water and a little wine, lay in the soft grass beside them.

He didn't know how he could have missed it. Rosalie was exhausted. She'd been so fierce and determined, willing to canvas relentlessly, jumping at Charlie without thought. Even after a faint and broken bones, she was on her feet ready to face off with him once more.

But she was taking on too much. Alcide should have known better than to support this combat.

She needed Ren to make her stronger, so be it. His body had been telling him what his heart was starting to discover. He wanted her. Badly.

Unlike everyone around her who took and took from her, he wanted to take care of her.

And here she was still sleeping after a full day's rest, broken only by a short bath at midday, where she had needed to redress her ribcage before falling into a deep sleep again.

He had wanted her outdoors for that special moment she needed from him, in that grassy place by the water's edge, with the fireflies and the song of the bullfrogs in the background, nature matching the wild essence of her wolf spirit that lay underneath her caretaker persona.

He leaned by her side, waiting for her to wake. He recalled the pretty gray wolf being mangled by her foe the night before and his heart almost stopped with fear for her. She was kind and nurturing but also persistent and brave. Yet she needed him.

The beauty of the night was thawing his soul and he vowed that he would stop fighting her wishes. She was his alpha and he was ready to be her mate so she could show her worth to her pack.

"*Ma reine…*" he whispered.

She stirred under the moonlight, her eyelashes fluttering against her cheeks, and he gently stroked her hair.

She opened her eyes and frowned at him. "Ren?"

He smiled. "Welcome back, sweetheart."

"Where am I?"

"Behind the cabin, by the river." He nodded at the water gleaming with the near full moon.

She looked down at her bandages under her tank top then rolled onto her side.

"The vampire," she exclaimed, both brows raising at once.

"Gone." He had buried the hunter's corpse somewhere deep in the woods. Emme and Justin would soon know that their torturer was finally dead and interred.

"I've slept for so long." She stretched cautiously. "What time is it?"

"How do you feel?" Despite her wolf healing nature

and Caro's gift, the nasty purple bruise on her shoulder remained.

She patted her ribs before looking up at him. "Healed, I think. There's no pain."

"That's good." He'd been extra careful carrying her. His gaze caught hers as he tried to read her emotions.

She bit her bottom lip, and he sensed her hesitation. What had been an easy choice right after her beating was now awkward. They were strangers yet both experienced this pull between them that would not be ignored.

It was fate. Their destiny. And they could no longer ignore it.

He tenderly scooped the back of her neck in his palm and bent down to take her lips. She tasted like summer and leisurely days.

As she reached out to slide a hand through his hair, he felt the tension in him ease. She wanted this as much as he did.

She arched back to meet his kiss deeper and rolled closer to flip one of her legs over his hip.

He groaned at the passion quickening through him and pressed her against his chest with hunger. His entire body yearned to be within her while his soul breathed in her essence, laying a balm of peacefulness over his loneliness. Banishing that resentment—that intense bitterness about life—that never quite left him.

This felt right. This *was* right. And beautiful.

Them, like this, together. How had he never understood what true affection felt like?

He leaned back, suddenly worried that he might be rushing into this. That she might not be ready. "Is this too soon?"

"We need this," she said. "We have to. I have to beat Charlie."

His heart sank a little. Of course, she had to. A small

voice wondered if she was still in love with her doctor. Hoping she no longer was.

But his body soon drowned out that dissenting belief. Why did it matter? It was him she was married to. It was him who had her in his arms right now and him she had to mate with to defeat her opponent. Not Beaumont.

She stripped off her pajama top and wiggled out of the cotton bottoms and in no time she was in his embrace wearing nothing but the bandages below her chest and a pair of white undies.

With a determined expression, she reached again to rake his hair back from his temple.

"Rose," he growled. Ren buried his face in her shoulder, inhaling her scent and kissing the soft valley of her flesh. She was all his for the night and nothing else mattered in that moment.

She moaned as his lips found her breast and she arched her back again to press her hips against his belly. He kissed down her sweet curve, trailing his tongue over the sensitive bud, and she gripped the strands of his hair with a hoarse cry.

His body was on fire, his cock hard for her, in a rush of pent-up need that spread from his crotch all the way up his back in an almost unnatural way. He had to have her.

"Do you still have the charm?" she breathed. "The little silk bag from Caro?"

"I do." It saddened him that this was all about the spell to make her stronger. He was dying to possess just a small amount of her heart. "Under the quilts."

But he had made his choice when he'd moved in with the wolves and pledged himself to Joseph-Marie's family, that he would live with their rules and their culture. And this, tonight, Rosalie's mating to acquire dominance over the pack, was part of that.

Seeing Alcide agree to have her fight had shaken his

commitment to the pack. But his pledge to her was unwavering.

Yet, he had a crazy wish that none of this mattered to her, that she responded to his kisses and touch just because she wanted him, the man, not the protector.

Oh, hells with all that. He shut down his innermost heart's desire.

He had been burnt alive by men, and now was at the service of wolves. He had made a pact. He might as well enjoy the ride for what it was.

He carefully flipped her over on her back and pressed his thighs against hers as he grazed his fangs along the flesh of her neck.

She jolted under him, and he sensed her hesitation. But then, as if she decided that this was now or never, she lifted his T-shirt up and over his shoulders, her palms skimming his sensitive skin in the process.

He growled with desire. *Let's do this.* Finally. His body had been calling for it for days.

He kneeled above her to remove his shirt before tackling his belt.

As he pulled his jeans down past his hips, she stretched under him. The sight of her naked chest, the skin glowing in the light of the torches, stoked the flames of his desire even higher.

He quickly removed the rest of his clothes and hooked his thumb into the band of her undies, peeling them off. He ran up his fingers along the inside of her thighs. She was wet and ready.

Yes, he would have her. Now.

"Do it, Ren." She parted her knees inviting him in. Any sense of propriety he'd ever held was gone in an instant.

Fangs out, cock hard as hell, and propped above her with one elbow, he dove down to seize her shoulder and went straight for her neck. The tender flesh of her skin tasted sweet under his tongue and right there, just like that, before even entering her body, he dug in to sample her blood. The wolf in her wanted his essence for more power, but not before the vampire in him had what it needed.

She jerked at the bite then settled as he drank from her, his saliva seeping into the wound and increasing her desire further. This was the one thing that always worked. Done right, the bite always drove their partner mad with passion.

"Ren..." Sighing with bliss into the warm air, and apparently fully recovered from the fight, she wrapped herself around him, legs at his hips, arms clutching his torso, tamed and eager in his embrace.

Her sweet blood was intoxicating, and he only wanted one thing, to be within her, slide himself in and out of her to subdue the pent-up cravings that had been driving him wild since he'd seen her so desirable in her wedding dress.

She was melting under him, moaning with each pull of her blood. He slid his palm between her legs to play with her and make her even more willing. She bucked against him as the pad of his fingers hit the right spot and she attempted to move her head for a kiss. But he had her pinned down, drinking deep from her, intensifying her cravings while teasing her without mercy to make her entirely his.

"Ren!" She cried his name and the beast in him almost relented his hold of her, but he was too far gone, driven purely by primal needs.

She wanted this and so did he. No matter the reasons behind it. This was nature's drive at its core.

His hard cock found her, and he slid deep inside her.

She moaned at the pressure. There was no chit-chat between them, no more bantering, no more questioning. They were one with each other in the wild, one with the nature around them, and with the primal creatures that lived within each of them, the she-wolf and the vampire. The alpha and the immortal.

He let go of her neck and greedily licked the blood at her wound.

He watched it heal and her delicate skin returned unblemished.

She pulled at him, and was shocked to witness her eyes, her pupils now eerily blue, a pure crystalline shade that he had never seen before. Even more striking than her father.

Was their mating now turning her into the alpha?

He didn't have time to ask before she dragged him down to her for a passionate kiss, her tongue searching his.

And there he lost himself within her. Sliding in and out as he worked his hand between their bodies to mount her pleasure with each of his hungry command of her hips.

And right as she screamed her own cravings for him, seconds away from a final release, he blinked and was hit with a vision that took his breath away.

The forest receded. Gone were the river, torchlights, and fireflies. Gone was Rosalie. He stood at the top of a mountain under a full moon and a starry sky. A womanly figure in a long shimmering silver dress faced him. The pelt affixed across her alabaster shoulders draped all the way to the ground.

"What…" he managed to articulate.

"You are to be bonded with one of my daughters, warrior," the dream said. "Are you willing to pledge yourself to her?"

"Who—"

"I am Selene, Daughter of the World Above and Insight Below. Queen of the Moon and Stars. Answer me, son of Ambrus and Lilith. Are you ready to be her life companion?"

Rendered speechless, he had no clue what this was all about. His mother's name was Charlotte, although he vaguely recalled that she had lived past lives. And he had never known his birth father Ambrus, the Exiled.

But all this didn't matter one bit right now. His body was tortured with cravings while his soul expanded toward the power of the being before him.

"Will you protect her?" the noble goddess asked, her voice dropping a notch, resonating with a measure of kindness that reminded him of Rosalie. "For eternity at your side. She will need you."

He swallowed, shock receding and awed at the solemnity of the moment. "I am."

"Then I bless you, my immortal son. You are one of her pack now."

The vision disappeared as a powerful orgasm shattered inside him, starting at the depth of his core and radiating all the way through his limbs. He sensed his fangs grow longer, his eyesight turned keener.

In his arms, Rosalie arched with a cry in her own fiery pleasure. A mark appeared at the top of her chest, just below the clavicle that had been broken earlier by Charlie. The seal was shaped like a Celtic crescent moon, filled with intertwined loops within the delicate curve and surrounded by tiny stars. He felt a burn on his chest in a similar spot.

Her eyes widened as she took in his mark. Her pupils, still of the brightest blue, turned glassy and he heard her growl. Not the groan of a woman in the throes of passion but a feral sound that came from beast and not human.

She shot him a wild gaze and wrenched herself away from him. And right there, he witnessed her transformation.

He had seen countless wolves shift, hells he had seen her do it just yesterday.

But this, this was something else. Bare skin turned into gleaming white-silver pelt, ears elongated, and spine lengthened into a fierce, proud tail. Her bandages lay shredded in the grass at her paws.

He swallowed with a mix of shock and wonder at the large, stunning creature before him. He had wanted to talk to her, comfort her, even, tell her about his vision, get closer to her.

But here she was, a fully formed wolf, twice her regular size and staring at him with a poised glacier-blue gaze. Caro had been right. The new Rosalie would be a fair match for Charlie.

Every fiber of his body had only one purpose—protect her, be with her. But he had no idea what to do with the huge and magnificent beast she had become.

"Rose," he called to her.

The animal continued to watch him. She took one step in his direction and his heart eased. She would shift back, and they would talk about what had just happened. Draw a plan together to kick Charlie and his gang out of town.

But she lifted her muzzle to the sky above and howled at the moon. The sound echoed ominous and mournful throughout the entire forest.

While he heard wolves howling in Briac Fall all the time, this call was so eerie it chilled him to the bone.

She finally turned her head to him and paused as if she wanted to tell him something. But she instead swiveled with the swift beat of her silver tail and took off into the woods leaving him behind and stunned.

A deep sorrow shrouded his soul.

They were mated for life, soulmates under the goddess Selene, and he had never felt more apart.

CHAPTER 24

The entire experience had shaken her to the core.

When she'd laid in Ren's arms, felt his power and succumbed to the ecstasy of the infamous vampire bite, she had thought she'd died and flown to the heavens. So many feelings had flooded her that she'd never wanted it to end.

She had wished to be forever connected to the lover who was both commending and thoughtful, who seemed to meet each of her needs by pure instinct.

But her bliss had quickly turned into something else—duty—as the goddess Selene had appeared to her to remind Rosalie of her responsibility to her people.

And as she now ran through Beaver Woods toward the center of town—her paws hitting the pine needles covering the dry soil of August, the fragrance of bark and moss filling her with purpose—she realized that this gift, the extra strength and stamina, carried with it a significant cost.

She had always known she'd had to put aside her own desire to fulfill her role in the hierarchy of the pack, but tonight her path was clear.

She alone had to defeat Charlie's intentions and whoever would come after him to destroy their harmony. She alone had to protect her siblings from the threat of returning to war.

As she considered the moon's rays lighting her way under the shadows of the majestic white spruces of her home, she was somewhat shaken that she wasn't given much of a choice in life.

But there was one thing that was all hers.

One place that *she* alone had created. And, overwhelmed by the feelings brought on by the intense connection she'd shared with Ren, feeling lost in it, she had needed to be there to find herself again.

As she reached the town, she snaked her way to the back of her new medical clinic.

All her own.

A dream she'd had ever since she started her nursing program four years ago.

Her heart fell at once. Would she be able to run it? Or would protecting her pack take her away from it all?

She would likely not have enough time to see everyone. She'd have to hire help. But she had to be able to do both.

She shook her pelt and shifted back to human.

And there in the dead of night, naked under the moonlight in the small gravel parking lot surrounded by evergreens, she stared down at her body. The soulmate symbol was still there upon her collarbone. A moon crescent of deep purple, with a speckle of tiny silver stars at the tip of its point.

Just like the one that had appeared on Ren's skin. They were mated to the depths of their souls. What did it even mean?

Uneasy about the whole thing, and not wanting to think about it yet, she rubbed the back of her neck before pushing open the rear door of the clinic. The workers hadn't bothered to lock it. No one ever worried about intruders here.

She padded up the carpeted stairs to the main floor, passed the reception desk and took the small hallway to her right. At the end was her office.

With more calm, back to being human and in her medical environment, crisp with the scent of fresh paint and new furniture, she ambled down to her sanctuary.

The contrast of her experience in the last hour was stark. One minute, she'd been having sex with a vampire under the stars, her own feral nature meeting his, and now she entered the efficient inner sanctum of Rosalie Gauthier, NP, owner of Briac Falls Medic.

Blond woods and tan leather conveyed a space that was both welcoming and serious. Her framed degree hung on the wall behind her desk, along with scenes of the mountain and cascades painted by local artists. Her tall windows lay open to let in the fresh night air to help the last layer of paint dry.

She opened the closet and found one of her lab coats, which she swiftly put on before sitting in her office chair.

She leaned back and lay her naked feet on the file cabinet beside her desk. Her heartbeat regulated as the warm, outdoor breeze filtered to her.

It will be okay, she told herself, as if she was one of her own patients. *I will survive this.*

She had assisted so many people. But Ren was right, aside from Caro, when had she ever let someone take care of her?

A flash of memory returned, her mother sitting by her bed, reading her favorite fairy tale, Snow White and the Seven Dwarfs. She smiled at recalling her young self, dreaming of being royalty.

Her mom had been warm and nurturing—Rosalie's role model. And when she passed, Rosalie had wanted to be just like her to Liam and Delphine. Life had seemed so simple listening to bedtime stories at her mother's side. A prince would come someday and sweep her away.

She did not have a prince. She inhaled deeply thinking of Ren and his powerful embrace. Of his arm strong around her hips as he took charge of her body.

She had a knight. A true warrior.

Who had pledged a lifetime to her. To assist her.

She suddenly stopped feeling sorry for herself and wondered about Ren's own sense of duty.

She thought of the legend recounting how he'd been attacked by a mob of humans and left for dead. And how her ancestor had rescued him. Pledging himself to serve their family had a whole new meaning when you were immortal. Yet, she had seen nothing but pure fealty in his eternal devotion to her kin. Never debating his own set of rules which, just like his life, were simple. She recalled how he'd restrained Charlie from her in his usual no-nonsense, unemotional manner.

A guardian to the end.

She had caught a glimpse of his repressed power as he'd drank from her tonight, with a hunger she hadn't recognized. Unleashed he would be a force of nature to be reckoned with.

Which was why Charlie was so scared of him. Why the bastard postured so hard around him. It was probably why her opponent had called in the mercenaries and had burnt that poor LeGall creature to a crisp.

Charlie feared Ren.

Deeply.

Ren who had been so gentle earlier as he stroked her hair to help her sleep. Ren who had known how to awaken passion in her weary body. Nothing could ever compare to what she had experienced with him.

Her soul was suddenly buoyed with an affection that engulfed her whole. He was her husband.

Her soulmate.

No, she did not want a divorce. She wanted *him*, by her side.

She wanted him to cheer her on as she defeated Charlie.

She wanted mornings watching the sun rise over the river and late nights in his bed tracing his strapping shoulders and sliding her hands over his wide muscular back.

She wanted him to run the woods with her—the vampire and his wolf under the full moon—and later find his palms, and his fangs, all over her own body as she lay naked under him after her shift back to human.

She swiveled and took her feet off her cabinet. She stared at a family picture taken years ago. Mom and Dad, so happy and young, with Liam a baby on Mom's hip, Delphine in a frilly dress and pigtails, while Rosalie stood beside her father, wearing jeans and sporting a brave face. Even then she understood the duty to her family.

Ren said he could not give her children. That they would have to divorce because of it. Had Dad thought of that when he planned the fake union?

Did it matter?

She'd always assumed she would carry her own child, but there were other means to be a mother. Orphans in their world had to be taken in by a wolf family, and news occasionally came from the Laurentian mountains or way up north that a young pup had lost his parents.

Her heart swelled. Yes, she could see herself raising an orphan wolf child with Ren. With his calm presence, steadfast rules, and sense of responsibility, he would make a fine father.

And what about love?

She had entered this arranged union not thinking

about feelings at all. In fact, all she had thought about was her dad. Making sure he recovered his health in peace.

She would have agreed to anything.

She'd seen and felt Ren's passion, no doubt he'd been physically attracted to her. But despite his teasing earlier, would he truly want her again?

Or would he think his mission accomplished, now that they were mated, and she'd gained that strength she coveted?

Would he set her free?

Did she *want* to be set free? She stood and looked out the window to inhale the forest scent that was always present in the air around these parts. The town was quiet at this hour, the streets empty in the middle of the night. This was her home, where she knew everyone.

Outsiders would often drive through here. Get gas at Ti-Jo Leclerc's station or stop by the Landrys' diner. There was only one place to stay overnight, Mrs. Beaulieu's bed and breakfast where François had spent the night. But that was it.

This was wolf territory. The Merciers were human, with their magical gift skipping every second generation. And so were the Leclercs and Thomas Chauvin. As well as Abbé David who officiated her wedding. But most families were shifters.

Wolf-shifters ran the ski lift and the guest lodge complex outside of town, which brought a substantial income from tourists each season. In the summer, too, when hikers took over for the winter sports fans. But none of these visitors ever stayed long-term in the town proper.

Just as this was no place for François, it was no place for strangers. Locals were polite when they came to Briac Falls but, by design, made no way to retain them.

They had managed like this for centuries, adapting with every political change. Alphas had been in turn sovereigns, governors, and provosts of their territory over the years, and now held a councilman position in the Domaine-Lassalle County.

And it all worked just fine.

She huffed as the motion sensor light of her office turned off, leaving her in darkness. This was not the time to think about her own life, Ren, or children. She had to do what she had been born to do.

Protect her pack.

She was mulling over different ways to take down Charlie in combat when she felt a shift in the air behind her.

Then a rich voice that she knew too well filled the room. "Are you scared?"

"Ren." She pivoted away from the window.

"You ran away." His tone held that sexy quality that always strummed deep within her core.

A moonbeam from the skylight above lit half of his face and gave him the aura of a lethal predator.

She blinked. "I'm not scared of you."

No, but she was terrified of the bond they shared.

He advanced toward her, and his woodsy essence hit her full force. The hormonal remnants of her shift made everything more palatable.

"That's good." He was upon her, and she had to crane her neck to look up at him. She had never quite realized before how tall he was next to her.

They had slept together, bonded, and he now made her nervous as hell.

"Then why did you leave?" Something sounded different in his timbre, talking as if he actually owned her.

She stared into the depths of his dark irises and felt the pull that existed between them. He wasn't even touching her, but the connection they shared was unmistakable.

She shrugged and took a step back to lean against the wall. "I don't know."

"You're my wife." He slid right in front of her, his expression grim. "*My* mate."

"And? Did I insult your manhood or something?" Unsure why, she found herself turning defiant at the ownership in his attitude.

He winced with hurt at her harsh words. "I was worried, *mon coeur*."

He anchored his palms on the window frame, trapping her between his arms as the turmoil in her increased.

She shook her head, trying to settle her hammering heart. She hated her weakness in this moment. "No need to worry about me. I can look after myself."

"Someone needs to." He cocked a brow at her. He was so close that she could feel his warm breath on her cheek. "And it looks like that someone is me."

She frowned at the pull his mere presence enacted on her. It was taking all her control not to reach for the back of his neck and draw him in for a kiss. She ached to taste his essence all over again.

"Are you going to follow me like this everywhere now that we're mated?" She didn't know why she kept mouthing at him like this. It was as if she wanted to push him away. It was not like her.

And his presence made clear why she had run away from him. She was filled with feelings for the handsome and fierce man she had married. Could she have fallen in love with him? The thought petrified her.

"Maybe." His lips stretched in a slow, proprietary smile.

She tilted her head back to study him.

He shifted his posture to lean one elbow on the wall beside her and hooked a finger at the edge of her lab coat to pull her to him.

"This is a cute outfit." Amusement twinkled in his gaze.

"I'm a nurse," she said with a shrug she hoped was casual.

"A nurse practitioner," he corrected her.

"You know the difference?"

"I looked it up when your dad asked me to marry you." His hungry expression softened.

"What else did you look up?" She was surprised he'd taken the time to learn more about her.

"I checked out the university where you got your degree, the hospital where you apprenticed, the street where you lived," he informed her, still holding her coat. "Quite a different life than this little sleepy town."

"Very."

"You want to go back?" He became serious as he released her and trailed a finger lightly along the collar of her lab coat. "End all this and return to your old life? To Dr. Beaumont and your life in the city?"

"No." She said the word simply, but it was with a certitude that resonated within her to the core. "This is home."

"With me," he affirmed.

She stated the obvious. "We're mated now."

"What does it actually mean?" Still supporting his bulk on the wall by her side, he carefully tucked a wayward strand of her hair behind her ear.

"We're together." She searched his gaze for any indication of his feelings toward her. They were mates yes, but how deeply did he care for her?

"Forever," he said.

"Yes."

"Forever my life or forever your life?"

"Huh?" She looked at him shocked. She hadn't thought about that.

"The goddess told me we would be mated for eternity. Sounds like my lifespan to me."

"Wait, what?"

"That's forever and ever." His brows raised to stress his point.

"You mean, I could be immortal." Oh wow, she actually had got herself much deeper than she'd originally thought.

"Didn't the goddess tell you?" He seemed confused.

She closed her eyes once, bringing forth her vision of Selene, just before she fell into a rush of pure ecstasy in his arms. "She said our life together."

"There you have it."

"Oh shit." Her eyes widened at the realization. She would care for him eternally.

"Really?" he smirked, surprised by her reaction.

"That's a really long time, Ren." Dad had not seen this one coming, neither did she. "If I'm immortal though, I don't feel any different."

"Well, maybe you're not. I'll ask my mother. She's the bloody Ice Witch. She should be able to figure this out."

"Wow."

"Too much?" He was still leaning over her. His expression now full of empathy and making her heart melt again. She and her dad had put him in this position, and he had been nothing but a gentleman.

"I don't know," she said. "I'm still processing tonight."

"It was...nice." He slid his finger along her jaw and the shiver that ran through her made her toes curl.

"Intense," she admitted.

"That too." He shot her another smile filled with hunger before peeking down the collar of her lab coat. Oh god, he did *still* want her. At least sexually.

"So we're together now," she told him.

He cast her a puzzled look. "Wasn't that the plan?"

"Yes," she said cautiously. But she had never thought that far until actually doing the deed. She'd been focused on fighting Charlie, without much thought of her relationship with Ren until just now.

"I really do care about you," he finally said, his expression serious.

"You do?" Could he truly fall for her?

"You worry about people." He reached to cup her cheek with tenderness. "You're kind, and persistent."

"Caro calls me stubborn."

He curled his lips with a tilt of his head. "Yes, you are. Your insistence in taking down Charlie all by yourself…"

She nodded.

"This place though…" He pushed himself off the wall to take in her office. "You built this."

"Yes. Well, Pelletier's team built it."

"And you did it to take care of your people. Just like Joseph-Marie took care of me when he found me at death's door." A shadow crossed his eyes as he stepped away from her to lean back on her desk.

"I never learned all the details of how you joined us," she pondered. "What actually happened to you?"

"I was burned alive." His mouth took a grim twist.

"What?"

"Tied to a tree and burned," he smirked with a dejected shrug. "The witch's son."

"But that's horrible," she cried, aghast at his fate. She was suddenly laden with guilt to have run away from him.

"I made the mistake of using magic to spark aflame an unlit candle at the public house one night," he explained without a trace of emotion. "A mob followed me and my human best friend when we hiked up to Beaver Woods to set some traps. They attacked us."

"Oh my god." She was filled with horror. And here she

had only thought of her own predicament, forgetting Ren had survived the worse.

"There were too many." He finally caught her gaze, and she detected the depth of the grief he carried. "They killed Pierre in front of my eyes as they lit the bonfire under my feet. Never quite trusted humans after that."

"Ren, that's despicable." Her heart breaking for him, she crossed the distance between them to reach out and run her fingers through his hair in a soothing gesture.

He closed his eyes for a moment and she felt his vulnerability. "I never told this to anyone—" His voice broke before he could continue. "The pain of burning alive was not the worst. What haunts me to this day is to not have been strong enough to save my friend."

"Oh Ren, I'm so sorry." She wrapped her arms around his stiff body and leaned her cheek on his shoulder. "It wasn't your fault. The blame rests solely on those who attacked you."

"Maybe." He eased into her embrace with a sigh. "Unlike turned vampires like LeGall, we immortals are not killed by fire. I was still alive when Joseph-Marie found me. I had to lay there under the dirt and ice for a full season to heal. Your ancestor had buried me, knowing even more than I did the ways of immortals. He saved my life."

"And you carried that trauma your whole existence?" She hugged him tighter.

"After I hunted them down and made those bastards pay for killing Pierre, I remained with your pack and vowed to protect your family so that no one would ever hurt any of you." His voice returned to the steady, certain tone it always held. "I failed Pierre, but I won't fail you, Rosalie. Never."

"Oh god," she suddenly realized. "It must have taken a lot of self-control not to jump at Charlie when he beat me at the *épluchette*."

"Self-control? Nah, I was ready to end him," he said with a chuckle, standing up and wrapping his arms around her waist. "Without my brother there, I would have. Griff stopped me."

"But you did save me that day." She snuggled closer against his chest. "You ripped him off me."

"My queen," he teased while resting his chin on top of her head. "I had to."

"My knight," she breathed. And for her it was not a joke. She grieved for him, how he had been so viciously attacked and had carried the blame his entire life.

She pulled back to admire his noble features, her heart swelling with emotions for him.

"My duty-bound handsome knight." She pressed a soft kiss on his lips before laying a gentle hand at his chest.

"Handsome?" He raised a brow at her.

"Very."

His lips curled into a half-smile, and he captured the back of her head in his palm. "You left our bed way too quickly, you know."

"I'm sorry."

"We should go back." His tone had turned to a sexy purr. "Continue where we were."

"Again?"

"We barely started." His gaze was filled with lust and more. A sense of ownership, sure, but with also a profound desire to be with her, only her.

"What about Charlie and the fight tomorrow." She wanted nothing more than to lay with him again, but she had to call upon her more rational side. "We should draw a plan."

"After."

"After what?

"You hurt my feelings, leaving me like that," he teased.

He was joking but she'd noticed the small undercurrent

in his voice. He was so large and strong and well, so every-thing, that she had never before thought he could actually have genuine feelings for her.

But now, after he shared his suffering with her, she saw the sweetness hidden deep inside him.

"I wasn't thinking, Ren," she confessed. "I was so over-whelmed. I had to shift and run."

"You have to make it up to me," he insisted, the amused smile carrying all the way to the corner of his eyes. "Our bed is lonely without you."

She relented with a laugh, his playfulness soothing the worries overwhelming her. "I suppose I can fix that prob-lem." He filled her with warmth and made her believe everything would be okay. "And Charlie?"

"Tomorrow, sweetheart, tomorrow. Right now, I'm taking you home."

CHAPTER 25

This was it. The night of Rosalie's combat was finally upon them.

Ren crossed his arms at his chest and leaned back on his heels as he surveyed the small group of allies gathered for the occasion on the back deck of his cabin.

With both elbows on the banister of the back porch, a beer bottle loose in her hands, Rosalie was facing the water and watching the sun setting behind the pine trees of the mountain across the river. Her friend Caro stood silently by her side.

The heat still hung uncomfortably in the air, making him even more restless.

They had mobilized their supporters here, to hack out a plan in case things turned sour. Her cousins Max and Don were sitting in Ren's deck chairs, holding a half-drunk beer can each, and looking unusually solemn. Nick Pelletier was there, too, hands in his pockets, his drink perched on the railing.

Caro had brought her mother, Mrs. Mercier, the housekeeper of Chateau Briac. The middle-aged woman was human, but she was the heart and soul of the village. Nothing much passed by that she didn't know. She was talking animatedly with Old Simon who had sworn he'd follow Rosalie to the end.

Rose… A shiver ran down his back just thinking of her and how she had felt in his arms this very morning. Soft and passionate at once.

Every fiber in him wanted to take her away from here. Away from his log cabin, away from Briac Falls and the impending combat, from the Domaine-Lasalle mountains that had always been his haven.

He could take her to Montreal with him. Start a life there in the original St-Amand family dwelling in the old part of town. Or go all the way to Lafourche Parish in Louisiana where his mother had made her home.

But he knew Rosalie wouldn't agree to leave. She had to stay. Fight for her family, for her people.

"You have doubts." Griff came to stand beside him, following his gaze on Rosalie who had turned away from the water to nod at something Caro said, her chestnut hair glistening in the moonlight as she moved.

"Doubts?" Ren peered over at his sibling. "Hells, I have a whole lot more than doubts, man."

"You don't think she can win?" Griff seemed genuinely surprised.

Ren rubbed his neck, the muscle stiff from tension. She looked too fragile in her denim cut-offs and ribbed tank top. He didn't want to entertain the thought of her defeat —she *had* to win.

"Rosie," her cousin Max called out from his seat. "Why isn't your dad here? Shouldn't he stick around to support you before your big night?"

She lowered her gaze to him with a composed expression. "He has to be at the field to greet everyone. Set the stage, so to speak."

"He's telling everybody you're going to take down the bastard," Nick added with a satisfied grin.

"He won't let her get injured," Mrs. Mercier reassured them. "We all know this."

"He does have faith in me." Rosalie's confident posture was one of a true queen about to face her enemy.

"It's not a question of faith," Ren retorted. "The odds are still against you."

"You don't think I can win this?"

He exhaled in a huff. "I think you'll get hurt," he grumbled.

"Shut up, Ren," Nick said. "Of course, she can beat him now. My brother saw her run through the woods last night. Holy shit, *fille*. You're one mighty alpha apparently."

"Matt saw me?" She shot Nick a surprised look.

"Oh yes, everyone knows you two…" He cast Caro, and then Ren, a deliberate glance. "You know…mated."

Caro gave Ren a quick smile as the memories of the last hours flooded him with warmth while Rosalie flushed a little at Nick's allusion.

After he'd brought her back home last night, they had plenty of time to bond, both physically and emotionally. And now that his lust for her had subdued, it was his heart that was involved.

"There's no question you're the one to lead us, coz," Max said. "Everybody is talking about it."

"Yeah, once they see you shift," Nick said. "There will be no uncertainty at all."

But Ren *did* have doubts. Sure, she was bigger now but so was Charlie.

She crossed the distance between them and cupped his cheek with a reassuring palm. "I can take him, honey. You don't have to worry."

The connection they shared now was unmistakable.

They should have been alone here, watching the sunset

together and discussing their future, not having drinks with a bunch of people eager to see her battling a foe set out to slay her.

"You keep saying that," he protested. "But he would have killed you had I not intervened."

"I'm stronger now," she insisted. "Because of you."

"You're not used to this new form." He couldn't rid himself of his fears for her. He still thought he should be the one fighting in her place. "You've been like this for what, twenty-four hours? What if your balance is all wrong?"

"I will take him." She pursed her lips in a thin line, and he detected the tiny strain of doubt in her expression. Damn, she was being brave for the others. He should have known.

And she would not let them see her fear.

He wrapped his arms around her and pulled her to his chest.

"I know, *mon coeur*. I know." He rested his chin on her head. "But we still need a plan B."

She pivoted in his embrace and looked at the small group before them.

"I can take Charlie," she told her allies. "But what about his cousins, Tom and Hubert? They're still devoted to him. What will they do during the fight?"

"Only what they *can* do," Nick stated. "They'll be watching like the rest of us."

"I need an eye on them all. Charlie fights dirty," she said. "If you guys know about my transformation, Charlie is probably aware too, and he's smarter than he lets on. He'll have something set up in case he can't take me down."

"Oh, don't you worry, Rosalie. We got your back," Old Simon said. "We'll keep tabs on his cousins and that whiny Lambert."

"What do you think, Mrs. Mercier?" Rosalie asked. "Will the townspeople rally behind me? The Fortins and the Savards? The Chauvins?"

"The Chauvins were always with you, they're human. As for the others, now that you're mated under the moon goddess, they'll see you can protect them. They won't interfere."

"And what about the hired outsiders?" She looked at him over her shoulder, her body stiff in his embrace.

Damn coyotes. His stomach clenched.

He had planned to watch over her during the combat. Jump into the arena as soon as Charlie gave signs of hurting her. He couldn't be watching for the mercenaries.

"Please?" she asked him. "You don't have to be there for me. I'm more worried about those hired shifters. They are not from the pack. Their loyalty is to Charlie alone."

"And his money," Ren grumbled but recognized her apprehension for the kind that had killed her mom.

"Alcide will stop the fight if he sees Charlie with the upper hand," Simon said.

"And you know that how?" Ren eyed the old veteran.

"I spent the better part of the morning shouting at him for getting Rosalie in danger."

Ren smiled. Those two went way back. Only Simon would have the guts to yell at Alcide. But Ren shared his sentiment entirely. He would still be yelling at him, too, if he hadn't seen the remorse in the alpha's eyes when he'd told him off after the tragic events at the *épluchette*.

"That was not necessary, Simon," Rosalie said. "I had a long talk with Dad earlier. He feels guilty enough for putting me in this situation."

She turned in Ren's arms. "And Simon's right. Dad will stop the fight if I get in serious danger."

"It didn't work the last time," he said, unable to contain his fears from her. "You'll get hurt."

Her spine straightened. "I'm a wolf, Ren. Blessed by Selene. I can take it."

But he didn't want her to take it. He didn't want one bit of her flesh tainted by that scumbag's claws.

"I'll get us some reinforcement," Griff said with a nod. "Just in case."

"And my siblings?" Rosalie asked. "You never know, he could arrange for someone to take Liam. He's just a kid."

"They'll be on the dais with your dad," Max said.

"So will I," Caro said. "I'll sit with Delphine. She's a mess. She thinks it's all her fault because Charlie assaulted her."

"That son of a bitch," Rosalie growled under her breath. "He won't get away with this."

Ren could sense her anger. And she needed to keep that fury close if she wanted to beat her opponent.

Ren never felt so helpless. This was a situation he could easily solve with one deep bite and a broken neck. Swoop in and deal with it. End the scum. Hells, Griff would likely be delighted to do this with him.

But he couldn't. Damn the wolf pack's bloody politics.

What had always looked so valid and simple for centuries no longer made sense to him. He longed for that gray area where his own immortal family dwelled, where they made up their own rules.

And then it dawned on him. He was no longer following the rules of the pack. That he was pledged only to Rosalie.

He loved her.

He knew this deep within his heart. It was crazy. He had only been with her for over a week. It had been lust at first sight, but her determination and compassion had touched his tortured soul.

And he would have to follow her wishes. Even if it killed him to do so.

"You're right. He won't get away with it, *mon coeur.*" He drew her closer to him and with deep hope, stared at their allies, each fiercely and equally loyal. "And I will be right with you when you take him down."

CHAPTER 26

*S*he was scared.

She hadn't wanted the others to see it at the log cabin but here she was, facing the bastard. The entire town was watching, most crammed in the bleachers erected for the event, others packed in a circle around the combat area.

She swallowed as she stood under the sports lights in the middle of the same field where he had nearly killed her at the *épluchette*. She could still feel his jaw sinking into her flesh, and the snap of her rib as he shook her senseless.

But not this time.

This time, she would shift, and the entire pack watching the fight would see her new size, see that she had been blessed by the moon goddess with the mating bond. They would all acknowledge her as the alpha.

And she would take that asshole down to prove it to them.

Charlie leered at her, rolling his shoulders and cracking the knuckles of his massive hands, one side at a time. One punch and she could be down for good.

Nimble on her feet, in old denim shorts and a T-shirt,

she kept her posture loose, ready to crouch in a defensive stance. She was eager to shift, right now.

But Charlie's fans wanted it differently. The whole shifting process would have to be part of the battle. They needed to see the two contenders fight as humans, then humanoid shifters before turning into full wolves.

She would have to stay out of Charlie's way for a few strikes before transforming into her new beast.

On restless toes, waiting for the horn calling their fight to start, she anxiously studied the spectators in the newly erected bleachers. The crowd was animated with anticipation. She was seeing some of her people in a whole new light. They were more bloodthirsty than she'd ever imagined.

She glanced at the dais where her family and Old Simon sat. Delphine was dressed in an unusually plain outfit and Liam stood at attention in a rarely seen focused posture. Her poor brother feared for her life.

Her siblings had known nothing but peace in their lives and she hated how witnessing this violence was shattering their protected existence. Bloody Charlie Bouchard!

Caro was right there at their side, sitting with *Grand-Maman Mercier*. The grandmother was stooped over herself in a floor-length black and gold paisley dress, her long white hair escaping from a glittering turban.

Her friend had her arm around Delphine's shoulder and Old Simon patted Liam's knee. Rosalie's tension eased a little.

Their family had plenty of allies.

She noticed Max and Nick farther to the left, not far from Charlie's minions. Her other cousin Don and his buddy Matt were standing guard at the entrance of the arena.

Ren, out of sight and perched in a tree somewhere at the edge of the forest, was surveying the whole area for outside trouble. She knew it was killing him to see her fight. When this combat was over, they would have time to explore their relationship further.

"You came for more, Rosalie?" Charlie sneered. "I knew you liked it."

"Freak." She smirked, eying him with disgust.

He waved at his supporters and turned back to her. "You liked being put in your place, sweet pea. Admit it. That's where you belong. Under a real man's thumb."

"Fuck you, Charlie." She was livid that he'd forced their entire town into this position. His ego had brought them to the brink of a civil war, with people who had been friends for decades now taking sides.

"Just like your sis over there." He leered at the dais. "She's a hot little thing. She'll make a great bride."

"She's underage, you creep." Her nose wrinkled with distaste as she moved in a wide arc around him.

"Me marrying a Gauthier. That'll be perfect." He wetted his lips and squinted at her. "No one will go against me."

"This will be over before you know it," she snapped. Her rage grew like a wildfire, urging her hormones to enact her change.

"Oh, your brand-new physique, you mean?" he said. "About that, did you think it would be your big surprise?"

She stopped circling to eye him with hatred.

"I know all about it, girlie. Sorry, but everyone saw you." He shrugged his massive shoulders. "I know you tried, but don't think I'll be impressed. It will be me in the end, *fille*. And we'll start with ridding the town from that Jérémie Landry and his human husband. Then we'll get Ti-Jo out. Always hated that guy."

She focused on his feet, trying to ignore his prattle. His confidence was rattling her, and she was starting to lose hers.

He was slow, like a huge rhino ready to charge.

But she could outlast a rhino. And once she had turned into her true wolf, he would have no chance.

She allowed the wrath at seeing his grip on her sister fuel her. She could let the insults about her slide, but his assault on her kin was something else.

Charlie was just a dirtbag. His neglect of the *Jardins* had caused Mrs. Savard's aunt's pneumonia. She had spent weeks in the hospital.

And little Matheo Landry had nearly broken his neck from a faulty step at the restaurant Bouchard owned in the ski village. The scum just didn't freakin' care!

Wrath was continuing to build inside her when the battle horn finally blew.

Charlie hollered for his fans. They were on.

She came down to the low, strong wolf stance her aunt had trained her into her entire life. She was more than ready.

He circled heavily around her, then exploded in an ominous, throaty evil laugh.

"My poor little wolf, you're so psyched, aren't you?"

She sure was. Keen to rip him apart, hands dying to go for a hit at his throat first.

"Not today, sweet pea, not today. There will be no fighting."

She froze at his words and suddenly noticed the quiet around them.

Something was wrong.

She turned to the entrance of the combat area and saw it. Oh God!

Don and Matt were being held up at gunpoint by two coyote mercenaries.

Charlie followed her gaze. "Look up, missy. Your old dad is done."

She glanced at the dais. Dad, along with her two

272

siblings, was surrounded by gunmen she had never seen before. They pointed military-grade weapons at her kin's head. Another had Caro by the neck, his hand on her face preventing her from carrying on any magic. A furious Simon was supporting *Grand-Maman* Mercier who was shaking her head in shock.

"Bring the family down here," Charlie barked, daring her to take one step in his direction. "Don't anyone move, or we start shooting."

"You fucking bastard!" she roared.

"What? Did you think I'd be honorable?" He cackled with a malevolent sneer. "I'm sorry sweetheart, but the Gauthiers reign is over now."

CHAPTER 27

*R*en had swooped down from the tree as soon as he'd seen Alcide being taken hostage.

He was torn for a moment, wanting to rescue her first. But he knew she would want her family safe. She could take on Charlie. But the kid Liam was defenseless.

From what he'd seen—the villagers arguing with each other under their breath at the sight of the captive Gauthier family—the town no longer liked the idea of Charlie. Darting fearful gazes at the hired guns, most had looked like this had gone way too far for them.

Taking their esteemed alpha and his kids hostage had been too much.

As Ren snaked his way through the dark forest, he could hear Charlie posturing and claiming victory, calling to Alcide who had so far remained silent. Damn son of a bitch.

Rosalie was swearing at Charlie with all her might. She hadn't yet shifted.

She had to be fearing for her family.

He really should have killed the fucking snake the first chance he'd had.

Again, he admitted the vampire way was better. Following rules had its limits when facing the true evils of this world.

He snatched his cell and texted a quick message to his brother Griff.

Get down here now, he told him.

As he pocketed his phone, he sent a fast prayer to Selene to protect his soulmate and was about to bolt toward the field when a sharp sting lanced his thigh.

"Where do you think you're going, punk?"

Fucking coyote. The filth had thrown a small blade into Ren's left leg, deflecting his jump. How had he not seen that one coming?

Pain radiated up to his hip as he yanked the damn thing out of his flesh.

He turned an annoyed scowl at his attacker. The shifter's stature was short but his body, in the olive-green military garb, was wiry and restless, ready to pounce. "You really want to do this, do you?"

"*We*, want to do this," the coyote snarled.

A bright flashlight suddenly blinded him. Ren's eyes readjusted and he noticed the company behind his assailant. *Shit*, five more gunmen, all decked out in the same war-ready outfits.

"Can I shoot him, boss?" one of them barked.

"Sure, go ahead," Ren's attacker urged with a sneer. "Mr. Bouchard will be pleased to see his head on a stick."

A volley of bullets buffeted Ren. He keeled over, flat on his back.

Fuck, that hurts. He hadn't been shot in decades.

He stayed immobile on the ground, eyes wide open to the moonlit sky, waiting to see what the idiots would do. Surely, they'd heard about immortals before.

"Good one, Corey."

"Yeah! That scum is dead," the shooter erupted in a sick laugh.

"I've been itching to shoot someone since we came to this podunk place."

"With the money we're making here, bud, I'll take us all to Havana for a joyride."

"Let's get his head," one of the scums shouted with glee. "Who's got a Bowie knife?"

"I do."

"Let Corey do it," the leader said. "He's the one who got the SOB."

Footsteps came closer to Ren and one of the coyotes straddled him, his foul breath permeating the air while Ren waited for his move.

The mercenary took a fistful of Ren's hair and cackled. "Yep, boss. Dead as a doornail."

Without another beat, Ren's arm shot straight out to grab him by the throat, causing the coyote's eyes to bulge in shock. "That'd be undead, idiot!"

Ren bolted to his feet. He crushed the coyote's windpipe in his grip.

"Oh fuck!" one of the coyotes yelped.

Ren stared at the remaining mercenaries and smirked. "Anyone else wants to take a shot at me?"

"You bastard," one of them exclaimed. "You killed him."

"Don't play with things you don't understand, buddy." Ren was fueled with fury. He had no sympathies for fuckers who took children hostage!

He flung away the inert mercenary while another coyote turned his gun at him. The few shots going through him barely hurt this time. His immortal revitalizing blood would soon dissolve any metal shards lodged in his body into nothingness.

Only one thing could kill him, and bullets and blades were definitely not one of them.

He leaped at the shooter, fangs fully out and ripped his throat open on the spot.

"That's two." His jaw dripping with blood, he growled at the others as another corpse hit the ground. "Let me pass or I kill the next one who comes at me."

The remaining three mercenary eyed him with both fear and horror in their eyes. They'd obviously never faced one of his kind before.

But dammit, he just didn't have it in him to murder a bunch of contractors who were just after money, no matter how sleazy they were.

He chose to spare them and raced past them at vamp speed through the forest. He soon reached the back of the erected bleachers and took one silent, giant leap all the way to the top.

No one saw him land, everyone eying the spectacle in the field below. Ren's throat closed in with dread at the scene.

Charlie and Rosalie were facing each other, surrounded by his minions. His cousin Tom taunted Rosalie.

"He's going to rip you apart, girl," he leered. "After having fun with you."

She ignored the creep, and stood her ground on her bare feet, fierce despite her smaller figure.

"You're too chicken to fight honorably, you bastard," she shouted at Charlie. "You had to bring in *coyotes*."

"Maybe we *should* have our combat after all," Charlie sneered at her. "So, they can really see that the Gauthiers are truly finished."

Dammit Rose, shift already. Ren mumbled to himself. Every part of him wanted to jump in the ring and fight for her.

But one look at the dais told him he couldn't. Charlie was ordering them down to the field.

Alcide had the barrel of a semiautomatic pressed to his head.

One of the mercenaries gave Liam a shove and the kid fell to his knees, dropping his portable game. The hired-gun eyed Alcide before crushing the kid's device under his large boot with a cruel laugh.

Liam let out a yelp as Delphine swooped in to grab her little brother and clutched him to her chest. She glared at the coyote in a death stare not unlike her older sister's.

Conflicted, he took one more look at Rosalie.

Fuck, he had no choice. He had to rescue Alcide and his kids.

He was taking one step down in their direction when three more coyotes appeared in front of him.

"Not so fast, buddy," one of them snarled, pointing his weapon to stop him.

Ren readied himself to pounce but noticed the fuel tank at the back of his crony a second too late.

Shit. A goddammed flamethrower.

A stream of fire blasted into him. The flames licked his chest and he fell backward on the aluminum bleacher.

Panic rushed through his veins and bile rose to the back of his throat. Cold fear seized control, and he could no longer think.

He was back two hundred years ago.

Frozen in place, he could do nothing but stare in horror at the vision of the ancient, agonizing blaze overtaking him.

CHAPTER 28

"This is perfect." Charlie burst into a maniacal, pleased cackle as screams and chaos erupted from the bleachers, some people pushing others to try to flee down the steps.

Nothing had prepared Rosalie for the horror she was witnessing. Ren engulfed in a blast of flames, toppled to his knees. With a look of pure horror contorting his face.

"No!" she screamed.

"Ok stop," Charlie ordered. "And bring that vampire over."

Her heart sped like mad as Ren picked himself up with a dazed expression and began to march down the steps, his face seemingly drained of blood. His plain shirt hung in scorched tatters, exposing the nasty blisters on his arms and chest.

She quashed a sob stuck in her throat. Her Ren. He'd been burned at the stake, body and soul eaten away by the flames. He'd carried the trauma for centuries. This, now had to be pure agony.

"See folks, this is how you dispose of a regime," Charlie boasted to his audience. "I did not only build my body but my mind. I've learned all about how strong leaders rule by watching biographies on the history channel."

The hired coyotes were motioning her family down toward the field, her father held at gunpoint and Liam buried within Delphine's arm. One of the mercenaries had Caro in a chokehold and forced her down the steps.

The rest of the crowd, with Old Simon supporting *Grand-Maman* Mercier, now silently watched it all with disbelief. This was no longer fun.

"You know it, Charlie!" His bootlicker cousin Tom chimed in. "You're the leader!"

Charlie gestured toward her father and siblings. "Bring them all down for a public display and judgment."

Judgment? What the fuck? She turned from her dad to Ren and back to her opponent. The bastard had truly gone mental.

"Don't move an inch, slut," Charlie snarled at her. "These are silver bullets at your dad's head. Don't let me kill more wolves than I have to. You say you want to do good for your town, now is your time to prove it."

"You fucker!" she uttered under her breath.

She was powerless. Her family and friends surrounded, her dad held by the back of his denim shirt with a gun to his head, and Ren subdued by the flames.

She racked her brain for a way out of this for them all.

"Come on, bring them down," Charlie barked with impatience.

She watched her family, along with Caro, being snaked down into the arena under the bright sports lights, her father's hatred palpable, her sister clutching her kid brother. Both were stiff with fear and repressed fury.

Ren soon followed down to her side, flanked by the hired coyotes, the muzzle of the flamethrower stuck close to his back.

No one in the crowd dared to move, cowed and not knowing what to do. The rivalry game was over, their alpha wouldn't save them. All were at Charlie's mercy now and they knew it.

"Kneel, alpha," Charlie instructed.

"You were never quite right in the head from the get-go, boy." Her dad spat at Charlie's feet, ignoring the gun to his head. "That grandmother of yours has filled your head with nonsense ever since your mom left."

"You shouldn't be worrying about me, old man. Your time has come." Charlie grabbed the weapon from his minion and rammed it into her dad's chest.

She tightened her fist hard. This could *not* be happening. She had to find a way.

She caught Ren's gaze on her. Her tension eased when he gave her a tiny nod, the color returning to his cheeks.

As long as that freakin' flamethrower was off, he was okay. She'd have to tackle that first.

They had to create a diversion and quick. She had Max, Don, and their squad somewhere in the crowd.

But right now, she had to be careful. Her father was in a precarious position and would be dead with one itchy pull of Charlie's trigger finger. That asshole was much too unpredictable. He was making this into some sort of event to prop up his ego.

She shuddered as he brought the handgun back to her dad's head.

"Alcide Joseph Gauthier, you have been found guilty of the crime of failing in your duty as the alpha of the Domaine-Lassalle pack." Charlie intoned in a fake version of her father's proclamations. "You are condemned to die by a single silver bullet to the head."

"Oh, fuck this, boy," her dad said.

"Kneel!" Charlie rammed the gun into her dad's

temple and Rosalie recognized the deadly look in her father's eyes—Dad was about to shift.

"Daddy, no!" a small, panicked voice cried.

Liam!

It happened so quickly. Her little brother broke free from the mercenary and lunged for Charlie. Liam grabbed the massive man by the arm with surprising might and tried to shake him off their father. "Let my dad go!"

Charlie shook Liam off him and for the very first time in his life, her brother shifted into a small brown wolf in front of their eyes.

"Liam!" Delphine shouted and shifted herself into her sleek silver wolf form as Liam leaped again at Charlie.

Teeth out, Rosalie's sister pounced for Charlie's throat before he could shift, forcing the scumbag to topple backward on the ground.

Shot cracked into the air as Charlie wrestled Delphine off him.

"Delphine, let go!" Rosalie yelled in a panic, trying to pry her sister off. She shouted at her brother nipping at Charlie's leg, "Liam, you and your sister, get away from here."

"Don't let them leave!" Charlie shoved Delphine off as everyone stayed still, watching the scene unfold, stunned.

Rosalie bolted to shield her two siblings with her body and called out over her shoulder. "Run, Delphine. You and Liam, go. Get out of here now!"

She sensed her sister hesitate, looking at their dad, still surrounded by men at arms. But he, too, had now shifted into his magnificent gray wolf shape.

Delphine nudged their little brother with her muzzle and they both ran off, side by side, toward the woods, the sleek silver protecting the smaller brown wolf.

The coyotes and Charlie's cousins hesitated, confused at what to do.

They were all at a stalemate, surrounded by the enemy —Ren with a weapon trained on him, Caro trapped in a mercenary's arms, and her dad, in wolf form, pacing in front of Charlie who had picked himself up from Delphine's attack.

"Oh, what the hell, just let the pups go," Charlie finally shouted at his crew with a shrug. "They're just kids. How far can they run? We've got the big ones."

The time for action was now.

Rosalie called to her goddess and, with one look at Ren, she shifted herself into her new shape.

Adrenaline rushed in a tide of raw power. Her vision turned keener. Her scent detected everything, from the sickly-sweet odor of her rival to the acrid fuel in the weapon holding Ren at bay. She furiously snapped her tail to and fro.

The crowd above cheered at her transformation.

"Oh shit," Tom Bouchard yelped. "Look at her."

"Shut up, Tom," Charlie barked.

He turned toward her dad, aimed, and without warning, fired his gun.

Dad caught the slug in the flank and toppled to the ground. The crowd cried out then held their breath.

No! Rosalie yowled with distress and burst to her father's side. With her heart hammering in her ribcage, she pushed her muzzle to his flesh and felt his faint pulse. He was breathing but remained limp on the field.

"You're next, Rosalie," Charlie boasted with zeal. "This is all your fault. If you had dropped your claim, you would both live."

She stared down the barrel of his gun and her stomach clenched. She had failed.

All this time, she had wanted to do good by her people and now they were at the mercy of a deranged pig driven by jealousy and power.

"Burn the immortal!" Charlie ordered.

Oh hells, no. She turned to Ren, readying herself to jump at the flamethrower when a low, trembling voice rose from the silent crowd, droning on ancient words. *A spell.*

"Koir idash, vyenrt aheir."

Rosalie looked up to *Grand-Maman* Mercier standing in the bleachers with her hands in the air, Old Simon propping her up with his arm under her shoulders.

A heavy wind blew over the arena as the old lady continued her incantation, shaking the spotlights and picking up dust.

"Grand-Maman!" Caro had managed to wrestle free of her captor, now distracted by the supernatural gale, and she joined in with her grandmother.

"Koir idash ith sinnsearachd. Noirceis!" The clear voice of her friend melded with the assertive tone of her elder.

"Koir idash, vyenrt aheir," the older *guériseuse* chanted along with her granddaughter, her voice steady. *"Koir idash colebex yth!"*

As the wind intensified, every single light exploded in a shower of glass.

A thick unnatural darkness descended over the field and the moon turned a misty gunmetal gray. The harsh wind lifted more dust from the dry ground, making visibility near impossible.

"Annehyentx!" Caro snapped into the electrified night.

Thunder suddenly shook the ground. Heavy rain fell, clearing the stiff air.

Jolted from the shock of seeing their alpha taken hostage and shot, everyone ran screaming for cover as the summer electric storm intensified.

"Get out of here," Simon shouted at the villagers as he helped *Grand-Maman* Mercier along.

Jérémie Landry and his partner helped lead the locals down and off the bleachers while Max and his squad jumped onto the middle of the field, some shifting into large gray wolves.

They pounced at Tom, Hubert, and the mercenaries—wolves and coyotes at each other's throats. Some holding to their guns, others shifting and fighting with teeth and claws.

Caro ran toward Rosalie and her father, who still lay unconscious on the damp field.

Her cousin Don, still in human shape, raced to them. He scooped her dad into his arms and slugged him over his shoulder. He nodded to Rosalie and fled the scene with Caro.

She turned to Charlie, who had now shifted into his massive wolf form as Ren stood his ground facing his flame-holding opponent.

The corrosive gas smell caught her throat as a blast of flames shot out in a torrent above them.

Everything seemed to recede from her vision except for the two threats coming for her and Ren—Charlie and a column of searing, white flames closing in on them.

CHAPTER 29

*D*amn that fucking fire! Ren forced himself to think past the scorching memories crawling up his skin as he stared at another blast of flames coming his way. He dug his hand into Rosalie's fur as he swiftly assessed the scene.

The Pelletier brothers, Nick and Matt, were fighting two of Charlie's minions in wolf form, while Max Gauthier and his buddy Gabe Beaulieu battled mercenaries further down the field.

Ren had the hired gun advancing to his side, blasting the goddammed flamethrower in intervals toward him, while Charlie, fully shifted, growled as he faced Rosalie. The massive dark wolf grinned foul teeth, saliva dripping as he snaked back and forth around them, his tail snapping like a whip.

Rosalie stood close to Ren's side. He could sense her heartbeat against his hip, her strong body coiled with power and strength. She was as big as Charlie, her sleek back reaching Ren's waist.

The memory of her, bloody and defeated on this very

same field three days ago, spurred his protective instincts. There was no way in hell he'd let her get killed!

"Rose, hold back." He didn't wait for her reaction and lunged into the massive form of Charlie's wolf, ramming into his flank with all his strength.

This time the bastard had anticipated the attack and stayed steady on his paws. As Ren attempted to sink his fangs into his monstrous neck, the son of a bitch managed to snap razor-sharp teeth deep into his arm.

Calvaire! A lancing pain radiated up to his shoulder.

Charlie shook him back and forth as Ren tried to get a grip on the large furry body. His bones creaked from the force.

Rosalie growled behind him.

Ren smashed his fist into Charlie's snout and with a grunt of pain, the shifter finally let go.

He jumped to his feet to see Tom Bouchard suddenly join them. He was strolling in human form, puffing his barreled chest with a satisfied smirk and pulled out a gun from the small of his back.

Rosalie snarled again, circling back and forth, looking for an opening to get past the flamethrower while Tom Bouchard took potshots at her.

Oh hells. Please don't be silver bullets, too.

"You're not so fast now, vampire trash." Tom took aim at him with a sneer.

Charlie erupted into a powerful howl behind him, chilling him to the core, followed by the telltale click of the flamethrower for another blast.

With his senses assaulted by the fuel's caustic scent and heat on his skin, Ren suddenly stared into the blaze.

And again, his mind left his body.

He was no longer facing the coyote's flamethrower but his own bonfire surrounding him from centuries ago.

And his fears were no longer for Rosalie but for Pierre.

As the pyre flames licked his flesh raw, scorching him into an agony too horrific to describe, the torture cutting his breath short and making him want to retch, he watched horrified at the vision of the settlers forcing his best friend to his knees.

And while Pierre knelt—the big, friendly man subdued by the mob, Ren called out a desperate prayer to the Almighty to save him. But he wasn't saved. The pitchfork plunged into his back.

Pierre's last words came out garbled and he caught Ren's gaze, his eyes filled with confusion.

Ren screamed his pain, unable to escape the guilt gnawing away at him. His friend was dying before his eyes for no reason other than being his companion. And Ren left burning for what felt like an eternity, his flesh calcinating into desiccated black.

"Renaud," a quiet voice resonated in his head.

Still bound to the tree trunk, he searched through his hallucination for the source of the calm. Had he finally died?

Renaud, my love.

He knew these words. He knew that voice. He'd heard them spoken in the throes of passion as they'd joined under the goddess' protection.

Rose?

I'm here for you, she was telling him. *Look.*

A giant golden moon suddenly materialized above his vision of Pierre breathing his last breath. And a shimmering halo settled over the scene and one by one, the tormentors were surrounded by a deep gilded haze before being absorbed into the ground in a gleaming shower of shiny drops.

There, from afar she appeared between the shadows of skeletal trees, in her majestic wolf form, with a gilded aura contouring her. *Rosalie.*

His soulmate.

As she strode toward him, she transformed into her beautiful human self, clad in a lustrous gown of gold. She stopped by Pierre, now slumped forward in death, and bent to him, her compassion infusing the whole nightmarish scene with peace and kindness.

The pitchfork dissolved at the touch of her finger, and she caught Ren's friend in her arms. She rested his body on the ground and his essence detached itself from the fallen corpse. The spirit of his friend peered at Ren with serenity in his gaze. He tilted his head in a near-imperceptible nod, as if to release Ren from his debilitating guilt.

Renaud, Rosalie said again in his vision. A deeply empathic look graced her features as Pierre's spirit dissolved into the sky to join with the heavy moon above. *It's okay. I'm here for you. Always.*

She walked toward him, waved a palm over the flames, and everything doused. She climbed the embers to embrace him and capture his bound hands in hers. His binds yielded and she kissed his cheek.

We are one, she told him.

His heart expanded as a feeling of love and peace like he had never felt in his three hundred years of existence settled down over him, making him whole.

Sensing her presence deep within him, he blinked a few times. The golden vision disappeared, and he was back in the Briac Falls arena.

The light summer rain pelted his skin, and Rosalie's wolf body pushed against him as together they faced the flames.

"Rose…" He had barely uttered her name.

She charged at the asshole with the flamethrower, which was still shooting out in all directions. The coyote toppled over, and a blast of fire swung erratically overhead. He struggled against Rosalie as she bit down on his wrist, thrashing his arm about, spurting ropes of fire all around them.

Panicked, Tom Bouchard discharged his gun wildly trying to shoot her down. With a growl, Charlie crouched to spring into her.

Dammit no! Ren swiftly grabbed Charlie by the scruff of his bristly back in midair, using the momentum to throw him down.

The large canine body hit the ground and rolled before coming to a stop. A wayward blazing stream crossed over Charlie catching his fur on fire.

"Holy shit!" Tom Bouchard stared in shock at his massive cousin who yelped and writhed as the fire spread across his coat. Flustered, he shot again at Rosalie. His last uncalculated shot hit the gas canister on the coyote's back.

Fuel leaked out as the hired gun swiveled around in panic, flinging it all everywhere. Splatters reached Charlie, magnifying the flames on his fur, and igniting the gas on the ground like a lit fuse.

"Rose!" Ren grabbed her by the middle and pulled her back.

Tom Bouchard dropped his gun and fled.

The blaze grew wider and engulfed both the big wolf-shifter and the underling coyote, who screamed in agony. A deep yelp echoed from the inferno, then nothing as the flames diminished.

Soon all that was left were two burnt corpses—one animal, one human.

Ren laid his palm upon Rosalie and took a long, slow inhale, trying to calm his hammering heart. Poor bastards, it didn't have to end this way.

"Holy shit, is that Charlie?" Max had appeared at their side, catching his breath as the rain subsided and the moonlight peeked behind the cloudy sky. Gabe joined him, dusting himself off.

"Yeah." Ren looked away from the dying fire as his gaze caught sight of Hubert, Julien, and the remaining coyotes scurrying into the woods, chased by Nick and Matt.

Rosalie shifted back to her human self, her bare skin glowing golden in the light of the moon fully appearing above them.

Ren accepted Max's offer of his flannel shirt and wrapped Rosalie in it.

"Charlie." She shook her head somberly, her expression filled with sorrow.

He remained silent and rubbed her back with sympathy, sensing her grief. He was a son of a bitch, but she'd known him her entire life.

"You threw yourself into that fire," he finally said. "You could have died."

"That coyote filth was about to burn you alive." She offered him a warm smile. "I had no choice."

"I had a vision." He drew her into the safety of his arms. "You were with me."

She nodded, her stare full of love. There was no mistaking the deep-felt connection. "Always."

"What the hell, bro!" A much too-familiar voice called out from the shadows. *Griff.*

"You're a bit late, man." Ren snorted. "You missed the party."

"Shit dude, what happened?" Cass was there, too.

Ren narrowed his eyes at the newcomers striding toward them in the field. His brothers were not alone. A small figure walked at their side, long dark hair cascading down over an elaborate dress of black velvet.

Calvaire. His mother was here.

"*Maman?*" He tightened his grip on Rosalie. "What the hell are you doing here?"

His family closed the distance between them, as Rosalie watched them silently.

"I know when my sons need me," his mother said, the short woman radiating with power, as usual.

"I could have used you a few minutes ago," he grumbled. His relationship with his immortal witch mother could only be described as complex. "Now, not so much."

"Renaud, *mon pitou*..." His mom gazed upon him fondly and his annoyance relented.

She had left them behind centuries ago. Hit with grief at the death of their mortal adoptive dad, she had departed Montreal to wander the American east coast. They had all reconnected a century later after she'd settled in Louisiana.

Rosalie slid her hand up his back and he let her quiet compassion fill him.

"Mrs. Callan St-Amand, I presume." With an easy smile, she switched to her old agreeable self as if she hadn't fought a deadly battle just moments ago.

"Charlotte, *ma chère*," his mother cooed. "Call me Charlotte."

"I'm Rosalie. Rosalie Gauthier, Alcide's daughter."

"Oh, of course. I remember you as a baby." With warmth, his mother reached out for Rosalie's hand. "Such a cute little thing."

"She's my wife, *Maman*," Ren stated. "And the new alpha of this pack. You better respect her."

"Why wouldn't I, *chéri?*" She gave him a mischievous eye before beaming back at Rosalie. "It's a pleasure to meet you, *chère*. I always knew what my Renaud needed was a strong woman by his side."

"You don't know anything, *M'man*," he moaned, falling into their usual banter. While their feelings had been complicated over the years, he grudgingly admitted that he still loved his mom dearly.

And she'd come all the way here for him. A powerful witch, she'd likely magicked herself here upon Griff's call.

Rosalie gave him a big bright smile, and he knew right there, that if someone could match his mother, it was her.

"So, Charlotte," she said, taking complete control of the conversation. "You're staying for the coronation?"

CHAPTER 30

"*Y*our mom is pretty formidable for a woman so small." Rosalie regarded Charlotte Callan conversing with Caro and her *grand-maman* on the porch of Ren's cabin in the dead of night. The trio of witches brought a mystical aura to Ren's rugged place in their shimmering dresses of velvet, lace, and gold paisley.

She leaned on the banister beside her husband, her hair still wet from the shower where she'd washed herself of the grime and nasty memories of the last few hours.

"No, *you* are," Ren insisted with a heated gaze on her. "You're incredible. The way you threw yourself at that coyote with the flamethrower was impressive."

"You finally got Charlie," she said, slowly nodding.

"*We* got Charlie," he said somberly. "Do you feel bad about that?"

"I don't feel guilty, no." She gave him a grim expression. "Once he had my dad at gunpoint, ready to execute him, I was set to end him."

She couldn't take pleasure at someone's demise, especially somebody she'd known since childhood. But relief flooded her to see her dad safe, healed from the silver bullet by Caro and her *grand-maman*, with a little help from Charlotte. He was now cheerfully talking with the other wolf-shifters, Max, Don, and their squad, while drawing Liam toward him in a fatherly hug, proud at his son's first shifting.

Delphine looked as pretty as ever, hiding her fierceness under her styled hair and trendsetting dress, while listening with her head prettily to the side as Old Simon recounted the battle.

Her siblings no longer needed her. They could fend for themselves just fine.

Ren dipped his chin. Fresh from the shower as well, he exuded an intoxicating scent of spicy aftershave and clean soap that made her bristle with emerging yearning.

"I always thought we could solve every problem with diplomacy," she said, "but you were right. Some people will stop at nothing to get what they want."

"Many could have died tonight." His voice had dropped to a low, comforting tone. "Your diplomacy will be needed."

"Yes, it will."

And suddenly her heavy heart lightened. She would get to do everything she had wanted. Open her clinic. Meet Rémi Desmarais and the other pack leaders next month. Finesse that boundary dispute with *Bois-Franc* and fix the dilapidated *Jardins du Domaine*.

"I wonder what will happen to the Bouchard compound, now," Ren pondered as he nodded at Cass hanging out with the shifters.

"Nick said someone inherits through Charlie's dad. His sister I think, who left town years ago when her brother died."

"Someone new coming to Briac Falls?"

"Yeah. We'll see," she said. "The *Fermières* are looking

after the place right now. It needs a major clean-up apparently. Tom and Hubert have left town."

"That whiny Julien Lambert is laying low, hiding at his parents, hoping we forget he sided with Bouchard," Ren informed her. "Danny Fortin had abandoned Charlie quickly. Simon told me he was right there helping him and *Grand-maman* Mercier when the coyotes took over."

"Dear old lady, she saved us all with that spell," Rosalie said with gratitude.

"The town loves you, Rose. They were all there for you."

"Yes." They may have been momentarily distracted by talks of war but seeing a hired militia ready to execute her dad had been too much. "They never wanted war."

"They want someone who cares." He gently brushed his knuckle along her jawline and tucked a lock of her damp hair behind her ear. "They want you."

The shiver of desire he drew with his touch ran all the way down her back and to her toes.

And there it was, their connection. She had felt him near her during the battle.

When she had doubted her ability, just before pouncing on the menacing coyote, and when she thought she wasn't strong enough, she had sensed him within her, filling her with confidence and strength.

He was her true soulmate. Forever.

And at this exact moment, she wanted to tell him that this marriage was not a charade, that it was real. That he completed her in ways that she had never felt.

Where her compassion sometimes blinded her to the dangers, he was right there to draw the line and take the hard, necessary path. When she neglected herself for others, *he* was the one who could see through her exhaustion and provide the solace she needed.

His simple, yet firm integrity made him the one for her. She would never doubt his intentions.

And right now, she wanted to tell him that she loved him.

Yes, loved him with all her heart.

She searched his dark expression, the chatter of their guests receding in the background. She had eyes only for him.

"Ren, I—"

"Rosalie!" Max shouted. "You got any more beers?"

"You can fetch them yourself, pal," Ren called back.

She smiled, partly relieved from the interruption. "I should go get some. Our first party."

"Is this what this is?" he teased with a raised brow. "Us hosting a party? Together?"

"Yeah." She turned to him with a hesitant look. "I think so."

"I see."

"I'll be right back."

She escaped to the kitchen and stood in front of the fan to cool off her heated skin along with her tumbling emotions.

All she had wanted to tell him remained caught in her throat. What if he didn't want her love? Sure, they had bonded. And he had performed his duty to her father by protecting her. And yes, she had felt him within her during the battle. They were mated under the goddess.

Sex between them was hot.

But neither had ever mentioned love.

And he was an immortal. A being centuries old, who had lived through many generations, probably loved multiple times. Why would he choose her?

He had introduced her as his wife to his mother but hadn't said anything about having her by his side forever.

She opened the fridge to take some beers out and propped them on the cheery lacquer serving tray she had brought to his house with her own things.

She had sex with Ren, fought alongside him. Heck, their opponents had perished in front of their eyes. All this and now she didn't know what to do. It had seemed so simple a few minutes ago, but now…

The heat felt clammy against her skin again and she snatched one of the cold beers to draw it on her forehead.

Later, she told herself. First, she had to tend to their guests. There would be time to deal with Ren and what they meant for each other.

A cold feeling dug inside her at the thought that they could be over now that no one opposed her. Still anxious, she picked up the tray and turned to head for the back deck.

She bumped directly into him, nearly tipping the bottles over.

"No need for the beer." He reached for her temple and drew his finger along her skin to rest on her bottom lip. "They're all gone."

"Wait, what?" she frowned. "Max really wanted that drink."

"I kicked them all out." He took the tray from her hands and sat it on the table amid the rest of the discarded party dishes.

"All of them?" She backed out from him to bump the kitchen table behind her.

"Yep. All of them."

"Even your mother?" she asked with surprise.

"Yes, even her."

"I needed to ask her about the immortality thing."

"Oh that." He smiled.

"I need to know," she insisted, suddenly nervous that

they were indeed alone in his house. Or was it *their* house, now?

"In good time." He took a step forward to trap her between him and the table.

"What did you tell them to make them leave so quickly?" She slowly pushed herself deeper into the edge of the table, his presence both enticing and making her heartbeat faster.

He raised a knowing brow at her. "I reminded everyone that this is our honeymoon."

"Oh." She nodded. "I'm pretty sure some of them know this is fake. Caro and Delphine, for a start."

"Is it?" he probed. "Are we fake?"

"Well…" She didn't know what to do with this. "You did want to divorce me."

"I did, yes." He pursed his lips, seemingly considering their initial conversation.

"We can do it now, you know."

"You're forgetting one thing."

"The mating."

"There's that." He bent closer to her, bringing a kiss dangerously close to her neck while his masculine scent overpowered her. "But this—us together—it's hot."

"It's the mating," she protested, not sure she wanted the lust without the emotions. "We don't have to act on it. Once we live far apart, we won't feel the physical part."

"So you still feel a physical thing?" he teased.

She bit down on her lip. "I do."

"Good."

She looked at him puzzled. "You think it's good?"

"Don't you?"

"I don't know," she admitted.

He pulled back from her, his expression drawn, sobering. "There's another thing you forget."

"And what is that?"

"I am bound to the alpha of the Domaine-Lassalle pack."

"Your oath?"

"I take it very seriously."

"Even after what happened with Charlie?" she wondered. "You're not disgusted by wolf politics?"

"Especially after what happened. He was not the first. He won't be the last."

"So you'd stay with me out of duty."

"It's more than duty, sweetheart." He stood solidly in front of her. "You know that."

"Like a pledged knight."

"To his queen, yes. To you," he added with a wide grin. "*Ma reine.*"

She stared at him and failed to notice any irony in his expression. He truly looked at her like she was some sort of monarch to whom he'd pledged his life.

"Ren, I have to be honest with you," she finally said, finding her courage. "I feel a lot more than gratefulness for your devotion to our family."

"Is that what you think this is? That I am here with you just because of a pledge?"

"I don't know."

"How can you not see it?" His lips turned into a hungry smile, and he seized the back of her head to give her a powerful kiss as a deep groan emerged from his throat.

She responded to his kiss with a matched passion. Everything suddenly felt right, just as it should.

With a low moan, she reached up to dig her fingers into his silky hair, craving for more.

He scooped her up to sit her on the table. "Rose…" he whispered against her lips. "You have no idea how I want you."

His lips trailed down the curve of her neck, her skin

coming alive with heated longing. Every fiber of her body wanted him, her heart swelling with the need to stay in his embrace forever.

"Ren, you don't understand."

"Uhm…" He slid the strap of her tank top down her shoulder and continued his descent, kissing his way to the edge of her bra. She quivered, desperately hanging on to what she needed him to know now.

"Ren, seriously, we have to talk about this," she protested feebly.

"Do we?" He pulled back, a strong arm remaining at her waist. His gaze was warm and filled with desire. His fangs slightly visible below the full lips. Damn, he was handsome. And she was on the cusp of letting him drink from her again.

"We do."

A proprietary gleam appeared in his eyes, making her hot with longing. His expression lit up with amusement as he snaked a hand behind her back to find the clasp of her bra under her top. "What is there to talk about?"

The usual self-contained bodyguard she knew had been replaced by a fun-loving, passionate man ready to take her.

She placed two hands over his shoulders, fighting her damnedest not to fall under the cravings drawn from his touch.

"What is this?" she asked with gravity. "Us? What are we to each other?"

"Us?" He had his palms fully at her back now, his warmth on her skin, making her feel both secure and full of yearning for more. "We're married, Rose."

"I know," she said. "But how real is this?"

He frowned for a second before shooting her a smile so wicked it made her core tumble with wild lust.

"As real as it gets," he said.

"You mean it?"

"Of course, *mon coeur*. Don't you see the effect you have on me?" He stroked her breast over her bra, catching her breath short as he cupped her.

"Uh-huh."

"Don't you like this?" He brushed his knuckles across her nipple, which pebbled hard against the cotton fabric.

She trembled at the sensations in her body, wondering if she would have the strength to keep this conversation going as he was slowly but surely overtaking her rational senses.

"And this?" His hand slipped under the bra to fondle her bare flesh.

Her hesitation flew right out the window, replaced by a pure animalistic rush of unbridled needs. She growled, the wolf in her responding to the touch of her mate.

So what if things remained unsaid for now. At this point, all she wanted was his body around hers. She wanted him on her, *in* her.

"Yes," she croaked. She stared into his deep brown irises before reaching for his belt and pulling him closer. "I like this."

He slid the tank top off her back and slowed down to peel off her bra, taking his time with each strap. His fingers lingered on the mating mark at her chest, tracing the crescent moon and pausing at the stars.

"My soulmate," he said, his tone turning serious.

"We can't escape it," she said, equally subdued despite the cravings rushing through her.

"The best trap I've ever been caught in." His smile had returned.

"You mean it?" She reached up to cup his face within her hands, searching for any trace of regret or strain.

"Of course, *ma belle*. I don't want to be anywhere but with you." He bent down to deposit a kiss at her forehead.

"Neither do I." She craned her neck back to capture his lips with tenderness.

"Oh god, you're so hot." He groaned, discarding his plaid shirt to the floor. The white tee soon followed.

Hungry, she slid her hands along his firm and sculpted chest, pausing with care at the old, burnt scar at his flank.

"Here?" She cast a quick glance around the kitchen.

"Yeah, here." He reached for his belt buckle in a gesture so manly, cravings pooled between her legs, her hormones overriding the last bit of resistance she had felt.

Before she knew it, his jeans and boxers were down to his ankles and her shorts were off.

He was naked in her embrace, naked and hot as hell, his thick cock rock-solid and ready to take her.

"*Calvaire*, Rose. I can't wait."

"Me neither." She scooted to the edge of the table and spread her knees wider. "I want you, Ren. I want you bad."

That was all he needed. He quickly helped her remove her panties before feeling her intimately, finding her slick and more than willing. Without much pause, he slid himself in her with a primal drive.

She gasped out his name.

"Rose, *mon amour*," he whispered against her throat.

His arms were around her, keeping her close, his cock deep inside her, not moving, just there, filling her with such intensity, such closeness, that she felt the connection deep inside her heart.

"Rose, I love you." He tightened his hold of her as if he never wanted to let her go. "I have loved you since the moment you walked into the church to marry me."

"Ren…" She suddenly found herself tongue-tied at the confession. At his body in and all over her. At his soul calling to her.

"It's not just our mating," he continued with a slow push inside her. "It's so much more."

She tried to pull back to look at him, but his clinch was too strong. He held her so tight, his need of her so deep, that she finally realized that what they shared was more than pure lust.

He had lived through a trauma that had never left him. That it had made him the stern man everyone knew. But he had let her in, past the unyielding barrier erected for centuries around his heart.

"Oh Ren. I love you. I love you so much."

"You do?" He turned his face so she could catch his gaze. And she saw him at his most vulnerable, the strong warrior letting her witness all of him. All the way down to his very soul.

"Yes, Renaud. I do. Ever since you rescued me from Charlie's awful cronies, I knew."

He gave her a crooked smile, tugging her hips into him, filling her some more. "You didn't seem to care for me helping you that day."

"It's what I love most about you, Ren. The ultimate protector. You brought me back to life after Charlie nearly killed me."

"I thought my heart had stopped. When I believed you could be dead…"

"I'm not dead." She leaned her cheek against his muscular shoulder.

"Not as long as I live."

"Which will be a long time."

"So will you. You're as immortal as I am."

"You think?"

"I know. I asked Mom and she confirmed it. I just didn't want to scare you. You've been through a lot tonight."

He touched her hair with tenderness, pulling out deliberately slow before driving himself deeper inside her, filling her with both longing and bliss.

"So did you," she said. "That flamethrower…"

"Yeah." He paused. "I'm not invincible after all."

"It brings it all back."

"A weakness of mine." He shrugged before dropping a kiss on her head. "I'm not proud of it."

"You're more human than you think, honey. It's normal to have fears."

"Just don't tell my brothers," he chortled.

"But you can tell me." She was still amazed that he trusted her with his secrets.

"Yes, I can. It's easy to tell you things, sweetheart. You have a kind heart."

"And here I thought it was because I was a badass fighter," she teased.

"You are that as well. But I've been around tough fighters for a long time. A truly compassionate person is rare." He clutched her rear tighter to bring her even closer. "I could stay like this forever."

She leaned back in his embrace and held the base of his neck with intertwined fingers. "Not me, Ren. I want all of you."

"You have me."

"Bite me."

"Again?"

"Yes, do it. I want both the man and the vampire."

His hold of her strengthened and she sensed his sharp fangs grazing her skin. Without further warning, he sank them deep into her flesh.

She jolted for a second. But as before, the sensation turned unbelievable.

She moaned his name as a tide of euphoria overcame her body.

Rocking against him, she mounted the desire within them with each thrust of her hip.

Soon she surrendered to the pull of his aphrodisiac bite

and let herself fall into pleasure as he moved with her in rhythm.

He pulled back slightly, and his fingers somehow found their way between them, right where she yearned for it.

She cried his name again, loudly this time, and released the back of his neck to secure her balance on the shaking table. She heard the crashing of glassware but didn't care, lost in the perfect moment with the man she loved.

He took his bite away from her and licked her wounds.

As he lifted his head from her shoulder, she caught his gaze and saw the pure surrender in his pupils. Everything was so real, so true. The fakeness of their marriage completely vanished as they met in pure harmony, baring their souls.

"Hells, I love you," he growled, his voice hoarse, his thumb on her needy spot drawing her closer and closer to a much-craved release.

"I love you too," she managed. And then her entire body succumbed to an overwhelming climax.

He plunged deeper and faster into her, until he too collapsed into pleasure over her.

He remained within her as their hearts hammered together in matching cadence while they caught their breath. Their sweaty bodies nestled against each other and for the first time since she met him in the St-Anne-des-Pins chapel, she found herself relaxing into safety and the glow of his love.

She rested her head on his shoulder and reveled in the bliss of their union.

"Oh mercy, look what we've done to this kitchen."

"You wanted it, *mon amour*," he chortled, kissing the tender part of her skin just below her ear.

"We should probably clean up," she said, not moving an inch from the comfort of his strapping embrace.

"Clean, up? Not now, *mon coeur!*" He kicked off his

boots and pants before scooping her into his arms in one swoop to whisk her away from the mess. "I'm in no way finished with you."

EPILOGUE

𝒩o one said a word as *Grand-Maman* Mercier lowered the laurel crown upon Rosalie's forehead while Alcide placed the blessed black oak scepter in her hand. With pride, Ren watched her from the side of the church's altar as her aunt Camille wrapped the cloak of ermine fur over her shoulder.

"*Rosalie Marie Gauthier, fille d'Alcide Joseph Gauthier et Rose-Aimée Boissonneault*, with the power given to me by the goddess Selene and under the protection of Morag of the Celtic Isles," the Mercier elder intoned, "I declare you leader of the Domaine-Lassalle pack. May your reign be peaceful and thriving for as long as you live."

Ste-Anne-des-Pins Chapel presented an entirely different look for the coronation. Gone were the white bows and flowers from their wedding ceremony. They'd been replaced by sheer drapes of silver and midnight blue. Tiny dancing fairy lights floated above the entire chapel—courtesy of his brother Griff.

Here was a place where magic was to be celebrated, not burnt to a crisp.

Rosalie cast him a warm smile. She was as beautiful as

the first time he'd seen her, walking down this very aisle. The power she held over everyone was unmistakable.

Ren glanced at the pew, catching his mother's pleased gaze. She had given his bride her own seal of approval and had indeed confirmed that Rosalie was as immortal as Ren was. With his mother's reincarnated lives many times over, dating back to the beginning of humankind, the ageless witch knew such things.

An eternity together, an eternity as their leader.

He wondered if she might actually pass the role onto another wolf when her generational time was over. He looked at her cousins Max and Don, sporting similar amber eyes, dark chestnut hair, and the Gauthier's noble posture. They appeared both satisfied with the latest outcome but maybe, yes, one of their children could take over one day.

His heart swelled with love as he looked at her again and he saw her warm gaze on him. They had a long, bright future ahead.

The passion between them was unquenchable. Their love as steadfast as ever.

He stepped forward and held his hand up to assist her from her throne of oak and ivy.

She caught his palm in a decisive but gentle grip and, as always when he was near her, he felt the turmoil in him recede.

He'd had doubt about his place among the wolves, but with her here at the lead, Briac Falls still remained his haven. His place as her protector still had meaning.

And despite her newly-found strength, he knew she needed him. Already asking for his input on how to approach the upcoming shifters council.

He smiled inwardly to think of her sitting at the table with the likes of Rémi Desmarais and cranky Jim Power from the Labrador pack. He vowed that no one would ever touch her again as Charles Bouchard had done. While he respected her authority, she knew that standing down as Charlie challenged her had killed him, and they had an implicit agreement that she would never stop him again from enacting justice on her behalf.

Bouchard's funerals had been brief but compassionate despite the circumstances of his death. His grandmother, surprisingly unfeeling and ranting that wolves had gone weak, had chosen to leave town to live with a distant niece.

As they took the steps down the altar, Mrs. Savard played the organ, the local children's choir assisting in singing a rich, traditional hymn. Rosalie nodded to her father and siblings on the front pew.

"Your family is all here." She tightened her grip on him. "Caro hasn't shut up about hanging out with Maisie Thibodeau last night."

He smiled. Ren had spent the previous night at the tavern with his brothers and Alcide's wolves, Nick, Max, Don, and the rest of the gang, and mutual respect between immortals and shifters had risen among them. A rare occasion for him to see his two worlds collide. He hoped he'd see more of it.

"Not everyone made it." He looked at the cluster of people around his mother, each more eclectic than the other. "Justin is still in London with Emme, but once Mom told everybody, the rest knew they had to be here."

"That elegant blonde there, that's Nyssa Vlahos, the real estate mogul?" she asked, mentioning the stylish woman his brother Mag was set to marry at Christmas. She and her little sister Cat had arrived in town in the morning, and he'd made a note to introduce the teen to Delphine. He felt the two girls would be kindred spirits.

He chuckled to himself, remembering how Mag used to rant about the woman who wanted to buy him out of his nightclub. The *Serpent Maudit* was still thriving, and Mag had turned into a faithful partner to Nyssa and devoted paternal figure to young Cat.

Ren nodded at Old Simon and Ti-Jo as they passed by them. The rest of the locals were all grinning and nodding with pleasure as Rosalie and Ren continued to walk down the aisle.

Everyone was relieved that the coyotes were gone. Mr. Fortin had heard from his son that Tom and Hubert Bouchard had crossed the border into the US, too embarrassed to face the pack.

"I'm surprised to see Cass here," Rosalie said, dipping her chin toward his brother, who sat in the pew beside Griff, just as they had less than two weeks ago for their wedding. "Hasn't the Montreal jazz festival started already? I thought his band was one of the big features."

"Not until next week. It's unusually late this year. And he wouldn't miss your coronation." He patted her hand with pride. "He's been rooting for you since the beginning."

"Really?"

"My brothers are very fond of you," he stated.

They finally exited the chapel into the moonlit night, church bells accompanying their steps. A fresh breeze swirled around them, fluttering the leaves of her crown and the folds of her elegant green dress. The heat wave was over, signaling the start of autumn.

"Do we really have to go to this big feast?" He slid a hand at her waist. "I had hoped to have you all to myself tonight."

"The *Fermières* would be upset if we don't," she explained. "Everyone expects it."

"Your duty."

"We can't escape duty." She shook her head.

"I'm not leaving your side. Ever," he told her. "It is *my* duty."

314

Her ancestor had saved his existence, but she had saved his soul. Soothing away the trauma and guilt he had carried for centuries.

"I don't expect you to always be there for social events." She leaned into him, taking in the crowd around her. "But please stay with me tonight. All these people, it's a lot right now."

"You got this, *mon coeur*." He nestled her against him. "Just this one event and we'll finally have our honeymoon. Bless your dad for suggesting he stays on as leader for one more week."

"An entire week alone at the cabin, just the two of us." She gave him a dreamy look. "No one else."

"Good thing I didn't really start on the addition yet. We still only have the one bed," he teased, dropping a kiss on the top of her head.

"As if I'd go anywhere else," she protested.

She gave him a loving look as the locals called out to her with insistence.

She was theirs now. They still had the ceremonial dinner where she'd answer to all their people, while he'd remain at her side, vigilant and silent.

But in a few hours, she'd be his only.

He'd take all her worries of the day away, just as her mere presence made him feel whole and at peace.

"I had Mom raise wards around the cabin's land." He bent to whisper in her ear. "No one will cross our property line unless we want them to."

"Alone for an entire week." She plastered on a bright and brave expression as she turned to the pack. A slender but steady figure in the white fur stole and laurel crown. "Mercy, I can't wait."

"It'll be just you and I." He shot her a proprietary smile as his soul heated with the need to take her again, his heart filled with love. "Just you and me. My queen."

Continue the St-Amand brothers quest for love with Cass's story in A VAMPIRE'S STAR. Find more at marieclaude-bourque.com/a-vampires-star/

Dear Readers,

I'm sure you won't be surprised to hear that a lot of authors put parts of their lives, consciously or not, in their story. This time, for Alcide's heart attack, it was completely unconscious on my part until I read the final manuscript for the last time and realized what I had done.

My father did pass from a sudden heart attack. A paleontologist—Dr. Pierre-André Bourque—my dad died in the arms of his colleague on the side of the road in the middle of the Moroccan desert while in the midst of a science expedition. He was only 65 years old. Shock, for my mother and myself, is a mild way to explain how it hit us. It's been over 15 years now and while grief never quite leaves us, we've learned to live it. But it's no surprise that I wrote a heroine whose father has a heart attack. And since I like happy ending, Rosalie's dad does survive. It does however really affect Rosalie and give her the motivation to protect his health at all costs, and yes even to marry a complete stranger. Although we have to agree, that one wasn't such a bad decision after all!

Thank you so much, wonderful reader, for continuing to be part of this Black Oak World journey with me. It is truly an honor to have you on board.

If you wish to be more involved in my writing process, see how my own heritage has a way of seeping into my writing, and discover which new tortured hero will finally find his true love, I invite you to join my Secret Circle where you will receive about two emails a month (usually on Mondays) with my latest progress, small giveaways and freebie reads.

You can join me here: www.subscribepage.com/mcbourque and as a thank you gift for your lovely support, you will receive your own exclusive copy of my American Title winner novel Ancient Whispers, where the elusive First Witch Morag Callan first makes her appearance into my world.

A true soulmate story and inspired by the ply of Acadians and Cajuns in North America, this award-winning novel, currently unavailable anywhere, will touch your soul, I promise.

As always, trust your heart,

Marie-Claude xoxo

A VAMPIRE'S HEART

A Witch-Vampire Meet Cute Paranormal Romance Prequel

To prove her worth as a leader to her coven, awkward witch Maisie Thibodeau must battle a horrible monster in front of the whole supernatural community. But the White Holly sorceresses are not the only ones watching.

Immortal Valerian St-Amand can't tear his eyes from the small but powerful witch as she battles a dangerous troll set on her small mystic town.

While he had vowed not to interfere in witches' business, his unexpected fear for her life makes it impossible for him to keep his distance.

Read on for a taste of *A Vampire's Heart*…

"Hey, it's her!" Mag elbowed him as the pub's door opened, letting some fresh air in.

"Who?" Val frowned as he continued to scan the room, casting a brief nod at the waitress bringing them their drinks.

"The girl from the shop," Mag explained with eagerness.

Val reluctantly looked to see what made his brother so enthusiastic. The young witch from the craft store stood there, a small figure in an anime logoed t-shirt, plain jeans, and faded sneakers. Her poker-straight black hair fanned against her cheek and down to her chest.

A little geeky, but yes, there was something about her. He felt a kinship in her awkwardness. She, too, didn't seem to want to be there.

She perused the crowd, waved at a few people, before settling her eyes on him.

His breath remained caught in his throat as her gaze of the deepest jade connected with his own. The contact disturbed something in him that had been dormant for centuries.

Seigneur!

The strange force stirring within him had gone straight to his core. His heartbeat pounded madly as a flush of warmth spread down to his groin.

Oh damn. Val instinctively searched for Sasha, who

was vigorously lapping water from his bowl at his feet. He couldn't remember ever feeling anything so intense before. He shook himself as he sunk his fingers into the fur of his loyal companion. This could mean trouble.

"I wonder if I should hit on her," Mag was saying.

Val moved his head bleakly as she broke their connection to survey the bar with her head held high before waving with animation at a group of women at the back.

"Sure, why not." He let out a slow exhale, his pulse now steadier, and leaned further back in his chair. He forced himself to look away from her and continue to study the patrons. But he couldn't shake the feeling that this young witch was something else.

And with his entire being, he strongly prayed that Mag would leave this one girl alone.

A VAMPIRE'S HEART, the prequel to *A VAMPIRE'S SPELL*, is available at
low cost on all storefronts…
and FREE to all
Secret Circle Subscribers
Get your copy today!

You probably wonder about some of the characters you met here... such as Charlotte Callan, Mrs. Mercier, Jérôme LeGall, as well as what happens to Ren's five brothers and Emmeline Dubois.

Here is the list of books current and to-be-released in the Black Oak world:

~ *Vampires of the Black Oak* ~

A Vampire's Heart (Val and Maisie's first meet cute): In this prequel to A Vampire's Spell, awkward witch Maisie Thibodeau must prove her worth as leader to her coven by battling a horrible monster in front of the whole supernatural community.

A Vampire's Spell (Val and Maisie): Guilt-ridden legacy vampire Valerian St-Amand teams with powerful witch Maisie Thibodeau to protect his city from a crazed scientist seeking immortality.

A Vampire's Sin (Mag and Nyssa): Immortal Montreal vampire Mag St-Amand teams up with ambitious real estate tycoon Nyssa Vlahos to rescue her kid sister from a child-trafficking ring run by a pack of daemons.

A Vampire's Soul (Emme and Justin): When female vampire Emmeline Dubois teams up with faithful immortal friend Justin St-Amand to escape a vicious hunter set to kill her, the centuries-old friendship turns into so much more than she'd anticipated.

A Vampire's Fate (Ren and Rosalie): When female wolf-shifter Rosalie Gauthier returns to her town to take on the leadership of her pack after her father's illness, her birthright is challenged by a tyrannic rival and marriage to powerful vampire Ren St-Amand is her only option to save her family's legacy.

A Vampire's Star (Cass and Tilly): Can an immortal truly father a child? That's what rock star Cass St-Amand finds out when Tilly Davenport, a strong-headed music producer banshee, shows up backstage at his latest concert claiming to be carrying his child.

A Vampire's Blood (Griff and Isabelle): Can you fall in love with your lifelong enemy? Griff St-Amand has his hands full when he finds himself having to rescue French supernatural hunter Isabelle LeGall despite her hatred for his family.

A Vampire's Christmas (Antoine and Charlotte): What best Christmas present can six vampire brothers give their mother but bring back from the death her true love— lost three hundred years ago. But is righteous man Antoine St-Amand ready for a new life with his immortal wife in this modern century, especially after she'd sworn to him never to use magic to keep him alive?

~ Warlocks of the Black Oak ~

A Warlock's Kiss (Diesel and Kera): Stoic warlock leader Diesel Stanford must convince his panther-shifter ex-girlfriend Kerala Clarke to return the only magical artifact that can cure his sister from a terrible hex.

A Sorcerer's Night (Sin and Celeste): Protective panther-shifter sorcerer Sinclair Clarke battles a powerful demon who holds hostage his fiancee, legacy witch Celeste Stanford.

An Alchemist's Desire (Thorn and Raven): Recluse alchemist Thornwood Huntington must help talented violinist Raven Giancola unlock the magic of her enchanted violin despite his vow to keep all things magic away from non-sorcerers.

An Archmage's Destiny (Knight and Bryce): With her reputation on the line, steadfast attorney Bryce Jackson must convince daredevil warlock Knightley Morgan to return to the folds of his powerful New England family or apply the devastating consequences herself.

A Spellbinder's Denial (Duke and Sloane): Riddled with guilt after his unleashed powers wrecked lives decades ago, billionaire warlock Duke Morgan still refuses to unlock his powers to make amends, but when savvy banshee Sloane Davenport crosses his path again, even his fortune won't be enough to protect her.

A Necromancer's Love (Mal and Harper): When vampires descend on his city, Seattle necromancer Malcolm Dunsmuir can no longer hide from the darkness of his demon side, especially when the enticing life-loving human Harper Grant tries her very best to bring him to the light.

A Warlock's Storm (Rey and Saira): Stranded on a boat in a haunted New England harbor, rugged warlock Rey Stanford and sassy female panther-shifter Saira Varma battle sea-monsters and revenants as they try to survive the night.

FRENCH-ENGLISH GLOSSARY

baptême - *Baptism, French Canadian curse*
Cercle des Fermières - *Circle of the Farm Women (an actual real-life organization in Québec)*
calvaire - *Calvary, French Canadian curse*
Chasseurs - *Hunters (as in Les Chasseurs, a group of supernatural hunters)*
chérie - *dear, endearment to a woman*
épluchette - *corn shucking party (in Québec)*
frère - *brother*
fille - *girl*
Fille d'Alcide Joseph Gauthier et Rose-Aimée Boissonneault - *daughter of Alcide Joseph Gauthier and Rose-Aimée Boissonneault.*
grand-maman - *grandmother*
Je le veux - *I do*
Jardins du Domaine - *The Estate's Garden*
ma chère - *dear, usually to a female friend*
ma p'tite - *kiddo — for a girl*
mon beau - *handsome, endearment to a man*
ma belle - *beautiful, endearment to a woman*

mon coeur - *sweetheart*
ma reine - *my queen*
Sanctuaire des Truands - *Sanctuary of the Sinful*
Serpent Maudit - *Cursed Serpent*

CAST OF MAIN CHARACTERS

Vampires:

Renaud (Ren) St-Amand: Mount-Royal Immortal and honorary member of the Domaine-Lassalle Wolf Pack. Brother to Val, Mag, Justin, Cass and Griff.

Cassiodore (Cass) St-Amand: Mount-Royal Immortal. Brother to Val, Mag, Justin, Ren and Griff.

Griffon (Griff) St-Amand: Mount-Royal Immortal and brother to Val, Mag, Justin, Ren and Cass.

Professor Justinien (Justin) St-Amand: Mount-Royal Immortal and professor of Astronomy at McDougall College in Montreal. Brother to Val, Mag, Ren, Cass and Griff.

Emmeline (Emme) Dubois (aka The Vampire of Ville-Marie): Montreal immortal vampire and former fiancée of Val St-Amand. Friend to the St-Amand brothers and Maisie Thibodeau.

Magnovald (Mag) St-Amand: Mount-Royal Immortal and owner of the *Serpent Maudit* night club in Montreal. Brother to Val, Justin, Ren, Cass and Griff.

Valerian (Val) St-Amand: Mount-Royal Immortal and

founder of the *Sanctuaire des Truands* shelter in Montreal. Brother to Mag, Justin, Ren, Cass and Griff.

Ambrus the Exiled: Birth father of Val, Mag, Justin, Ren, Cass and Griff. Impregnated their mother in the late seventeenth century before disappearing from their lives.

Wolf Shifters - Gauthiers:

Rosalie (Rosie, Rose) Gauthier: Grey Wolf shifter, daughter of Alcide Gauthier and wife of Ren St-Amand.

Alcide Gauthier: Grey Wolf shifter and alpha of the Domaine-Lassalle Pack. Friend and ally to the St-Amand brothers.

Delphine Gauthier: Grey Wolf shifter and younger sister of Rosalie Gauthier.

Liam Gauthier: Grey Wolf shifter and youngest brother of Rosalie Gauthier.

Maxime (Max) Gauthier: Grey Wolf shifter and cousin to Rosalie Gauthier. Son of Camille Gauthier.

Donatien (Don) Gauthier Grey Wolf shifter and cousin to Rosalie Gauthier. Son of Camille Gauthier.

Camille Gauthier (née Boissonneault): Grey Wolf shifter and aunt of Rosalie Gauthier. Sister of Rose-Aimée Gauthier and widow to the late brother of Alcide Gauthier. Owner of the Briac Falls local Wolf Kung-Fu dojo.

Hugo Gauthier: Grey Wolf shifter child and distant cousin of Rosalie Gauthier.

Joseph-Marie Gauthier: Grey Wolf shifter, alpha of the Domaine-Lassalle Pack in the late eighteenth century.

Rose-Aimée Gauthier (née Boissonneault) Grey Wolf shifter and late mother of Rosalie Gauthier.

Rosaire Gauthier: Grey Wolf shifter and late grandfather of Rosalie Gauthier.

Adalie Gauthier (née Beaulieu): Grey Wolf shifter and late grandmother of Rosalie Gauthier.

Wolf Shifters - Bouchards:

Charles (Charlie) Bouchard: Grey Wolf shifter and antagonist to the Gauthier and St-Amand families.

Tom Bouchard Grey Wolf shifter and cousin of Charlie Bouchard.

Hubert Bouchard Grey Wolf shifter and cousin of Charlie Bouchard.

Doris Bouchard Grey Wolf shifter and grandmother of Charlie Bouchard.

Johnny Bouchard Grey Wolf shifter and late father of Charlie Bouchard.

Wolf Shifters - Pelletiers:

Nicholas (Nick) Pelletier: Grey Wolf shifter and best friend of Max Gauthier.

Mathieu (Matt) Pelletier: Grey Wolf shifter and best friend of Max Gauthier.

Jacob Pelletier: Grey Wolf shifter and construction worker in Briac Falls.

Léa Pelletier: Grey Wolf shifter and waitstaff at Alcide's Tavern in Briac Falls.

Marie-Christine Pelletier: Grey Wolf shifter and brief lover of Ren St-Amand in the nineteenth century.

Wolf-Shifter - Other Families:

Simon (Old Simon) Tremblay: Grey Wolf shifter, war veteran and Briac Falls local postman. Friend of Alcide Gauthier and Ren St-Amand.

Danny Fortin: Grey Wolf shifter and follower of Charlie Bouchard.

Emilie Fortin: Grey Wolf shifter and high school friend of Rosalie Gauthier.

Mr and Mrs. Fortin: Grey wolf shifters, owner of Briac Falls general store and parents of Danny Fortin.

Dick Fortin: Grey Wolf shifter and Briac Falls local accountant.

Myriam Lambert: Grey Wolf shifter and friend of Rosalie Gauthier.

Julien Lambert: Wolf shifter and follower of Charlie Bouchard.

Ed Beaulieu: Grey Wolf shifter and local Briac Falls construction worker.

Mrs. Beaulieu: Grey Wolf Shifter and owner of Briac Falls local bed and breakfast.

Gabriel (Gabe) Beaulieu: Grey Wolf Shifter and best friend of Max Gauthier.

Noah Landry: Grey Wolf shifter teenager and love interest of Delphine Gauthier.

Jérémie Landry: Grey Wolf shifter and owner of Briac Falls local collectible shop. Husband of Thomas Chauvin.

Marie-Pier Landry: Grey Wolf shifter and friend of Rosalie Gauthier.

Matheo Landry: Grey Wolf shifter and Briac Falls local child.

Maika: Grey Wolf shifter and friend of Delphine Gauthier.

Elise: Grey Wolf shifter and friend of Delphine Gauthier.

Chantal Aubry: Grey Wolf shifter, widow and brief lover of Ren St-Amand in the late nineties.

Wolf-Shifters - Other Packs

Rémi Desmarais: Grey Wolf shifter and alpha of the Val d'Or Pack.

Nicole Desmarais: Grey Wolf shifter. Mother of Rémi Desmarais and former alpha of the Val D'Or pack.

Jim Power: Labrador Wolf shifter and alpha of the Labrador Pack.

Witches, Warlocks and Healers:

Caroline (Caro) Mercier: Seer and Healer for the Domaine-Lassalle Pack. Daughter of Fabienne and George Mercier.

Charlotte Callan (aka The Ice Witch): Ancient witch of the Callanish tradition and mother of the Mount-Royal Immortals.

Maisie Thibodeau: Witch of the White Holly Coven in Berwick Hollow. Wife of Valerian St-Amand and best friend to Emmeline Dubois

Diesel Stanford: Warlock and leader of the Order of the Black Oak. Resides in Seaport with his wife panther-shifter Kerala Clarke and their young son Sai Stanford.

Morag of the Celtic Isles (aka The First Witch): Immortal Celtic witch and High Priestess of the Callanish Coven in the Outer Hebrides of Scotland.

LeGall Hunters:

Jérôme LeGall: Supernatural hunter tasked to eliminate Emmeline Dubois, Vampire of Ville-Marie. Turned cursed vampire by Justin St-Amand.

Disciples of Nostredame:

Father Grégoire: Oldest disciple of Nostredame, living

at the *Sanctuaire des Truands* in Montreal and assigned to Val St-Amand.

Humans - Briac Falls

Mrs. Fabienne Mercier: Housekeeper at Chateau Briac for Justin St-Amand. Mother of Caro Mercier.
Ti-Jo and Louise Leclerc: married couple, owner of the Briac Falls local gas station.
Jade Leclerc: friend of Rosalie Gauthier.
Abbé David: cleric of the St-Anne-des-Pins chapel and officiant of Ren St-Amand and Rosalie Gauthier's wedding.
Dr. François Beaumont: Toronto doctor and former boyfriend of Rosalie Gauthier.
Thomas Chauvin: husband of Briac Falls collectible shop owner Jérémie Laundry.
Mrs. Savard: local Briac Falls widow and future receptionist of Rosalie Gauthier medical clinic.
Suzie Savard: local Briac Falls hairstylist.

Humans - Montreal

Antoine (Papa Antoine) St-Amand: Adopted father to the Mount-Royal Immortals. Husband to Charlotte St-Amand. Died of rabies in 1690.
Nyssa Vlahos: CEO of Vlahos Enterprise and fiancée of Mag St-Amand.
Catalina (Cat) Vlahos: teenager and half-sister to Nyssa Vlahos.
Captain Akande: Female police officer and Captain of the Sureté du Québec provincial police. Mag St-Amand's loyal friend.

ACKNOWLEDGEMENTS

I want to thank all of you, wonderful readers, for your constant support during the writing of this story. It means a lot of me.

Thank you also to coach Jess Michael to keep me on track through the worse of writing this book and to my Seattle friend and Trope Queen, Jennifer Hilt, for her help and support.

As always, I am also very grateful to talented romance author, friend and amazing editor Jenn Bray-Webber who helped turn this book into my vision. Thank you also to Charity Chimni for the detailed copy editing and to Frauke Spanuth for another great cover design.

Marie-Claude Bourque is a Montreal-born Seattle-based author of slow-burn paranormal romance and the winner of the American Title V award with her first novel ANCIENT WHISPERS.

Her writing features modern-day fantasy skillfully weaved into infinitely romantic stories between smart strong women and complex passionate heroes.
Happily Ever After always absolutely guaranteed!
Find more at www.marieclaudebourque.com

To be first to hear about her latest book, win free copies and more, subscribe to
Marie-Claude's Secret Circle

Or connect directly with her at
www.facebook.com/mcbourque

facebook.com/mcbourque

amazon.com/author/marieclaudebourque

goodreads.com/mcbourque

bookbub.com/profile/marie-claude-bourque

www.ingramcontent.com/pod-product-compliance
Lightning Source LLC
Chambersburg PA
CBHW030920260626
47169CB00002B/339